VERITY'S CHOICE

Ladies of Munro, Book 3

Elizabeth Donne

ARE YOU SIGNED UP FOR DRAGONBLADE'S BLOG?

You'll get the latest news and information on exclusive giveaways, exclusive excerpts, coming releases, sales, free books, cover reveals and more.

Check out our complete list of authors, too!

No spam, no junk. That's a promise!

Sign Up Here

www.dragonbladepublishing.com

Dearest Reader;

Thank you for your support of a small press. At Dragonblade Publishing, we strive to bring you the highest quality Historical Romance from some of the best authors in the business. Without your support, there is no 'us', so we sincerely hope you adore these stories and find some new favorite authors along the way.

Happy Reading!

CEO, Dragonblade Publishing

Additional Dragonblade books by Author Elizabeth Donne

Ladies of Munro Series
Sophia's Letter (Book 1)
Ellena's Secret (Book 2)
Verity's Choice (Book 3)

Dedicated to my husband, Alan,
the one who chose me

CHAPTER ONE

Fernbridge, October 1814

VERITY LOCKHART'S TOES sank into the mud with a satisfying squelch. A youthful giggle that belied her eighteen years bubbled up in her throat. *If Mother could see me now!* Her eyes cast quickly in the direction of the vicarage. No, she was safe, out of sight, and deliciously alone.

The hem of her dress dipped into the pond water and she hastily raised it higher, draping it over her arm, her pale knees exposed in a most shocking fashion. She didn't think the frogs minded. They were used to her knees by now.

Her focus turned to the dragonfly perched on a sunny rock a few feet away. She carefully lowered her net. Her toes felt their way through the chilly water as she edged forward. Slowly, slowly.

The dragonfly shifted as her shadow fell over it, and Verity threw her arm out just in time. The hoop of the net encircled the creature's flight and the collapsing netting downed the insect while it struggled.

"There, there," she soothed, gathering the net and its flailing prisoner up with gentle fingers. "Don't fight so. I am only going to sketch you, and then you'll be free again."

She hastened to the grassy verge, dropped her skirts against her damp legs, and reached for a glass jar that lay waiting. A *bzzt* of frustration, and the dragonfly was in the jar, the cork stopper sealing it in.

"Come on," she said conversationally as she carried the jar and its occupant to a bench nearby. "This won't take long. You'll soon be off on your adventures again." The dragonfly did not respond. Verity considered its silence somewhat accusatory. She tucked a straggling lock of white-blonde hair behind her ear and dropped her gaze. "You don't understand. I have no adventures. None at all. But I will keep a memory of you in my sketches. Later, I will add water colors. Do you see? Whenever I look at them, I will think of what you may be getting up to, somewhere beyond the meadow, perhaps even crossing distant rivers."

The dragonfly pulsed its wings. Verity sighed.

"All right, let's begin."

She opened a leather portfolio of loose pages and removed a clean sheet. Verity squinted at the jar, then her pencil began to shift with confident strokes as the dragonfly took shape, first in outline, then in exquisite detail. Her feet rubbed against each other as the early autumn afternoon began to cool. But she wouldn't stop to put on her stockings and shoes, not until her little muse was free again.

It was while she was jotting down notes about the colors to be added later that she heard the faint voice.

"Miss Lo-o-o-ck-ha-a-art!" it called.

Verity knew to whom the voice belonged, even though its owner had not yet appeared over the rise.

"Tch, what is it now?" she grumbled to herself. "I have barely been gone an hour."

She packed away her sketch and pencil, slotting the leather tongue of the portfolio through its buckle. A deft bend and twist deposited her footwear out of sight under the bench, where her bare feet were tucked away from view. Just in time, too, as the calling refrain had changed suddenly to "Oh, there you are! I don't know why I look anywhere else. If you're not at the stream by the church, you are always here."

The voice was accompanied by a degree of puffing as a plump

young woman approached the bench.

She stopped to catch her breath, her gaze following Verity's across the shallow pond, buzzing with insects.

"My, but it is a lovely view. I can see why it draws you here, miss."

Verity smiled down at the glass jar. One of her mother's maids would never understand how the strange and wonderful denizens of the waterways caught Verity's heart far more than flowering fields and dales.

"I suppose my mother is looking for me." Verity's tone suggested this was nothing new.

"Yes, miss. There is a visitor come. A young man from the village."

"And what has that to do with me? He has surely come to discuss something with my father. Some church matter or the like."

"I couldn't say, miss. I only know that Mrs. Lockhart said you are to come, and to make yourself presentable."

Verity's naked toes wriggled guiltily beneath the bench.

"Does this young man have a name?" she asked.

"I didn't catch what it was." Nellie's nose wrinkled as she tried to remember, without success. Then she grinned. "He was awfully handsome, though. I wouldn't complain if he came calling on *me*."

"Why, Nellie Brown!" Verity laughed. "I'm not at all certain these are appropriate thoughts for a young lady to have."

"Oh, miss, I suspect these are exactly the thoughts your mother hopes you will have when you see him." Nellie's eyes twinkled knowingly.

"Hmm. I'm afraid you may be right, Nellie. My mother could never be accused of subtlety. But I am not quite ready to fall for the first handsome face that graces our parlor."

Nellie shrugged. "That is not for me to say, miss."

Verity's lips curled into a mischievous smile. "Shall I put in a good word for you with our mysterious visitor?"

The young maid's eyes grew wide. "Oh, *no*, Miss Lockhart. He is far too grand a gentleman for the likes of me."

"A grand gentleman from the village, and you don't know who he is?" Verity tapped her chin. "Who can he be?"

"Best to come and find out, miss, before Mrs. Lockhart becomes impatient."

"I suppose you're right. Go ahead without me, Nellie. I will be there soon, I promise."

Nellie hesitated, but—short of dragging her young mistress along by the arm—there was nothing she could do.

"Mrs. Lockhart won't be happy if you take too long," she warned.

"I know, Nellie. Tell her I am going to my room to fix my hair and I will be right down."

The maidservant turned, and her stout legs fought the rise of the hill. With her back to the pond, she did not see Verity uncork the jar and watch the shimmering wings of a dragonfly reclaiming its freedom.

❊

WITH SHOES AND stockings in hand, Verity snuck into the house through the back entrance. Cook took one look at her and shooed her back out again.

"You'll not be tracking your mud through my kitchen, young lady," she said, pointing a long, wooden spoon in her direction. "Nellie, bring her a jug of water and a cloth to clean up before the mistress sees her. Honestly, as if I don't have enough to do!"

"Sorry, Mrs. MacTavish, it won't happen again," Verity mumbled from the back step.

Cook snorted, wiping her hands on her bleached apron. "I find that hard to believe." She lowered her voice, but Verity could hear her mutter, "Her poor mother. She'll never get that wild thing married."

Verity stiffened. She had heard it before. It was her mother's constant refrain. And because it was true, it was hard to hear. She did try her best to be everything they wanted of her, but, well, all of that just wasn't *her*.

There was no time to dwell on it now. She rose to her newly-clean feet and raced up the stairs, two at a time. She was barely through the door of her bedroom when she began to tug at her wet-hemmed dress, pulling it off over her head. It fell on the floor, and she stepped over it to collect a new one from the wardrobe. With stockings clipped neatly in place once more, she slipped into her shoes and ran a brush through her hair—like starlight, her father had described it when she'd been little—almost colorless and yet agleam with reflected light. There wasn't time to pin it fashionably. A tidy bun would have to do. At least her fringe had not lost much of its curl. Whoever their visitor was, he was not worth fussing for any further.

She adjusted her skirts so that their deep-green folds fell smoothly, then she descended the staircase rather more demurely. It was time to be the vicar's daughter everyone expected.

The bottom landing creaked as she stepped onto it. Her father had wanted to replace the warped board, but her mother enjoyed knowing when someone approached the parlor. Unsurprisingly, therefore, Verity now heard her mother's voice declare, "I do believe that is our daughter at last." A clatter of china suggested Mrs. Lockhart had set down her tea. "Verity," she called, "come in here, dear."

As if I would greet a guest anywhere else. She wished she could *be* anywhere else. With that option not currently available, Verity now stepped into the parlor, her hands clasped together, her head lowered.

A movement across the room made her look up. Their guest had risen to greet her. Verity sucked in her breath. He was—there was no other word for it—*magnificent*. Nellie had not exaggerated at all. His frame was neat and slender, his clothes tailored to perfection. The eyes of the stranger were dark and penetrating beneath his black, short-cropped hair, and his mouth lifted slightly at the corners in a secretive smile.

Verity caught herself staring.

Mrs. Lockhart proceeded briskly with introductions. "Verity, I wonder if you remember Mr. William Cole. You played together as children. Of course, that was a long time ago. Perhaps you do not recognize him now."

William Cole. Verity's heart sank. Why did this sublime creature have to be William Cole?

Her mother continued, as if the disparity between the Williams, past and present, mattered not a jot.

"The last time you saw each other must have been, what, about five years ago?"

Mr. Cole nodded. "Before I left for university." His voice was soft and deep and seductive. It was impossible not to notice. But Verity remembered a different version of him. One that was not nearly as irresistible.

"You were the last to leave," she stated flatly.

"And you never did," he remarked.

"Not yet," her mother added, a teasing lilt to her voice. "But she has just turned eighteen, and she will be sure to make her own little nest." She smiled meaningfully at their guest, her intelligent eyes bright, her mind no doubt plotting as usual.

"If I were a boy, I would be at university," Verity said with a hint of sourness.

Mr. Cole raised an eyebrow. "Indeed. Is that what you would have preferred?"

"What nonsense," tutted Mrs. Lockhart, placing a hand on her full bosom. "There is no talk of our daughter doing any such thing. Is there, Mr. Lockhart?"

Her mother turned to her father, who was quietly submerged in his favorite chair. She did not wait for him to answer but instead continued with her usual momentum. "It is unheard of. Her days are filled to the brim already around the home and within the community. What more could a woman wish for?"

Mr. Cole looked pointedly at Verity, as if he expected her to answer that question.

She was taken aback. The William Cole she had known had never cared for her opinion.

He was nearly three years older. In their childhood, that had been a lifetime of difference. When the children of Fernbridge had gathered to play at picnics or festivals, William had been—not counting herself—the youngest. And he had wanted very much to be included. It had been an almost desperate need to be liked by the others. He had used his natural intelligence to banter and play the fool for their amusement. It had been a little sad, really. But it had also meant that Verity, being younger still, had been utterly discarded.

It hadn't bothered her as much as it would have bothered him, had that been his fate. She was used to being ignored. Both her siblings were much older and always too busy for her childish needs. So, she would watch them play for a while and then wander off by herself to observe new things.

That was how she had found the butterfly. Its wing had been torn. She had expected it to fly away as she'd approached. Instead, it had fluttered haphazardly onto a leaf, perhaps hoping concealment could protect it when flight could not.

Verity had stood quite still, not to alarm it. She'd admired the design of its membranous wings and the way the segments had shone like plate-glass windows. It had been such a pity it would never fly properly again. Unless… What if she cut a piece of tissue paper and attached it with a little glue paste? But how would she keep the butterfly still while the glue dried?

She had been standing thus, in a pose of contemplation, when the jostling crowd of children had pushed past her, brushing the branch on which the invalid insect had been perched and knocking it down in a hail of knees and elbows. Verity had thrown herself to the ground to shield the helpless thing, but it had been too late. A cry of dismay had torn from her throat.

William Cole, always five steps behind the others, had

stopped to see what was the matter. He'd peered over her shoulder at the battered shape in the trampled grass and scowled. "Oh, it's just a stupid butterfly," he'd declared. And he'd run on to find the others.

Verity had felt the air being sucked from her lungs. He hadn't cared. None of them had. As far as they'd been concerned, the butterfly had been discardable, just like her. But it hadn't been. It had been fascinating, and alluring, and… and… then it had been gone.

That evening, all those years ago, Verity had drawn her first sketch of many. It had been a rough attempt, but she'd persevered. She'd needed to capture what had made the butterfly special. So that it would have been truly *seen*.

Was that what Mr. Cole was doing now? Here, five years later? Was he really seeing her for the first time? Could she say things to him that no other man had wanted to hear—how she loved time alone at the pond? Or that she hid notebooks under her bed, filled with complicated diagrams and scientific studies copied from the library?

She didn't think so.

"A woman finds fulfilment in her home and family," she found herself saying. And she hated herself for it.

Did she imagine it, or did Mr. Cole look disappointed?

Her mother, however, would allow no opportunity for contemplation and began at once to fuss.

"Sit, sit, everyone." Mrs. Lockhart waved her hands about. She proceeded to place herself in the middle of the settee so that Verity was obliged to take the only remaining chair—which just happened to be adjacent to Mr. Cole.

But if her mother had hoped to create a little *tête-à-tête* between them, her father had not been informed.

"How is my dear friend Marcus?" he asked their guest.

"My father is well, thank you, sir."

"And business at the bank is thriving, I hope?"

"Certainly, I have not heard otherwise."

"And your brother, Lawrence, he is to take the helm one day, I assume."

"Yes, sir. They already work together as equals." Mr. Cole looked at his hands. "My father is very pleased with my brother."

"I am told your sister is married and in Munro."

"Yes. Charlotte has a son and another child on the way."

"Good, good." The vicar nodded. "I am glad to hear it. It seems your parents, like ourselves, have just one nestling left to push out into the world. Speaking of which, I believe you are interested in joining the clergy. A very fine occupation. But then, of course, my opinion on the matter is biased."

Mr. Cole did not answer at once. When he did, it was merely to say, "That has not yet been decided."

"Oh, my dear!" Mrs. Lockhart threw her hand to her bosom once more. "You cannot wait! A young man must keep busy, or he will fall into bad habits for want of better things to do. See how happy and content Mr. Lockhart is."

Mr. Cole was obliged to do just that. He turned to Verity's father, who sat amicably in his deep, upholstered chair, his light-brown hair a little long and wild, belying his calm nature. Beside him lay a small stack of books with spectacles resting on top. Across his lap lay a warm, woolen coverlet. Truly, he was the very picture of contentment.

As if satisfied that Mr. Cole had seen enough, Verity's mother added, "No, indeed, sir, the church is the very thing!"

Mr. Cole shook his head. "If I were made of the good stuff that Mr. Lockhart has in abundance, I would agree. I know it is what my father wants for me. However, I am not convinced that I am suited for it."

"'Not suited'?" Mrs. Lockhart waved a hand dismissively. "Fiddlesticks! You can speak well enough to deliver a sermon. Mr. Lockhart simply reads them from the books the diocese publishes." Her eyes glanced at her husband and then looked hard at Mr. Cole. "You have two strong arms and I daresay a healthy pair of legs with which to serve your neighbors. What more is there to it?"

Mr. Cole looked at the floor.

Verity took pity on him. "Is there something else you would rather do, Mr. Cole?"

He looked up, his face shining, only to drop his gaze to his hands and say, "I did consider the military."

"The military!" Mrs. Lockhart whipped around to face her husband. "Did you hear that, Mr. Lockhart? All that marching up and down in the mud when he could have a nice, clean pulpit once a week. Who would not rather have a congregation that loves him instead of an enemy trying to murder him?" She turned her attention suddenly to her daughter. "Verity, dear, do tell him he is being silly."

Verity wanted to declare, *"I will do no such thing! The man should follow his dreams!"* Instead, she bit her feelings back and said, "I do not think it is my place to speak to him so."

"You're in want of a good wife, Mr. Cole." Her mother scolded him since Verity would not. "If you had a fine woman to come home to of an evening, you would not be so keen to run off to war."

"No doubt you are right, ma'am," their visitor said, mostly to his boots. His soft voice had grown quieter still. Then, with alarming abruptness, he stood. "I'm afraid I must be on my way. I had only meant to stop and look in on you as I passed."

"I say, my boy," protested the vicar, "you will not stay even ten minutes more?"

"No. You will have to forgive me. Thank you for your hospitality, but I must take my leave at once."

"Well!" Mrs. Lockhart breathed out heavily. "I will not say it pleases me. But of course, if you are expected elsewhere… Perhaps we will see you again soon?"

Mr. Cole bowed stiffly. "We will no doubt see each other with great regularity, now that I am returned to Fernbridge."

"Ah, well, that is good. Will we see you at church on Sunday, then?"

Mr. Cole's face tightened. "My father will likely insist."

And with these words, he turned and walked his long legs to the front door. With a curt "Good day," he was out and into the garden, striding toward the gate post, where his horse was tethered.

Mrs. Lockhart looked at her husband. "Well, I never! How strange he has grown. And will you look at that? He has forgotten his hat. Verity, run and take it to him. Quickly now, before his head catches a cold."

Verity took the hat in hand and stepped lightly onto the path, reaching Mr. Cole before he had mounted his horse.

"Here," she called, making him turn, "you left your hat."

The man's eyebrows rose from a frown into high arches, his mouth softening and parting slightly.

"Ah, so I did. Thank you." He tipped the hat onto his head and was about to resume his departure when Verity gasped.

"What is it?" he asked, his eyes darkening with concern.

"Your hat…" Verity pointed to the curved brim. "It's a red admiral."

William relaxed into a smile. "I have never heard the style described as such. As far as I am aware, it is a simple top hat."

"No, no… *on* your hat. It is a red admiral butterfly! They're not usually this far north in October. I haven't seen any for several weeks now."

"And you have been looking out for them, have you?"

Verity blushed. "I just notice things."

Mr. Cole's smile wrinkled with bemusement. "Yes, you do, Miss Lockhart."

He lowered his hat again with great care and they both gazed at their winged guest. It did not seem to mind the attention, and it rested for several moments before flitting off in movements that were, at once, both lurching and graceful.

"Thank you," said Verity. "That was very kind."

"What? Holding my hat for you to see your red captain better? If that is all, may I say you have very low expectations, Miss

Lockhart." He offered a lopsided smile to soften the comment.

"It's a red *admiral.* And yes, you are probably right. I don't expect much and am usually the happier for it. But I did think it a great kindness that you lingered for my sake when you had been in such a hurry only moments earlier."

"Oh." Mr. Cole straightened up. "That." He placed the hat back upon his head. "Yes. I had best be off then, hadn't I?"

The smile had fallen from his face once more, and the dimples in his cheeks had dissolved. Verity was sorry for it. When his eyes were lit with mirth and mischief, he was almost unbearably attractive. All she could admire now was his dark-blue coat and the way it spanned across his back as he mounted his horse.

He turned and touched his finger to his hat before spurring his horse onward down the lane. Verity remained at the gate, watching his figure recede into the distance. She was oddly sad to see him go. Perhaps it was simply because he had offered a little distraction from her predictable life.

From the doorway, her mother's voice rang clear and high with energy. She was sure to have plenty to say about their visitor, and Verity resigned herself to a half hour of relentless commentary. She cast one last look down the stony path, but Mr. Cole was out of sight. Taking a deep, bolstering breath, she closed the gate behind her and walked back along the path.

"My goodness, you certainly took your time," Mrs. Lockhart noted as Verity approached the front door. Verity would have told her about the butterfly, but her mother was bound to answer it with *that look,* the one that expressed disapproval and disappointment without need for words. Instead, Verity merely said, "Did I?" and walked on into the house.

"It is very odd that Mr. Cole should wait with such patience for you to arrive so that he may renew the acquaintance and then scuttle away the moment he had done so," Mrs. Lockhart declared.

But Verity wasn't listening. She rarely did. Oh, she would nod and make sounds of encouragement, but her thoughts would always drift to her latest discovery. Today, it was the red admiral and the delight of seeing one again before winter came.

If she were honest, however, she would confess that her mind was not only on the painted black wings, but on a dark-blue coat and the eyes that danced above it.

CHAPTER TWO

Too soon. It was too soon. What had he been thinking? He should never have let his father talk him into it.

William urged his horse into a gallop, but it didn't help. The truth stayed with him.

"If you had a fine woman to come home to of an evening…" That was what Mrs. Lockhart had said. He knew she had meant her daughter. After all, wasn't that why he had come?

And would it really be that bad? Miss Lockhart had done a lot of growing up. The dull, little mouse he had strived to avoid as a child was now rather more intriguing. She still had that odd fascination with insects, but at least she was pleasing to look at. Her features were delicate, her hair almost a silvery blonde, her pale-blue eyes intelligent.

But she could not hold his gaze like Ellena did.

Heat rose in his chest as he remembered Ellena's warm-chestnut hair and the way she would look at him with bold honesty. He missed how she could match his wit, their banter driving away the emptiness that always struggled to overwhelm him.

Ellena was everything he yearned for. Yes, indeed, a fine woman to come home to of an evening. Only… she would never be his. William thought back with deep bitterness to their last conversation. How he had misjudged the situation! He had never stood a chance. He had risked much and lost everything. And now he had to settle for this life he never wanted: as a country vicar, married to a vicar's daughter.

He should have waited, let his wounds heal a little. It might have made the choice—or lack thereof—more bearable. But his father had grown impatient. Even a good man has his limits.

The northern city of Munro and its bittersweet memories were scarcely a week behind him. And it would take far longer than a few days to shake his heart free of Ellena.

No—not Ellena. Lady Howell. He must remember that. No more lively conversations with Miss Trenton. For she was Miss Trenton no more. She was utterly lost to him, forever the wife of that pompous viscount. The man had won, taken the one thing in the world William had been sure of.

His horse slowed to a trot as it recognized the hedge adjacent to its stable. He gave the animal its head, and it immediately lowered its neck and folded its lips around the last of the year's dandelions. William let it finish a mouthful, then clicked his tongue. "Walk on," he coaxed, steering the way to the stalls with gentle pressure from his calves.

He left his horse in the care of the stable hand and crossed the yard to the east entrance, knocking clods of mud from his boots with his whip as he walked. He smiled ruefully as he thought of the location of his rooms. "Facing east, so you may rise with the sun," his father had said. Mr. Marcus Cole had assumed his younger son would be just like Lawrence—hardworking, dedicated, predictable. Well, he couldn't *always* be right.

Leaning against the door frame, William tugged at his boots until his stockinged feet were free. He left the dirty articles there to be fetched and cleaned and padded across the thick rug to the inner door that led to his drawing room. His eyes fell to the writing desk, but there was no post awaiting him.

He threw himself onto the settee. There was nothing to *do* in Fernbridge. He could go riding, of course. But as for the rest, the options were small pickings: an afternoon aimlessly browsing the library; tea with his mother's friends; some project his father wanted to involve him in. Or dinner with Lawrence and his brood of children. That was arguably the worst—an evening in the company of the golden son, with his delightful wife and charming children. Oh, he was happy for them, of course. But it was just too sickeningly perfect. At least when he visited Charlotte in Munro, his sister was not a constant reminder of everything he had failed to be.

A knock on the door shook him from his thoughts.

"Come," he summoned.

A timid young woman in a starched uniform entered.

"Please, sir, I am to say the master wants you. He is in his study."

"How does he know...?" William began, then bethought himself. Mr. Cole had no doubt told the stableboy to report when his youngest had returned to the house. Even so, his father had an uncanny grasp on everything that happened under his roof.

William sighed. "I am on my way."

"Yes, sir. Although if I may say, sir?"

"Yes?"

"Um... you might want to put on some shoes."

William looked down at his feet, then back at the maidservant, who was blushing deeply.

"Thank you. That will be all."

"Yes, sir."

The maid fled, and William rose from his chair to collect the needed items from his dressing room. Then he sauntered casually down the corridor—a subtle rebellion against his father's summons.

"You wanted to see me?" he asked from the doorway of the study.

Marcus Cole looked up from a very neat pile of papers. His greying hair curled around his ears and neck, softening the long oval of his face.

"Ah, William, come in. Take a seat. Tell me all about your

visit with the Lockharts."

William grimaced. *Time to report.* He sat down reluctantly.

"What do you wish to know?"

"Don't be coy, William. You and I both know what we're about."

"Mr. Lockhart is well and asked after you," came the evasive reply.

"William." Mr. Cole's voice had an edge of warning to it.

William sighed and leaned back in his chair.

"Miss Lockhart is pleasant enough, if that is any recommendation."

"Good. I told you she is no longer the scrawny lass you remembered."

"She still has some odd notions."

Mr. Cole furrowed his brow. "Such as?"

William pictured Verity's pout at not being able to study further. Somehow, it seemed a betrayal to lay her secret desires bare to his father's scrutiny. Instead, he chose another, lesser flaw for a woman to have.

"She is preoccupied with the study of butterflies."

Mr. Cole gave a gruff laugh. "If that is her only fault, William, you have little cause for complaint."

"It was but a first meeting since childhood."

Mr. Cole pressed his lips firmly together. "I suppose you will make sure to visit just frequently enough to find something unacceptable about her."

"It shouldn't take long."

Mr. Cole rose from his chair and rapidly crossed the floor toward his son.

William flinched. He had gone too far. But his father had never been a violent man. Surely, he wouldn't...

Mr. Cole strode past him. He pulled the door closed with a soft click, then turned to face his son.

"William, let us speak plainly. You are a man now. But you are a man without purpose. You do not serve your king or country as a good Englishman should. You offer nothing back to your community, nor do you provide for a family. In short, you do nothing but gamble with your friends, flirt shamelessly, and ride about the countryside. What value is there in such a pointless existence?"

Ah, there it was. The speech of the long-suffering parent. A reminder of how worthless he was.

"Well, do you have nothing to say for yourself?"

"What would be the point?"

"The *point*, William, would be that you actually cared what happened to you!"

"Why bother when everyone else has such firmly decided plans for me? You tell me to find a wife, but you already have one in mind for me…"

Mr. Cole interrupted with an exasperated wave of his hands. "We only suggested Miss Lockhart because you spent an entire summer in Steeples, supposedly looking for a bride, but came home empty-handed! Even your little detour to visit your sister in Munro brought you no new prospects. Honestly, William, are you even trying?"

William was silenced by these words. He had believed Munro held the answer—a life with Ellena, the one woman for whom he would willingly be the better man. But it had ended badly. His sudden return to Fernbridge had not been his choice.

At least this one failure had been successfully hidden from his family. He suspected that his father's tolerance, though extensive, would find its limit if he knew the circumstances surrounding his departure from Munro.

Perhaps he should at least offer a semblance of effort. It would not do to test his parents to a breaking point.

He forced the words from his lips. "I will try, Father. If you wish, I will return to the Lockharts tomorrow."

His father breathed out his visible relief. It was at once re-placed with caution.

"No, no, that would lack propriety. You are not officially

courting Miss Lockhart yet and should not seem overly eager. But she turned eighteen last month, and her parents have indicated she will soon be allowed to come out into society. A visit to the family once a week would be neighborly and indicate a general interest for when the time is right. Besides, you could learn more about the duties of a vicar and what will be expected of you when Mr. Lockhart retires."

William bit his tongue. This was not the time to argue. He had gained a few weeks' reprieve. A handful of visits enduring Mrs. Lockhart's chatter was a small price for perhaps a month of freedom. And then? He had no idea. But he suspected that young Miss Lockhart would hold the key.

CHAPTER THREE

THE WEEK FLEW by, except for the interminable church service on Sunday morning. Mr. Lockhart was very sincere in his teachings, but he erred on the side of thoroughness. William's bottom was numb after three hours of sitting. He wondered if, as vicar, standing for as long was any better. He dreaded having to find out.

By Wednesday, he could delay no more. Exactly seven days had passed, and he knew he had to keep his side of the bargain. But the thought of sitting in Mrs. Lockhart's parlor, sipping tea, and making small talk for half an hour felt like a rare punishment indeed.

It was such a beautiful day too. Although it was mid-October, the afternoon chill had not set in. It really was better weather for riding than socializing indoors. Perhaps that was exactly what he should do. He could take the back route, across the meadow beyond the church. A good, hard canter was just what he needed to rid himself of his frustration.

The smell of earth and musty fallen leaves soon revived his senses, dulled from lounging about the house all day. A long stretch of green countryside spread before him and he shifted his leg to urge his horse into the rhythm of a canter. It picked up the pace, hooves thudding a beat onto the damp grass. William felt his cares fall away, his whole body releasing itself to the freedom of motion.

Perspiration began to form on his skin, the rushing air cooling it as they drove onward. A warning sounded in his head. He could not arrive at the Lockharts' door a sweaty guest. Reluctantly, he eased his mount into a trot and then a walk.

But he was not yet ready for company. If he remembered correctly, there was a pond at the bottom of the hill that signaled the end of the meadow. The vicarage was on the other side, out of sight. He could let his horse have a drink while he procrastinated. It was only a short walk to the Lockharts when he was ready.

William took the route through a copse of trees, pausing to enjoy the solitude of the shadows. He dismounted, removing his hat to allow the gentle breeze to dry his damp hair. He walked his horse beneath the canopy of leafy branches, with no one to answer to but himself, in an idyll of shade and freedom.

But when he emerged from the seclusion of the trees, he found he was not alone. William tightened his grip on his horse's trailing reins. There was a girl standing ankle-deep in the shallow water near the edge of the pond, unaware of his arrival. She made a strange picture, carrying a butterfly net and stalking something among the rushes. The edges of her dress were muddy and her hair was coming undone.

Her white-blonde hair.

"Miss Lockhart?" William asked with no small surprise.

She whipped around, her face flushed, guilt and horror in her eyes. They darted quickly to a bench a little way off, where stockings, shoes, a glass jar, and a sketchbook were gathered in a messy pile.

"Oh," she said. "Mr. Cole. You startled me."

"What are you doing here all alone?" William inquired, though he realized it was a foolish question. She was obviously catching butterflies.

"I am catching a tansy beetle."

Taken aback, William was driven to ask another question to

which the answer should have been clear. "But why are you in the water?"

Miss Lockhart offered him a quizzical look. "Because that is the easiest way to reach the beetle."

To his own amazement, William now found himself saying, "Do you need any help?"

She seemed to consider this. "That is very kind, but then who would hold your horse?"

William looked down at the reins in his hand, then up at the horse's soft muzzle. "Ah. Yes. My horse." He smiled. "It would seem I can be of no help, after all, except to watch over your... erm... belongings."

Miss Lockhart's pale skin took on a deep-pink hue.

"That won't be necessary. They are in no immediate danger."

She glanced back at the rushes.

"Is it still there?" William wanted to know, interested in spite of himself.

She nodded. Without taking her eyes from the object of her intent, she remarked, "I will be perfectly fine on my own. There is no need for you to hang about."

William squared his shoulders. "Am I to understand that you are trying to get rid of me, Miss Lockhart?"

She ignored him and carefully lifted her net over a section of the vegetation. With utmost concentration, she leaned forward, her arm sweeping down and across in a shallow dip. She straightened triumphantly and grabbed the net to seal in her little captive. Her dress dragged a few inches in the water as she waded back to shore.

She walked right past William, dripping unceremoniously, and deposited her catch in the glass jar with delicate fingers. Then, at last, she turned to him.

"Mr. Cole, I appreciate your gallantry in wishing to watch over me. But has it occurred to you that we would need watching ourselves if we were to remain here alone?"

"Well, that is very inconvenient." He frowned. "I should like to stay. My horse needs a drink, and the pond is right there."

"Our house is over the hill. Your horse could be cared for there just as easily."

"True, but then I would be announcing my arrival for a visit, and your mother would no doubt send for you to join us. So you see, Miss Lockhart, we both benefit from lingering here."

She stood still for some time, pondering the situation. Then she shrugged.

"Very well, I designate your horse as chaperone. While you are holding the reins, I do not see how you can get up to any mischief."

William grinned. "If you were any other woman, I might consider that a challenge."

She pressed her lips together primly. "I believe you, Mr. Cole. You have quite the reputation among the ladies."

"It is only ever harmless fun, I assure you," William protested, surprised at his sudden urge to defend himself. What did it matter what she thought of him?

"And you are certain all of your companions feel the same way—that it is harmless and fun?"

William felt a little irked. "I've never heard any complaints." Was it his imagination, or did his necktie feel oddly tight?

Miss Lockhart's icy-blue eyes bored into his. "You may be certain, Mr. Cole, that if a gentleman were to toy with my affections, I would voice my disapproval unequivocally."

"That… is good," William heard himself say.

"Right, then." She resumed the conversation in a more chatty manner, as if, with this understanding between them, they could now proceed pleasantly. "Would you like to know more about the tansy beetle?" She held up the jar for him to see.

"Er… yes." William felt off-kilter. Somehow, he had been scolded without taking the usual offense, and now he had agreed to study an insect instead of admiring the nape of the young lady's neck. It was all very unsettling.

"It should be burrowing underground now to hibernate," she

explained, looking at the emerald-shelled creature with what could only be described as genuine admiration. "But we've had such unseasonably good weather, I suppose their schedule is a little off. In the spring, you can see their eggs, like yellow rice grains, on the underside of tansy leaves. Here, look closely. You will notice that its antennae resemble a string of beads. They really are quite beautiful."

William, to be honest, was not as much awed by the beetle as he was intrigued by the flush of excitement in Miss Lockhart's cheeks as she spoke. Her eyes sparkled with fascination. She was, put simply, truly happy. And the way it lit up her face turned her pleasant features into radiant beauty.

"… and that is why I sketch them," she concluded, several sentences having been lost to William as his thoughts had wandered. But he could imagine the general tenet of her speech—she was a collector. After all, did she not say she had wished to study further? She was clearly drawn to the sciences. And, while he did not share her interests, he discovered that he now wished to encourage her.

A thought took hold of him—a way to establish rapport with her. He had promised his father to make an effort. It would involve some research, but he had little else to occupy his time. He smiled with satisfaction at his idea.

Miss Lockhart returned the smile shyly.

"I must say, Mr. Cole, I did not think you would appreciate my sentiments on the matter." She swallowed hard. "I am grateful that you do." Her smile faltered. "No one has ever grasped the importance this holds for me."

Her lip trembled and she turned away.

William was moved by her depth of feeling. There was so much more to the quiet Miss Lockhart than he had expected. In a surge of compassion, he reached out and touched her gently on the shoulder.

"Do not be sad, Miss Lockhart. Look, your daisy beetle is waiting to be immortalized. I… I shall leave you to your sketch while I let my horse satisfy his thirst."

"Tansy beetle," she corrected, wiping her eyes as she turned around.

"What?"

"You said, 'daisy beetle.' It's a tansy beetle."

"Tansy beetle."

"Yes," Miss Lockhart confirmed, putting down the jar and gathering up her sketchbook and pencil.

"I will try to remember that." William's voice was soft and sincere.

She looked up at him. "Thank you, Mr. Cole. This has been a rare conversation for me, and I will cherish it."

William cleared his throat.

"You may find comfort in knowing, Miss Lockhart, that you are not the only one whose dreams clash with their reality."

Embarrassed by his impulsive revelation, William tugged at the horse's reins and stepped down to the marshy water's edge. He did not turn around. He did not want Miss Lockhart to ask him to explain. It was with some relief that he heard the scratching of a pencil on paper.

He lingered by the soggy embankment, focusing on the browning grasses and the occasional plop of a frog. Try as he might, he could not understand the allure of all the buzzing, flapping activity of the wetland creatures that so successfully held Miss Lockhart's attention. But, then again, his father could not grasp why he felt more at home with the military than the church. To each his own, he supposed.

After several long minutes, Miss Lockhart called, "I'm done. Would you like to see?"

With horse once more in tow, William approached the bench. He took the proffered page and prepared to make some idle exclamation of praise. But the drawing needed no flattery. It was good work—excellent, even. The minutest of detail had been captured. The shading was masterful. Scribbled notes on the side made record of the date, as well as coloring to be added.

"You will paint this?" he asked.

"Yes. In my room. I cannot carry my easel and paints with me here. That would make it impossible for me to sneak away at all." Her gaze lowered. "You will not mention any of this to my parents, will you? It upsets them that I pursue this hobby. They consider it… unladylike."

"I assure you," William replied, "it will remain our secret."

He rather liked that they shared a confidence. It created a deeper connection between them. And the clandestine element was undeniably thrilling.

She flashed him a grateful smile but quickly grew serious again.

"It is best if I head home now. No one has seen us, but it would be… difficult to explain if someone did. Could you allow me ten minutes to achieve some semblance of decorum in my attire before you knock at our door? It would please my mother if, for once, she did not have to send Nellie in search of me."

William grinned and offered her a conspiratorial wink. "I will leave when you do and take the long way around the village. Anyone who knows you visit the pond with some regularity might wonder at me approaching from this direction and assume we must have met. Let us take every precaution."

Verity folded her arms. "You're enjoying this a little too much, Mr. Cole."

"You would not deny a man his little pleasures, Miss Lockhart."

"I am glad my discomfort provides you with amusement."

William would have teased her further, but he did not believe it would be well received. Instead, he offered a suggestion.

"Why do you not simply bring a maid or friend as chaperone so that you may paint at leisure? Your parents can surely not object to their daughter pursuing the arts. A few landscapes amongst your sketches of insects should provide ample excuse for your presence here."

She shook her head. "It is too late to convince my parents

that my interest lies elsewhere. I would not be fooling anyone."

"Well, then, perhaps it is time to stand your ground. If it is that important to you, you should not have to hide it."

Her sudden burst of ironic laughter startled him.

"I would have thought it was obvious to you." Miss Lockhart gestured at herself with a sweeping motion of her arm. "I am not a man," she said wryly. "Rebelling openly is not in the nature of a woman. Besides"—she cocked her head to the side as she looked at him—"I imagine you would not be here"—she indicated toward her home—"if you were able to stand up to *your* parents."

Her words should have cut him to the core. Rather, he marveled at her audacity. It reminded him of Ellena—bold, honest, forthright. He had not thought he would ever find someone with any qualities to compare. And yet Miss Lockhart seemed to have integrity by the bucketload.

Not only that, but she saw right through him. And called him out on it. William perked up at the thought. He liked a challenge. Not the mind-numbing challenge of enduring a dull partner, but the thrilling contest of matched wills. And Miss Lockhart, to his surprise and delight, was offering him just that.

"Fair point, Miss Lockhart," he answered. "But I still believe I have the advantage. My parents may have—shall we say—*suggested* sound prospects in this general direction. And perhaps I have not, until now, shared their inclination. But I find I am discerning their wisdom in this...*ahem*... venture."

"Come now, Mr. Cole, I think you mislead yourself. You do not strike me as a likely candidate for a clergyman. Why, on Sunday, you were fairly dozing in the pew. Shouldn't a future vicar at least have a passing interest in the service?"

William's eyes twinkled. "So, you were paying special attention to my actions on Sunday, were you? Should you not have been attending to your father's sermon instead? Or perhaps you were equally bored, and spying on me offered you some distraction."

"So you admit you were bored!"

"No more than any other warm-blooded soul after two hours of preaching," William countered. "You cannot tell me you recall a word of what was said in the second half of the service."

"I… Well… All right, yes, Father does go on a bit. But his heart is in the right place. You, on the other hand, would only offer a shorter service so that you could tend once more to your own interests. Being a vicar is more than words from the pulpit, you know. Father really cares about the community."

William's planned retort died on his lips. She had hit the nail on the head. He really did not feel much for the poor and the sick and the elderly. He was young and vibrant and wanted to live life to the fullest. A uniform, a sword, a horse—these were the images that arose when he thought of service. Young women swooning at his tales of battle. Old women wishing they were young again at the sight of him in his ceremonial dress. It was service to his country, yes, but also service to himself. He would not deny it.

Still, he was not discouraged. Perhaps Miss Lockhart was prize enough for his parents. If he found a wife from such decent stock, they might feel he was well on his way to respectability. Perhaps they would even reconsider his hopes of attaining a commission in the infantry. And, with any luck, he would be posted some distance from Fernbridge so he would not have to endure his father-in-law's endless sermons.

His optimism greatly bolstered by these thoughts, William decided it was time to put his best foot forward.

"Your father is a good man. He sets a fine example. I promise to be on my best behavior and try to learn from him. Will that suffice for afternoon tea?"

She frowned. "It will do for tea. But you should know, Mr. Cole, that I am not impressed by posturing. It is better to be yourself, with all your faults, and allow others to decide if they will accept you as you are."

"You do not wish me to be a better man?"

"Better than what?"

William scratched his forehead. "I don't know. Just better in general, I suppose. Isn't that what all women want—to improve upon men? It seems to be a favorite pastime among ladies."

Miss Lockhart shook her head. "That is the last thing I would want. If you are not motivated within yourself to achieve all you are able to, then a woman will not be able to create such an impetus within you. You will only resent her if she tries. Besides, I have just as great a desire to be accepted as *I* am. Perhaps it is another's voice that urges you to reach for what you do not want. It certainly is not mine."

Silence followed her words. Miss Lockhart was quite different to other young women her age, William noticed. Almost old in her wisdom. And yet her features glowed with youth—skin, mouth, neck—all so inviting. If she would take him as he was, he could be content. She was not Ellena, but she might be enough.

"Shall we go, then?" she asked, and for the first time, William noticed that she was shivering. Her damp dress and bare legs offered no warmth against the cooler autumn air, even with the sun bright in the sky.

"I wish I could lend you my coat, but it is not a feasible offer under the circumstances. There would be questions."

"Thank you," Miss Lockhart replied, clasping her arms about her to stave off the cold. "However, I will be home very shortly and there will be a fire in the drawing room. The chill will soon wear off. Go ahead. I must just gather my things, and I will be on my way."

"You are certain I should not wait?"

"There is no need. I will be but a few moments."

"Very well. I will see you soon then."

"Yes, very soon."

William walked his horse to the bench and—careful not to knock mud from his boots onto the young lady's belongings—he stepped up onto the wooden seat and slung himself into the saddle.

He turned to make sure his companion was on her way, but

she was not. Instead, she was removing the cork from the jar and watching as the dai... the *tansy* beetle flew out and across the water. There was something almost sacred in the way she watched its flight.

Feeling that he was intruding upon a private moment, William tapped his heel against the horse's side and moved on. He resisted the urge to look back.

There was no need. For the face of Miss Verity Lockhart was now ever before him.

CHAPTER FOUR

VERITY SAT ON her bed, poring over an engraving of caterpillars in the book *Erucarum Ortus*. The door was locked. What her mother didn't know could not upset her.

She was quite sure the assistant at the circulating library believed her father to be an avid entomologist, based on the frequency with which Verity fetched books for him on the subject. Fortunately, the vicar was always occupied with parish matters and did not have time to select anything for himself, relying on Verity's good taste. Thus, amongst biographies of great church leaders, or a treatise on sound economic management, there would be a book on zoological classification or the like, which was quickly slipped into Verity's shawl before being smuggled into her room.

This latest volume was the author's final work and reflected the usual high standards of Maria Sibylla Merian. However, Verity could not help but experience an odd discomfort whenever she considered Merian's work. Their lives were strangely similar, despite being separated by a full century. Both were artists and naturalists. Merian had been married at eighteen, and Verity knew her mother harbored similar hopes for her. But Merian's marriage had ended in divorce, and her life had been filled with financial struggle and resistance to her work. Fears that her own hopes might have a similar outcome lay shallow in Verity's heart.

She closed the book with a *thud*. She jumped when another *thump* echoed it.

"Verity? Are you resting, dear?"

Another knock on the door.

Verity sighed. If she *had* been resting, that would now have come to an abrupt end.

She slid the unsanctioned book under her bed and crossed the floor to the door. Unlocking it, she swung it open to find her mother with knuckles raised and a round "o" of surprise on her lips.

"You're awake!"

"I was reading."

"A novel?" Mrs. Lockhart asked suspiciously.

"A collection of art." Verity indicated the decoy book that lay upon her writing desk.

"Isn't that the same book you were looking at last week?"

"It's very good. I am learning much from studying it in greater detail."

Mrs. Lockhart sighed as her eyes lifted from the writing desk to the walls.

They were covered in watercolors of insects.

Verity was certain that every fiber in her mother's being willed her to take them all down. After all, they only encouraged an unsuitable hobby. And yet she said not a word. Although Verity steadily added more and more each month, until there was scarcely room to pin up even one new painting, her mother did nothing about it. Perhaps she knew that, as accommodating as Verity tended to be, there was a limit to her compliance. If her parents had forced her to remove the colored sketches, it would have made her miserable. It was the line in the sand, and they would not cross it.

But there was more to it than that. As Verity watched, her mother studied the collection on the wall, her expression fluctuating between a frown and naked admiration. Verity's heart pinched with pity. It had to be hard to have a daughter who did not follow the beaten path. She knew her mother loved her. Very much, in fact. And it was that love that kept her from doing what she knew would cause her daughter anguish. So the paintings stayed.

Today, there was something else on her mother's mind. Verity could see the sadness as she pulled her attention away from the pictures and focused once again on her daughter.

"Verity, dear, we need to talk."

It was inevitable. She was amazed it had taken her mother this long.

"All right," Verity answered, resuming her seat on the bed.

Her mother sat quite suddenly, as if the weight of the subject matter overwhelmed her. She had taken the chair at the writing desk, and her fingers absentmindedly stroked the cover of the book of art masters. Then her hands slid into her lap, where they appeared to hold her full attention for some time. Eventually, her head lifted, and she looked with renewed determination at her daughter.

"Verity, you know your father and I are getting on in years."

A rush of ice surged through Verity's veins. "Are you unwell?"

"No, no, thanks be to God. But, as you know, you came into our lives a little later than expected."

Verity breathed a sigh of relief. This information was nothing new.

"You were a lovely surprise to us in our... more mature years. But it also means we are slowing down a bit."

Verity bit back a grin. *Slowing down* was not a phrase easily applied to her mother.

"Your father wishes to retire—to take on a curate to assume his duties—so that he may enjoy a degree of complacency for once. After decades of devoted service, I think he has earned it."

Mrs. Lockhart paused and cleared her throat.

"The expense of a curate would necessitate greater economy for us. Unless... Unless you were safely tucked into a household of your own."

"And I suppose you have someone in mind to do this tuck-ing."

"Young Mr. Cole seems to have taken interest in visiting us of late…"

She saw the look on Verity's face and added hastily, "He could assume the role of curate immediately, and you could take your time with a courtship, get to know each other again. If something were to happen to your father and me, Mr. Cole's position as vicar would be secured—Sir Walter has said as much—and you would have the familiarity of your childhood home as the vicar's wife."

Verity laced her fingers. "I see you have given this a great deal of thought."

"We must be pragmatic at our age."

Pragmatic. That was what it boiled down to. Her dreams, her desires, were to be neatly set aside for pragmatism. Not only hers, but Mr. Cole's too.

"You should know," she informed her mother, "that Mr. Cole is not nearly as convinced about the clergy as you are on his behalf. Equally, I am not persuaded we are a good match. He is certainly charming. But he is more superficial than I should like in a man. I cannot, in good conscience, enter into matrimony with someone I do not fully respect."

"He is young. In time, he may surprise you."

"And if he does not? Let him surprise me first, and then I may reconsider. Besides, I am content on my own. I do not need new dresses or hats. Surely, I do not consume so great a portion of food that I will bankrupt you if I remain unwed a little longer?"

Mrs. Lockhart looked up the walls.

"Paper is expensive," she remarked pointedly.

Verity followed her gaze. "I will paint on the reverse sides. I can last months without new supplies. Please, Mother, let me find a better match. In my own time."

Her mother sighed. "You know full well your father and I

would never choose for you. But we are worried. Some of your choices thus far have not been in your best interests. You keep to yourself too much. And your fascination with insects is not… attractive."

Verity crossed her arms. "You mean attractive to men."

"Yes."

"Surely, not all men are discouraged by a woman with a mind." Verity pouted.

"No, dear. There is no shame in being a clever wife who can assist her husband in his duties. I believe your father has greatly appreciated my contributions over the years. But your endeavors are not practical, Verity. Even a man of science will want his wife to run his home, not be a partner in his studies."

"Don't say that!" Verity's head jerked up in alarm. Her mother's words had stabbed at all the truths she feared most. "If I cannot do what makes me happy when I am married, it is best I do not wed at all!"

"That is not sensible," her mother scolded. Then her voice softened. "Have you thought about your future when we are gone?"

"I don't want to," Verity declared unreasonably.

"If you have no husband, you will depend on your siblings in your spinsterhood. Would you prefer to cling to selfish interests and make yourself a burden to them?"

Verity hung her head. "No, Mother, I would not like that."

Mrs. Lockhart rose from her chair and came to sit beside Verity. She took her daughter's hand in hers and squeezed it gently.

"You are our precious child, and we want you to be happy. But happiness comes in more forms than you are willing to consider. Promise me you will think on what I have said."

Verity nodded.

"In the end," Mrs. Lockhart continued, "it is your choice. Just make sure that you are at peace with the consequences."

Her mother patted her hand and released it, rising to leave

the room. At the door, she glanced round, first at Verity, then at the walls papered with her daughter's passion. She shook her head and left the room.

A strangled scream rose in Verity's throat, and she fought it back. Fought it back like all the other things she had left unsaid.

Why couldn't life be easier? Why couldn't she have what she wanted? Choice! What a laugh! She could be a burden to her family or a servant to her husband's wishes. It was no choice at all.

Angry tears stung her eyes. She let them come. *It is my choice to cry*, she thought bitterly. Her heart swelled with rebellion. Her hands tightened into fists. She launched onto her feet and paced the room. Her paintings taunted her, reminders of stolen moments of joy and freedom. She pinned her gaze to the floor instead.

But Verity was not made to hold such rage, and the feelings soon seeped from her, leaving her exhausted. She curled up on her bed, hugging her arms about her. *Please, please, don't let Mr. Cole ask*. The words became a desperate mantra. For she knew—despite the illusion of choice—that if Mr. Cole asked for her hand, she would say *yes*.

CHAPTER FIVE

WILLIAM DISMOUNTED AT the gate. For the first time, he was looking forward to his visit with the Lockharts.

Removing the carefully wrapped package from his saddlebag, he patted the suede cloth that protected it and beamed boyishly. It was one of his prouder moments. William had written to the Entomological Society in Munro with a very specific request, and they had more than met his expectations. Miss Lockhart was in for a big surprise.

It had cost a pretty penny. Not much of his allowance remained for an evening of cards with the lads. But it would be worth it to see her face when she received her gift.

He straightened his cravat and ran his fingers through his hair. His throat was a little dry, and he swallowed to moisten it. When he knocked on the door, his heart pounded along with the sound.

The stout, young maidservant let him in, her attention at once on the mysterious item in his possession.

"Shall I take your coat, sir?" She accepted it from him, her focus lingering on his hands and what they held.

The maid led him to the parlor, then left to return to her duties. William sat down, placing the parcel on the seat next to him, but stood again immediately as the family arrived in the cozy room.

The parcel received curious glances. However, they were all too polite to inquire after the contents. Instead, Mrs. Lockhart called for tea, and Miss Lockhart resumed the embroidery she had left on the chair.

"It is so good to have you visit with us again," Mrs. Lockhart began. "Mr. Lockhart has benefitted immensely from having the company of a gentleman for a change, especially when it has not required his attention on some parish matter. A hearty conversation is always invigorating, is it not?"

"Certainly," William agreed, though he did wonder if the vicar's few quietly spoken sentences over the past several weeks qualified as conversation. Of course, he was not complaining. He had expected lectures regarding the life of a clergyman and the responsibilities he might come to expect if he entered the church. But Mr. Lockhart had not re-introduced the topic that William had expressed such doubts over. Maybe he could see what his wife could not. Or, perhaps, he simply couldn't get a word in edgeways.

Mrs. Lockhart pressed on. "We did not see you in church this past Sunday. I hope you were not ill."

"I was a little under the weather, but it was nothing serious."

William remembered that headache all too well. It had been the result of a bottle of poor brandy and a very late night, or rather, an early morning. His father had been furious when William's valet could not rouse him and had only paused in his admonishment to attend the service himself. The only good that had come of it was an exasperated comment that perhaps, after all, the military life would teach him discipline.

William looked across at Miss Lockhart. Had she noticed his absence too? Had she wanted to share a knowing smile that they were both thoroughly bored by the second hour of the sermon?

She was strangely quiet today. In truth, it was hard to be chatty when Mrs. Lockhart offered such strong competition. But her mother usually drew her into the conversation, and she always complied. Today, however, Miss Lockhart was focused entirely on her embroidery. It was currently on a circular frame, though what its ultimate purpose would be, William could not guess. The domestic activities of ladies were something of a mystery to him. Be that as it may, Miss Lockhart gave all of her attention to the careful stitches she made and none at all to him.

Normally, William would find a way to coax a young lady's focus to be trained on him. He might comment on her handiwork, then compliment her skill, his eyes lingering on her fingers as he praised her fine touch. Soon, he would draw a delicate blush from her cheeks, and she would be thinking only of him and his subtle cues.

He was considering whether Miss Lockhart would permit such playfulness or view it as inappropriate, when he noticed the pattern she was stitching. It had started as a series of leaves, their curves winding along the edge of the small hoop. But two of the leaves were now side by side like wings, and sprouting between them was the unmistakable segmented form of an antenna.

Too late, he found himself staring.

Mrs. Lockhart noticed at once.

"Oh, you see what a talent our daughter has with a needle, Mr. Cole. She really has quite the gift for…"

She spied the design.

"Ah… aha ha… I see you are creating leaves on a *twig*, dearest," she declared, though her flustered manner suggested she knew it was no floral scene, but a beetle being brought forth. "How… original," she concluded weakly.

The clattering of cups on a tray signaled the arrival of Nellie with the tea. While the men looked up at the plate of biscuits, an urgent scuffle ensued among the women. William only just noticed Miss Lockhart's embroidery disappearing behind her mother's pillow.

"Mr. Cole," came the flustered voice of his hostess, "will you take sugar?"

Out of the corner of his eye, William could see her daughter quietly fuming. But, as always, she kept her thoughts to herself.

He knew that feeling. He understood it. He wanted Miss Lockhart to see he understood.

"I won't take tea just yet, thank you." He turned to pick up the package. "With your permission, there is something I would like to give Miss Lockhart."

Mrs. Lockhart's raised eyebrows met his request.

"That is very kind of you," Mrs. Lockhart said with a slightly worried smile, turning uncertainly to her husband. "I don't know if…"

"It's all right," Mr. Lockhart reassured her. "Mr. Cole would not stoop to offend our household with an inappropriate token. We may be certain of his good intentions." Still, the good-natured vicar paid rather more close attention to his guest's actions as William leaned forward and handed the gift to Miss Lockhart.

She sat for several moments, contemplating the unwrapped parcel.

"Well, go on, open it," said her mother, apparently more eager to see the gift than its recipient was.

Miss Lockhart's fingers began to unfold the suede cloth that covered it, revealing a shallow, rectangular box. She pulled off the lid and reached inside to lift out the contents. There was a soft rustle as she did so. She discovered several layers of paper tissue wrapping, and these, in turn, she carefully removed. At last, the corner of a frame peeked through the final layer of paper, hinting that the mystery would soon be solved.

From the depths of the many protective layers, Miss Lockhart pulled a boxed frame with a glass front. Within, there was a large butterfly, nearly two inches across. Expertly mounted, its powder-blue shape was on full display, showing its black edging and several black speckles on its front wings.

A bronze plate at the bottom of the frame gave the butterfly's Latin name.

"*Maculinea arion*," she whispered. "It's a large blue."

"A large, blue what?" her mother wanted to know.

"I believe that is its common name," William explained. "I

purchased it from the Entomological Society in Munro. They sent a detailed letter, explaining its name and habitat and observed behaviors. I must say, it was most informative. I can bring the letter with me on my next visit. But I suspect Miss Lockhart might already know a great deal on the subject."

"It certainly is a fine specimen," Mr. Lockhart commented, craning his neck to see the object in his daughter's hands.

She stared blankly at it.

"It's dead." Her voice was strained.

"Well, yes," said William, somewhat miffed by her response. To be honest, he had expected excitement, gratitude… *something*. He had thought to bring that flush of joy upon her face that he had seen at the pond.

"I thought you could add it to your collection," he said, his confidence in pleasing her greatly diminished.

"My 'collection'?" She lifted her head and looked at him with doleful eyes. "I have no such collection."

"Yes, you do. You have your paintings. But I thought…"

His voice trailed off. He had given up a secret—their secret. He should not have known about her paintings. He had never been in her room, and her mother discouraged all conversation on the topic when in company. He cursed himself for his careless speech. Now there would surely be awkward questions.

But Miss Lockhart did not even seem to notice the slip. Her attention was somewhere else entirely.

"You think I collect the… the… *bodies* of these beautiful creatures?"

A warning shot up William's spine. Something was very wrong. He just didn't know exactly what it was.

"I know you are a student of nature," he explained. "I thought you would be pleased to observe this specimen more closely. I understand it is quite rare."

Miss Lockhart trembled at his words.

"Yes, it is rare. And now there is one fewer of them to brighten the world."

William was taken aback. He had not thought of that.

"Perhaps the collector simply found it," he said hopefully.

She shook her head. "Such a perfect specimen did not die naturally." Her lips tightened. "Someone was very pleased to discover it and could not wait to boast of their achievement. I imagine it was the subject of a talk offered at the Society's next meeting." She looked down at the frame in her hands. "But, for all their discussion, they did not really *see* it."

"Verity, dear," Mrs. Lockhart said to intervene, "I don't think we can hold poor Mr. Cole responsible for how the butterfly was acquired. It was still very thoughtful of him to encourage you where others might not have."

Her meaning was clear, and her daughter lifted her head in answer.

"I don't want to be encouraged. I want to be understood!" She whipped her head about to face him. "I thought *you* understood!"

Her face burned with emotion—anger, betrayal, loss. William faltered in response.

"I... I thought I did."

Miss Lockhart bit her lip. Tears welled in her eyes.

"You don't understand what really matters to me. Maybe no one ever will."

Her words rang in his ears. He had heard them before. They were almost Ellena's exact words. The same accusation. The same shock to his very core.

How had it come to this? How had he made the same mistake twice? Every time he sought a deeper connection, everything fell apart.

"Verity," came the surprisingly quiet voice of Mrs. Lockhart, "I think you are judging Mr. Cole rather harshly. He has hardly had a chance to know you at all, and I'm sure that..."

Miss Lockhart stood abruptly, placing the controversial gift firmly on the chair as a clear rejection.

"Please excuse me," she said. "I do not feel well."

Before her parents could protest, she fled the room, a stifled sob audible as she reached the staircase.

Mrs. Lockhart wrinkled her brow, her hands clasped tightly together. But no words came.

Her husband rubbed his hand across his face and huffed out a deep breath. "I apologize for our daughter, Mr. Cole. She is more passionate than most people realize. But that does not excuse her behavior here today. I assure you it will not happen again."

But William did not want his assurances. He did not care for any of this. He had never desired Miss Verity Lockhart in the first place. She was just as much trouble as Ellena, with just as little reward for his efforts.

He should never have let his father bully him into considering this match, this family. He had known what he wanted, and this had certainly not been it. But he had tried. His father could not say he hadn't kept his promise. And she had rejected him.

Well, perhaps now his father would finally hear him. It was good riddance to Miss Verity Lockhart, and welcome to his life as a soldier. Maybe she had even done him a favor.

He became aware that Mrs. Lockhart was staring at him. It was not a particularly friendly stare. She seemed to be making up her mind about something.

"Mr. Cole," she said eventually, "I know that Verity's ideas can be challenging. I also believe that the right person could meet that challenge. It would be a pity to give up before one has truly started."

Was she judging him? William's chest swelled with indignation. Of all the nerve! It was her daughter who was making things difficult. Miss Lockhart was clearly disinterested in him. If she liked him at all, she would have loved his gift, appreciated his effort. Why should he pursue her like some lovesick puppy, only to have her kick at him in her own misery?

He had thought they had something in common. Enough to explore a future together. But she was a self-absorbed child. And her parents indulged her. She was not for him.

He stood and bowed to them. A final civility.

"I think it is best if I were on my way. My presence here only causes discomfort."

"Not at all, my good fellow!" exclaimed the vicar. "You are most welcome in our home. Verity's reaction was unfortunate, I'll admit, but she would not wish you away. Young women will have their little moods. It will pass."

Mrs. Lockhart did not look at her husband. Her silence condemned him.

That was where their daughter had gotten her stubbornness from. William could see it now. The last thing he wanted was a wife like Mrs. Lockhart—all bluster and opinion.

"Thank you, sir," he replied with some pity for his host, "but I will take my leave. It would be easier for Miss Lockhart to settle without my presence to frustrate her."

"You must do as you see fit," Mrs. Lockhart said primly before her husband could interject. "Please send our regards to your parents."

"Gladly," he replied without an ounce of gladness.

William collected his hat and coat from the entrance. He was seen to the door by both Lockharts—a strained farewell. Dissatisfied muttering echoed after him as he strode down the path to the gate. He did not look back. He would never look back. The Lockharts had seen the last of him.

A bee buzzed about his head as he mounted his horse. He waved it away with his hat. No more need to pretend an interest in miscellaneous flying things. No more need to woo a strange, pale slip of a girl.

And yet he felt strangely empty without her blue eyes looking into his soul. She had seen what was there—and not run.

Not until today.

She had seemed so lost, and he had not known how to reach her…

He shook himself mentally. No, no, no. He was better off without her. She was too much work. What he needed was a simple life: a uniform, a horse, a sword.

His father would just have to understand.

CHAPTER SIX

VERITY SAT CROSS-LEGGED in the disused attic room. She had not meant to be here this long. But lately, nothing was turning out as expected.

She threw a glance toward the framed butterfly that had caused all the trouble. It lay—wrapped up once again, shrouded in its suede cloth—on a pile of dusty, empty hat-boxes. She had a good mind to bury it. It was a dead thing, and she didn't want it. But it was a costly item, and Verity had a frugal mind. It really should be returned to Mr. Cole. She owed him that much.

More importantly, she owed him an apology. He had meant well. She knew that. It wasn't his fault that she had lived a lie for years now, pushing her feelings down, out of reach. It was exhausting. Her conversation with her mother had heightened her frustration. Verity felt she was living on a knife's edge, about to fall and slay herself on the altar of everyone else's expectations. If her nerves had not been so jangled during Mr. Cole's visit—if she could have found the words there and then—she would have explained all of this to him.

She couldn't blame her mother, either. She had meant well too. Everyone had meant well. That made it so much worse. If they had been unreasonable or mean-spirited, she could rage against them. That, at least, would offer some relief from the relentless suppression of her own desires—the plans no one else approved of.

Mr. Cole could relate to this. That much she knew. At the pond, she had gained the impression he'd understood more. It had been a profound moment, a sense of coming home. Here was someone who could see who she was at her very core. For once, she hadn't felt a need to defend herself. He had grasped the essence of her and accepted it. Or so she'd thought.

His gift told her differently. He'd thought she was a collector! How could he have so thoroughly misjudged her? It was true that she wanted to capture the beauty and mystery of these tiny creatures. But she would never destroy them and put them on display for her own selfish pleasure. She recalled the image of the pinned butterfly with a shudder. Why did Mr. Cole not see the horror of it?

Men were—Verity decided—a bizarre species. Their need to kill things and present trophies of their conquests were concepts utterly alien to her. But men seemed to think women should find it all very flattering. She rubbed her brow with her fingertips. It was no different when they spoke. Or courted. It was all about displaying their prowess. Just like peacocks, fanning their best qualities for a peahen's attention. She had to admit, with some embarrassment, that most women apparently liked it.

Take these letters, for example. She held one open in her lap. She didn't quite know what to make of it. Several others lay scattered on the floor about her. She had been searching for a place to store the butterfly specimen where its presence would not torment her until it could be returned to Mr. Cole. However, instead of a convenient corner of space in this old travel trunk, she had found a stack of letters. All addressed to her mother. All signed with the rather cryptic initials "T.L."

Verity knew no one with these initials—something for which she was grateful. If she had known the gentleman who wrote so… so *intimately* to her mother, she would have been too mortified to look him in the eye. Whoever he was, she was in no doubt that they had been in love. Passionately so. At first, the contents had rather alarmed Verity, until the date had confirmed that they had been written before her parents had been wed.

But where had the gentleman gone? Why had they not made a life together? His words expressed such devotion and exclamations of romance that Verity could not imagine he had run off and deserted her. Had he died? Had his or her parents forbidden their match? Why, when there was such a man pining for her, would her mother have married a vicar? Verity's father was a devoted husband, but he was not inclined to declarations of affection. His flame was more a steady glow of embers, offering comfort.

Verity re-read the page in her hands.

My Dorothy, my dearest, my own sweet love.

It has been two hours since last I saw you, held your delicate fingers in mine, cupped your hand to my cheek. Its warmth lingers.

A similar heat crept up Verity's neck and bloomed upon her face.

I cannot believe your parents would spirit you away to Steeples for a full fortnight! The cruelty of your absence is almost impossible to bear. Every minute is an eternity.

Verity rolled her eyes at the hyperbole. The gentleman's prose was rather excessive for her taste. But she kept on reading, fascinated.

I pass by your house, knowing your laughter does not brighten its rooms. It is now the good fortune of the people of Steeples to share your company and find joy in it. I know you have promised your heart to me, but how can any man resist you? Will you still belong to me when two long weeks have crawled by?

Verity detected a hint of jealousy in his ardor. Had the young

Dorothy sensed it too—felt cautious of it? Had it festered, ultimately severing their bond?

It was very bothersome not to know. However, she did not feel it right to question her mother on the topic. These letters had been concealed, the gentleman never mentioned—not even in a fond, nostalgic way. And yet her mother had kept the letters. There were words here she had not wanted to forget.

Had she had a choice, Verity wondered, in marrying the young vicar, John Lockhart?

It shouldn't have mattered. Their situation had likely been very different to her own. But it *did* matter. Perhaps her mother understood what she was struggling with better than Verity had realized.

Suddenly, it became very important for Verity to know. She began to gather up the letters, folding them up and stacking them once again into a neat pile, the time-bleached ribbon binding them together with a bow. She would present them to her mother, demand an explanation for the stranger's initials, drag the story from her.

Verity stood up, took three confident steps toward the door, and paused.

What right had she to stir up old hurts? Her mother was not unhappy now. The letters were likely forgotten after all these years. But seeing them might awaken pain, long buried. Verity wanted answers, but not at the expense of someone else's peace of mind.

She turned slowly and retraced her steps. Kneeling, she lifted the heavy lid of the trunk and returned the letters to their hiding place. Beside them, perched on the hatboxes, the shrouded butterfly rested.

She missed William Cole. She wished he were here to talk to. She wanted to clear the air, yes, but she also wanted to talk with him about the letters. And regret. And hope.

There was much she wished to confide in him. With the ease they had known by the pond. Before the gift. Before she had run from the room like a wounded child. This time, she would make him understand everything. She needed him. His irreverence for predictability. His effort always to jest so that no one could see how he struggled. He was wonderfully flawed. She had no need to pretend with him.

Just a few more days, and he would be back. She would keep an eye out for him, intercept him at the gate. By the time they reached the house, all would be well between them. They would be the greatest of friends. All would be well.

With this refrain echoing in her soul, she all but skipped down the stairs. Even her mother's reminder to practice the pianoforte did not dull her mood. The next day, she took baskets of provisions to the poor and did not once think to visit the pond instead. Mr. Cole's visit would be distraction enough when it came.

Even when he was absent from church once again, she gave it little thought. Perhaps his father had eased some of the pressure on his youngest son. Likewise, Monday and Tuesday were of no consequence. It was only when Wednesday arrived—the day he always chose to call—that Verity began to experience the first pang of nerves. Still, she told herself, it was silly to fret so. In a matter of hours, all would be well.

CHAPTER SEVEN

Fernbridge, November 1814

MARCUS COLE PACED irately across the floor of his study. His wife lingered beside his desk, her hands clasped at her narrow waist, anxious eyes upon their son.

William stood waiting like a soldier at ease. His fists flexed behind his back, but his face showed no emotion.

"What do you mean, you won't go back?" his father demanded. "You promised to call on them every week. It's already Thursday. They will be expecting you."

"I don't see the point."

"You don't see the..." Mr. Cole turned to his wife, an arm waving in agitation. "Do you hear that, Harriet? He doesn't see the point."

"William," his mother responded in her usual dulcet tone, her voice several degrees calmer, but concern equally evident in her tone. "Miss Lockhart is about to come out, at which time you may court her formally. It will be much easier then. You could enjoy a ride alone—in an open carriage, of course. You could discuss your future together. You will see. It will not be so awkward."

"Honestly, Mother, I cannot imagine anything *more* awkward."

"What can you mean, William? You have never been uncomfortable around young women before."

"I haven't considered marriage to any of them before, either." *Except Ellena.* But they never needed to know that.

"You haven't considered marriage because you never take anything seriously," his father grumbled. "In six months, you will be of age, but you still act like a schoolboy. You lark about all day with not the slightest direction in your life."

William clenched his jaw. "I have asked if I might apply for a military commission through my uncle, but you will not hear of it."

"The military is just another of your schemes to play at being a man. It's all about riding your horse and carousing with the men."

"I would be serving king and country. Is that not what you expect of me?"

William's mother clutched his arm so suddenly, it startled him.

"Please don't speak of going to war." Her eyes were wide and pleading. "Some of our lads don't even reach the American continent and are drowned at sea. Many others fight and die on foreign soil." She shook her head sadly. "So many good lives have been lost."

"I suppose I am quite safe, then," William answered, "since you are both convinced I have no redeeming qualities."

His mother flinched. "Do not say such things. You are our own, dear boy." Her chin began to tremble. "We would never want any harm to come to you."

"Which is why," his father added, "we are trying to save you from yourself. It is time you settled into respectability. Marriage and a dignified occupation will develop in you a greater soberness of character. Without it, you are likely to fritter away your youth on gambling and womanizing." He rubbed the back of his neck and let out a long sigh. "Quite frankly, I do not understand how you have allowed yourself to succumb to all manner of decadence. We have given you careful example, taught you the value of virtue."

A sneer slid across William's lips. "You mean, I have not behaved like Lawrence. Surely, with such perfection in one son, you might have expected disappointment in the other."

William's father halted his patrolling of the floor. He looked hard at his youngest child, as if searching for the truth.

"Your brother is not perfect," he said eventually. "He has made errors of judgment over the years. But he has learned from his mistakes. If only you could…"

"Be half the man he is?" William asked bitterly.

His father straightened to his full height, which was not particularly tall. But the motion was one William knew well. It was always the precursor to an indignant lecture on his terrible attitude. He held up his hand to stop his father's inevitable speech.

"Don't bother. I've heard it all before—I should know better; I should reach higher. I am an unmitigated mystery to you. Lawrence learned these lessons, so why can't I? Well, I'll tell you why, Father. I am not Lawrence. I have different interests, different needs. I want to take the road less traveled, for better or worse. You think that if I enter the clergy, I will conform to your pious expectations. But I won't. I will merely be a terrible vicar. And everyone in the community will know I am a terrible vicar. They will resent me for it because they could have had someone who cared, but I was too unprincipled to resist your wishes. That, you see, is the extent of my good character—to know my weaknesses and not foist them on others."

A long silence followed these words. William was amazed there was no immediate retort from his father. His mother would not have spoken while his father scolded. But, even now, while her husband remained mute, she, too, said nothing. William's earlier rash words had injured her deeply. He'd known they would. But he was sick of holding back the resentment that bubbled and frothed within. He would make amends to her later. She deserved as much. But right here and now, he would stand his ground.

He watched his father, expecting the flood waters to burst any moment. The air in the room thickened.

Mr. Cole stood motionless at first. Then, with a slow collapse of his shoulders, his gaze fell. His mouth softened. His breathing slowed. His entire body gave in to a gradual resignation. "I see you cannot be persuaded," he murmured. He turned, found the arm of a chair and, reaching down, allowed it to guide him into the seat. "Very well," he said, "I will write to your uncle. If a commission can be purchased, we will see that it is done."

William held his breath. It was happening. It was finally happening! He wanted to rush forward and embrace his parents with joy and gratitude. But they were so downcast, he resisted the urge. No matter, no matter. They would soon recover. They would see his excitement as he prepared for the life he wanted. They would realize the wisdom of their decision. At last, he was free of all restrictive expectations!

"But what of Miss Lockhart?"

William's soaring relief came crashing to the ground at his mother's question. Numb disappointment echoed in his voice.

"I had assumed you only recommended the match because she was the vicar's daughter. Now that I am no longer entering the church... she is not... It's just..." He drew a steadying breath. "I thought to look elsewhere for a match of my own choosing."

"Why?" His mother's brow pleated. "I thought you were getting along pleasantly enough."

William hesitated. "I do not think that sufficient reason to propose marriage."

"Then you do not have an understanding? She is not expecting to begin a formal courtship with you shortly?"

"Quite the opposite. Even if I asked, I do not think she would have me."

Mr. Cole muttered from behind his wife, "Even this you have managed poorly. She has all but been offered to you on a plate."

William stepped to the side so that he might address his father face-to-face.

"She is not the easy prize you might think. I did my best, whether you believe it or not. If she will not have me, what am I to do?"

His mother's frown deepened. "And you are certain of this? You have spoken to her and she has made her feelings known to you? I must say, William, such premature actions are not proper. Not only should the subject of courtship not have come up, but how have you managed to speak so intimately to her? Surely, her parents have not allowed you to visit without appropriate supervision?"

There were no suitable answers to these questions, William knew. The conversation by the pond was a secret, at Miss Lockhart's request. He was not about to betray her confidence. And the whole butterfly debacle was too painful to relive. Besides, his parents would tell him he was overreacting—anything to get him back in line with their expectations of him. No, he was not going to marry Miss Lockhart. And that was final.

"No, Mother," he replied, "nothing happened to shame either of our families. In short, Miss Lockhart has had no enthusiasm for my visits. She is very studious and quiet. No doubt she senses in me the very same concerning traits Father has so frequently pointed out. There seems little purpose in pursuing someone who does not wish to be pursued."

A sudden inspiration cheered him, and he spoke it aloud before stopping to think. "Perhaps I will find a wife in the Americas. My military career might prove even more successful than hoped."

At the mention of the war-ravaged continent, Mrs. Cole grew quiet once again. Her husband stood and placed his arm gently about her shoulder. She lifted her hand to touch his, leaning her head toward him. They stood for several moments, brows touching, in a cocoon of unspoken reassurance. Then Mr. Cole looked up at his son.

"It is no secret that we do not want this for you. We have always assumed our children would take after us and make choices that we see the wisdom of. We do not agree with the path you are treading, nor the future you seek for yourself." He took a deep breath and released it heavily. "However, there is one thing you have failed to grasp. Despite the fact that our hopes and yours diverge on almost every point, we still only want your happiness. We worry that the course of action you have sought will ultimately cause you sorrow instead. But there comes a time when one must release the reins of parenthood and pray the horse does not break his leg."

His face grew flushed. William was amazed to see a film of tears form in his father's eyes. He watched in confusion as the man—who had only ever shown restraint and composure—now fought to control the tremor in his voice.

"It is essential—especially with you heading into the jaws of danger—that you fully understand your worth to us. You seem convinced we prize one son over the other. This is simply not true. You are not alike, certainly. But that is a matter of personality, not value. We love you equally, William. However, we do worry for you more, and perhaps I have erred by expressing that with some frustration. For that, I am sorry."

William did not know what to say. He was spared an uncomfortable silence when his mother grabbed his hands, pulled them to her cheek, and shed warm tears onto them.

"Oh, William, our dear, sweet boy. You must come back to us safely. I do not care if it is with a bride or not. Only come home all in one piece."

William smiled gently. "I haven't left yet, Mother. And there will be several weeks—possibly months—of training before I do. Perhaps the war will be done before I set sail, and I will be obliged to fritter away my time attending dances and picnics with eligible ladies in good old England."

"I should like that." She sniffed. She fished a handkerchief from her sleeve and held it delicately beneath her nose. Her husband, who had regained his composure, patted their son on the back.

"I shall write to your uncle today," Mr. Cole said, a measure of his businesslike self returning. "It will take some time for the request to go through the proper channels. The sooner we begin the process, the sooner we will know whether this endeavor can succeed."

Something of a grin spread across his face. It was not an expression he had often had cause to display. William was mildly taken aback by the sight of it, until his father's speech followed with equal warmth.

"That should give your mother ample opportunity to fuss over you and spoil you. You will be home for at least another month. Let us make the most of it as a family. What do you say?"

William basked in the new mood of optimism that had sprung up between them.

"I could not ask for more," he replied.

"Hmm, I expect you will get more, whether you ask for it or not. Your mother will likely have you fattened up on all your favorite dishes. Cook is going to have her hands full."

With good relations restored, they parted amicably for the afternoon. William's father returned to his desk to begin the promised letter, and his mother—no doubt inspired by her husband's teasing comment—went to speak to Cook.

William, free for the first time to do exactly as he pleased, fetched his horse. It wasn't long before they were galloping across the meadow, the grass a blur beneath them. Exhilaration flooded through his entire body, and his horse sensed it, pulsing its hooves on the turf, its stride lengthening as it reached for more speed. On and on they raced, released from all care.

After two wonderful, invigorating miles, the animal slowed, and William led it to a stream for a refreshing drink. He swung down from the saddle and stooped to splash a cupped handful of the icy water onto his face.

"*Ribbit*," said a frog, disturbed by his presence.

"And a good afternoon to you too, my fine fellow," William replied, tipping his hat to the amphibian. "Shouldn't you be off taking your winter's rest?"

As if reminded of this very idea by his visitor, the frog slowly hopped toward a patch of damp, fallen leaves.

The horse nickered. William looked up briefly, saw all was well, and returned his focus to the patch of leaves. The frog was gone.

Or was it?

William stared hard. The tiniest shifting motion alerted him that the little creature was exactly where he had last seen it, its outline barely visible against the shading of the background that masked it. Mottled browns and greens blended perfectly with the decaying vegetation.

"Well, aren't you clever!" he marveled. "I'm certain Miss Lockhart would love to paint you."

He pulled up, scowling. Now why had he thought of her? He had seen any number of frogs in his life. They had certainly never made him think of a woman before. And he particularly did not want to think of *her*. But there she was, edging in on his subconscious.

This would not do. Already, Ellena haunted him. He did not need another piece of his heart twisted with regret.

A nagging voice reminded him that Miss Lockhart could still be his, if he but persisted. He pushed it away. He did not want her. She was too strange. Too hard to figure out. Those piercing-blue eyes saw too much, demanded too much.

Even now, he felt them reaching, reaching, into his soul. They called to him. He could see her, dripping from the pond, not a care in the world, blue eyes focused on a tansy beetle. She had shared her most secret self with him, cried with joy to have someone truly know her.

But he didn't, did he? He had missed some critical element that made all the difference. No, she was better off turning her deep gaze upon someone else. That gaze that cut right through him, peeled back the layers, made him feel exposed. And yet at the same time, it was oddly comforting to be seen like that. No pretense. No games.

No, no. It was too hard. He needed the games, the chase. Her honesty was too brutal. He needed masking, like the frog. He wasn't ready to be vulnerable again.

Time. He needed time.

With a surge of irritability, he leaped onto his horse, urging it once more into a canter, then a gallop. It was a frenzied flight. Away from her. Away from Ellena. Away from himself. But he outran none of his accusers. And when he returned to the stables, it was without the triumph and satisfaction he had known when he had left.

He ate his dinner without enthusiasm, retiring early to his room. The bed held no hope of relief, and he imagined himself tossing about, the sheets wrapping about his legs like weeds in a pond.

He sat, trying to read, then stood and paced and sat again. Eventually, he donned his coat and hat and strode agitatedly to the stables, where he saddled his horse himself. Within minutes, he was riding down the lane in the deepening night.

Within the heart of the village, music filtered from the carriage inn. There would be several men willing for a game of cards, ready to drink and laugh and not talk of feelings. Or failures. Already, William felt the pressure lift from his chest.

Ah, this is more like it.

He handed his horse to the ready hands of a servant boy and stepped inside the bright room. The door closed behind him. It shut out all thoughts of hair like moonlight, or clever hands that painted frogs.

The noise of laughter and conversation was deafening compared to the silent night beyond the doors. The numbness of his ears spread to his heart.

William pulled up a chair. And exhaled.

CHAPTER EIGHT

VERITY WAITED IN vain for Mr. Cole's return. After a week, she stopped waiting.

So, he was done with her. She could hardly blame him. She hadn't made it easy. She had never been very good at pretending. He could not possibly have been under any illusion that they were a love match. Seeing him flounder in his attempt to please her had only driven that home. To be honest, there was a measure of relief in his rejection.

Still, she had hoped for the possibility of friendship. They could both use a little of that—some support rather than further demands. Though ill-suited to each other for marriage, they still had enough in common for something simpler and, in her opinion, more meaningful. She wished she had had a chance to tell him that.

Despite that awful moment in the parlor, when the words had stuck in her throat, she had come to think of William Cole as the one gentleman with whom she could speak freely. That was a privilege she did not want to lose. She had planned an apology and an explanation and the polite return of his gift. Perhaps he could recoup a decent portion of his money—he should not be out of pocket for her sake. She did not want to be the cause of any further regret for Mr. Cole.

But his continued absence told her it was too late for any of that. Clearly, he did not have the stomach for her.

He'd been markedly absent at the little party her parents had hosted after church for her coming out. She had not wanted anything glamorous. What was the point if she did not seek a match? She did not hope for a dance as an excuse to touch hands. Nor did she desire to be presented before eager potential mothers-in-law at a large dinner. Her parents had insisted that *some* sort of event should mark the occasion, and Verity had relented at the offer of a small tea for close friends and neighbors.

Mr. and Mrs. Cole had attended, though their shame at their wayward son's absence had been clear. *"A little under the weather"* was the excuse they'd offered for the lack of his company. Only Verity and her parents had known this to be a lie. So they'd offered their sympathies and wished him a speedy recovery as if, they, too, had believed him to be ill.

It seemed, however, that his "illness" persevered.

"Should I not at least send the butterfly back?" she asked her mother when another week had passed. "He knows I do not want it. I could offer my regret for my reaction on that day and try to heal some wounds."

Her mother looked up from her sewing.

"Returning his gift would renew the injury," she said firmly. "You have bruised his sensibilities, Daughter. And, I suspect, even if he did return, you would do it again, however unintentionally. Unless you intend to welcome him into your heart without reservation, you should not offer him hope."

"I don't want to encourage a romance," Verity replied firmly. "I only wanted to undo some of the harm I did. I hadn't meant to offend him."

Mrs. Lockhart put the shirt she had been stitching down upon her lap.

"Verity, as unlikely as it seems, there exists the possibility that young Mr. Cole is taking his time licking his wounds, but that he may return to us now that you are out in society. The idea of courting you more formally might be all the encouragement he needs. If he is willing to brave the obstacles that your eccentricities present, would you not be willing to at least give him a chance?"

Verity felt the panic rise in her throat. *He mustn't. He can't!* The words burbled up before she could stop them.

"No, Mama! It wouldn't be right!"

Her mother sighed. "What is it you want, then?"

"Just to be myself."

"Is it not possible to be yourself and find happiness with a family of your own?"

"I don't know. I think I will know when it feels right. And it doesn't now."

"How can something feel right when you don't let anyone in?" Her mother's voice had taken on a slight edge to it.

"What do you mean?" Verity was already tiring of the conversation. Her mother could go on so!

"If you don't give anyone a chance, how can they win your heart?"

"They might break it instead."

"Or you could be missing out on the one great love of your life because you did not recognize it in its infancy."

"Like you did?" Verity answered sulkily.

"Pardon?" Her mother tilted her head sharply.

There was a note of warning in her voice, but Verity ignored it. She was sick, sick, sick of the constant harassment. Her mother had let her own parents talk her out of being with the man she loved because they'd wanted her to marry someone more respectable. She was sure of it. Nothing else made sense. And here she was, lecturing Verity on making a similar mistake. Well, she wasn't having it. Concern for her well-being was one thing. Hypocrisy was something else entirely.

"I saw your letters," she blurted out. "The ones from a man with the initials T.L. The man you loved before you married Father. You cannot tell me to open my heart when you closed it so firmly to him all those years ago."

Her mother's face froze. "You read my letters?"

"Yes."

"My private correspondence?"

Verity swallowed. Some of her bravado was already slipping away.

"It was in the storage room, up in the attic. I didn't know they were such... intimate letters until I began reading them."

"You saw something that did not belong to you. Yet you helped yourself to its contents out of idle curiosity." The warning was still there. Verity's courage was failing fast.

"I'm sorry, Mother. I know it was wrong." And then a little flare of rebellion... "But you can't deny the truth. Before you married Father, you loved someone whose initials were T.L. You loved him deeply, but you married Father instead. Why? Why did you not follow your heart?"

Mrs. Lockhart leaned back in her chair. "You haven't the faintest idea what you are talking about, my dear child."

But Verity remained resolute. "I have eyes. I know what I read. I know what you gave up. And you would tell me to do the same as you—to marry someone I do not love because it is practical."

Mrs. Lockhart turned her full gaze upon her daughter, anchoring Verity with the weight of it. "Have you observed anything in all these years to suggest your father and I are unhappy?"

"No, but you were married for many years before I was born. You had already grown fond of each other before you had me. But in the beginning, it must have been difficult."

Her mother picked at a stray thread on her cuff before folding her hands on her lap. "It might surprise you to know that I was fond of your father from the start."

"Oh." Verity's confidence deflated somewhat. "But Father is so... you know... *staid*. He is not a very passionate man. Not like the gentleman in the letters."

A smile quirked about her mother's lips. "It might interest

you to know—not that it is any of your business, and I really feel you have overstepped the mark in the whole affair, Verity—that the passionate gentleman who wrote those letters is, in fact, your own dear papa."

Verity's small world exploded.

"It can't be!" she spluttered. "Father is nothing like that!"

Her mother sighed. "We were young. That is how the young go about things—all wild abandon and unfettered swooning. It lasts a while. Long enough to marry and have children and become busy, distracted. Then you settle into a familiar pattern. Less exciting, to be sure. But not less meaningful."

"But," protested Verity, still quite unable to come to terms with this new information, "Father's initials are not T.L. He is John Lockhart. There is no 'T.'"

"Ah, that. He was ever the romantic, my John. 'T.L.' stands for True Love, for that is what he has always been to me. Though we grow old and grey and tired, we have loved each other since our youth, and no one else."

Verity suspected that such news should have pleased her. For one, it meant her mother had not made a terrible sacrifice in marrying her father. And for another, it proved that the young Dorothy had indeed been true to herself and followed her heart. Both these discoveries should have offered relief, even encouragement. Why, then, was she dissatisfied with the outcome?

Mrs. Lockhart looked with pity upon her daughter. "I rather think you would have preferred a scandal. Your father and I have not provided the escape you sought from your own doubts."

Yes! That was it! How wise her mother was. And how horribly, awfully right.

Verity fiddled with her fingers, her eyes unable to lift to meet her mother's. "You believe," she began in a small voice, "I am capable of finding a lasting love like yours. Why... Why would you think that?"

"Oh, my dear!" Mrs. Lockhart threw her sewing down. In one fluid movement, she was beside Verity, wrapping her arms about her and cradling her head against her shoulder.

"You do make things impossible for yourself, my precious, foolish child. All that pining after little creatures, and endless hours spent painting in your room. This is not the way to love. You will have to give a greater measure of yourself to receive more in return."

Verity lifted her head and pulled a face. Her mother had just described everything that she did not want to hear.

"Now, now, do not look at me so. You know I am right. You are not ready to hear it, but I must say it nevertheless. Perhaps what you need is…"

Her mother's speech stalled. Verity could picture the cogs turning in the mechanisms of her mind. That did not bode well. Whenever her mother had a *brilliant idea*, it was usually mortifyingly embarrassing for Verity.

"What is it, Mother?" she asked, dreading the answer.

"Oh, nothing."

Nothing. That was the worst possible reply. It meant her mother knew she would not like the plan and was keeping it under wraps until she was ready to spring it on her.

Verity pulled herself free of her mother's embrace.

"Tell me."

"There is nothing to tell. I merely had a thought. That is all."

Verity closed one eye and squinted suspiciously. "Will this thought become a reality in the near future?"

"I cannot possibly say."

Verity groaned. Her mother—despite being a habitual gossip—could be utterly tight-lipped if she chose to be. There was no use in attempting to pry anything from her which she did not wish to share. The only way Verity was going to discover her latest epiphany was when her mother chose to reveal it.

So that was it. She could now stop fretting about William Cole and the courtship that had ended before it had quite begun. Instead, her mother had given her an entirely different cause for concern.

Just marvelous.

Her worries were further exacerbated when Mrs. Lockhart rose with quiet determination and murmured something about a letter she needed to write. And would Verity mind putting her sewing away in the basket for her?

An alarm sounded in Verity's brain. Her mother hated writing letters. She often dictated them to Verity, declaring herself too easily worn out by the demands of the quill. But this particular correspondence was to be written by Mrs. Lockhart's own hand.

Verity watched her mother leave the room. A cloud of doom settled over her as she imagined the private scribblings and to whom they might be addressed. What scheme was brewing in her mother's mind?

The room grew close. It stifled her. Outside, the branches swayed under a cold wind. There was no escape to the pond. So, painting it was, then.

Verity plodded up to her room, the weight of decision upon her. Which of her pictures would she have to give up looking at so as to paint upon the back of it? She scrutinized the multitude of choices. A ladybird upon a daisy drew her attention. It looked a little lost in the middle of the otherwise-empty page. She could fill in the background with more detail. The existing picture could remain, only better.

She began to set up the colors she would need. She did not want to overwhelm the image of the ladybird. It was still the focus. The flowers and leaves she would add would be small, delicate. She selected white, yellow, and green. These would offer a suitable backdrop for the bright-red shell of the beetle.

She pulled an old, stained smock from a drawer and drew it over her bodice, tying it deftly behind her waist. Choosing a fine-tipped brush, she captured her first new stroke upon the paper. The glass jar tinkled softly as she swirled her brush in water to rinse it before dipping the hairs into a darker shade of green.

A minute slipped by. It was enough. Her thoughts stayed only on the brush and the paper. All other cares slid from her.

An hour passed. A blessed hour with only her painting for company. It restored her equilibrium. When her mother called her to come downstairs and read to her, she did not mind. She thought no more about what schemes were being concocted on her behalf. For the rest of the evening, Verity knew peace.

CHAPTER NINE

Fernbridge, December 1814

DECEMBER BROUGHT SNOW and bitter cold. The pond was frozen, the insects hidden from sight, buried under soil and leaves and logs, some paused in their life cycle as eggs or larvae. Verity found the winter difficult. The days were short and dull. The family stayed near the hearth. They rarely ventured from the sitting room, let alone the house, except to go to church or take baskets of bread and jars of stewing apples to the poor.

There was nothing new to paint. Sewing and music and reading were all that stood between Verity and absolute *ennui*. And, of course, the occasional letter.

It was a particularly dreary, drizzly day that brought a lovely, thick stack of post from the village. Mr. Lockhart—as much affected by the lack of activity and purpose as the ladies of the house—had donned his great coat, scarf, and gloves and made the pilgrimage to the postmaster's office. A worthwhile endeavor, as it turned out.

While he braved the weather, his wife was inspired to catch up on her correspondence. After all, there would be friends who likewise sought relief from the mundane drudgery of winter days with a cheery bit of news from Fernbridge. It also meant Verity had work to do.

"Oh, how these quills vex me!" came the usual complaint almost immediately after Mrs. Lockhart had seated herself by the writing desk. "Not as nimble as a needle, nor as stout as a ladle. I cannot comprehend why I should struggle so. We are living in the nineteenth century. Why is there no clever man who can improve upon its design?" she wailed.

"Perhaps it will be a clever woman," Verity muttered under her breath. She instantly regretted it, for her mother turned at the sound and thrust the offending article at her.

"Here," she said, evidently pleased to have found a solution to her frustration. "You will write and I will dictate."

Verity took the quill without a word. It was pointless to argue. Besides, there was nothing else to do. Writing was as good an occupation for her listless spirit as any.

"Address it to Mrs. Fotheringhay. You know the details."

In a careful hand, Verity complied. When she was done, she sat back, waiting in readiness for the sentences to follow.

"I hope this letter finds you well." Mrs. Lockhart spoke. Verity dipped the nib in ink and scratched the words upon the paper. "I imagine you suffer in the cold as much as we do. The north has such an unforgiving clime and Fernbridge feels it. However, being in Scotland, you bear the worst of it." *Scratch, scratch.* "Mind you, last winter, the Thames froze quite solid and I recall they led an elephant upon its surface at the Frost Fair. If London and the south cannot escape such severe temperatures, I do not see how we may be spared."

She paused a while for Verity to catch up, then resumed her dictation.

"We have recently had the pleasure of reacquaintance with Mr. William Cole, whose father, you may remember, heads the bank in our local borough. He returned from his summer in Steeples two months ago and has since visited us a number of times, which we thought most civilized of him."

Verity's neck grew warm as she penned her mother's thoughts. She hoped this short reference would be news enough of Mr. Cole's family. Instead, her mother paused and contemplated the subject for what felt like a small eternity.

"Do you know, Verity," her mother said in that thoughtful voice that screamed *brilliant idea*, "I think you could add something here of your own. You express yourself far better than I do."

It was such a barefaced lie that Verity was amazed her mother did not blush with the shame of it.

"I have nothing to say," she insisted.

But Mrs. Lockhart waved her hand in a dismissive gesture. "I'm sure you will think of something. Only, do hurry. I have more to tell Mrs. Fotheringhay and do not wish to forget my thoughts."

Verity tapped a knuckle against her forehead, trying to coax the words from her mind. This was silly. It wasn't as if Mrs. Fotheringhay even knew Mr. Cole. She would not care if little was said of him.

Perhaps one sentence would be sufficient. "We see less of him now that the weather has turned." There. The end. No more need to discuss Mr. William Cole.

"Read what you have written," her mother commanded. Verity obeyed. Mrs. Lockhart rolled her eyes and grabbed the quill. "Move aside, Verity," she instructed, seating herself so quickly, Verity scarcely had time to vacate the chair.

Mrs. Lockhart gripped the writing tool awkwardly, her brow creasing with concentration. She wrote carefully, scowling repeatedly at the pen as though its existence offended her. Finally, she sat back, satisfied.

"There! That's more like it." She rose once more and indicated the empty seat. "Now you continue."

"But, Mama," Verity protested, "won't Mrs. Fotheringhay wonder at the two sets of handwriting? It does look rather odd."

"Oh, no, not at all," came the reply. "The old dear is as blind as a bat. She will have one of her children read it to her, and you know how they struggle with their letters. They will hardly notice which hand the words are in."

Verity perused her mother's written additions. She groaned

inwardly. "Why do you mention that he is handsome? Or that he brought me a gift? Mrs. Fotheringhay will draw all the wrong conclusions!"

"Perhaps they are not wrong," her mother said, cocking her head in an attitude of what could only be feigned innocence. "You would not deny that Mr. Cole is pleasing to the eye."

"No, but..."

"And he did bring you a gift."

"Yes, I know. It's just..."

"And if you had not been such a ninny about it, he would likely have brought you more."

"*Mother!*"

"Yes, yes, don't fuss so. I know you want nothing to do with the helpless fellow." She grinned. "But Mrs. Fotheringhay does not need to know that. Not yet, anyway. Maybe now she will stop asking about your prospects. At least for a while."

Verity's protest was silenced. It had not occurred to her that her mother was trying to protect her. She only wished she did not need protecting.

A stomping sound alerted them to the return of Mr. Lockhart.

Mrs. Lockhart darted from the room, crying, "He will shake the snow all over the floor!"

Verity allowed herself a knowing smile. Her father had a habit of dusting off his hat and coat in the foyer, shedding snowflakes that soon turned to small puddles upon the floor. Nellie and a mop would be sent for, with Mrs. Lockhart complaining that Nellie already had enough to do, and that a more thoughtful husband would have sorted himself before coming inside.

Today, however, Mrs. Lockhart uttered a cry of delight instead.

"Post! And so much of it! Verity, look how many letters," she called as she came back into the room, waving the stack in her hand. Mr. Lockhart followed, beaming, and took up position nearest the fire.

"Nellie!" cried his wife, to which footsteps hastily responded.

"Yes?" the maid answered, slightly out of breath.

"Bring Mr. Lockhart a hot cup of tea. And those special biscuits."

"Certainly, ma'am. And would you like me to tend to the foyer?" She cast a glance at Mr. Lockhart, who looked decidedly drier than the foyer surely did.

"Tea first, Nellie."

"Yes, ma'am."

While they waited for the refreshments that Mr. Lockhart had earned, his wife sorted through the correspondence.

"Oh, look, here is something from the bishop. Pass this on to your father, Verity. Now, let's see… What else?"

She stopped and stared at a familiar hand, twisting the letter to better catch the light and see the address.

"Who is it from, Mama?"

"Mrs. Cole."

The letter was all but torn open, and Verity held her breath while her mother's eyes raced across the page.

"Oh, my!" was all she said. And then, "Foolish boy!" and some tutting.

"Bad news?" inquired Mr. Lockhart.

His wife lowered the letter into her lap.

"Young William has joined the infantry. Apparently, his uncle helped him acquire a lieutenant's commission. He left a few days ago for Munro to receive training with his new regiment."

"He's gone?" Verity whispered.

"Yes." Mrs. Lockhart shook her head slowly. "His poor mother. She is beside herself with worry."

"It seems he has found his purpose at last," commented Mr. Lockhart.

His wife gave him a *look*. "You men. You break our hearts at every turn. What with England constantly at war, poor Harriet might never see her son again. Why could he not settle here in the country? He didn't have to take on the vicarage. There were other avenues open to him. Why did he have to throw himself in harm's way?"

"It is unlikely that he will be posted abroad before the spring," her husband reassured her.

"Winter. Spring. What difference does it make? It is a soldier's duty to fight. Without a war, he has no purpose. And with a war, he has terrible risk."

Verity had not thought of that. She had supported Mr. Cole in his goals, believing that, like her, he nurtured dreams others did not understand. She had imagined him, devilishly dashing in his uniform, going forth to conquer his enemies. But in her mind, the enemies had been his parents and anyone else who held him back. She had not considered the battlefield, with cannon fire and bayonets. These were not topics a young woman was encouraged to ponder.

Now the image of his handsome face grew strange in her mind. Bright blood spattered his uniform while his skin paled, cold in death. An icy hand touched her spine and she shivered. The room took on a ghostly chill.

"That window still lets in a draft," Mr. Lockhart grumbled, looking up. "I'll ask the Jones boy to have a look at it tomorrow. He is very handy with odd jobs."

"At least Mr. Cole will have officer's quarters," Mrs. Lockhart thought aloud. "I cannot think that the tents for the rank and file would offer much comfort in this weather."

The room grew quiet.

Mr. Lockhart shifted in his chair. "Let us have another letter, my dear. Different news will take our minds from such somber topics."

His wife sifted through the little stack on the table. She hesitated a moment, her hand pausing on a particular correspondence. Then she slipped the paper into her pocket.

That was odd, thought Verity. *What sort of correspondence needed to be hidden?*

Quickly resuming her browsing, her mother selected another letter with a satisfied exclamation.

"Mrs. Harris! Well, now, I haven't heard from her in a long time. Verity, you read it to us. My eyes grow tired."

Verity did as bidden, but her mind could not focus on the words before her. Thoughts of Mr. Cole—worried thoughts— would not withdraw from her troubled imagination. And then there was the matter of the letter her mother had not wanted to share. She was up to something. It couldn't have been worse than Mr. Cole's news, though, could it? Then again, Mr. Cole's choices wouldn't affect her directly. Her mother's plans, on the other hand, were aimed squarely in her direction. Of that she had no doubt.

And yet… And yet… The idea of Mr. Cole being hurt was doing funny things to her stomach. He wasn't a nameless soldier. At the very least, he was their neighbor. A very charming neighbor. And a bold one too. One whose eyes were not afraid to look. At her body. At her soul.

Verity stumbled over a sentence for the umpteenth time.

"My goodness," remarked Mrs. Lockhart. "I do not recall Mrs. Harris writing so poorly that you should struggle this much to read it. Is something amiss? Do you feel unwell?"

Verity wanted to say *yes*. But then her parents would fret and send her to bed. She would be alone with her troubled thoughts. At least here, with family and a pile of correspondence, there were distractions. So she merely cleared her throat and said, "I am fine, Mama. Perhaps if I turn toward the window, I will see more clearly what is written on the page."

She adjusted the angle of her posture accordingly and began to read once more, forcing herself to focus on each word and allow nothing else to enter her mind. In this way, a pleasant hour passed until the little heap of letters was depleted.

A second cup of tea and a sandwich added fortitude against the darkening afternoon. Mr. Lockhart dozed off in his chair. Verity returned to her sewing, a lamp offering guidance to her fingers.

"I will fetch my book from my room," Mrs. Lockhart announced suddenly as she stood.

"I can get it for you, Mama."

"No, indeed, it will do me good to stretch my legs a little. I will be right back."

She disappeared out the door. A creak of the floorboard told Verity her mother had reached the stairs.

A few minutes later, Verity's thread ran out. She recalled there was an extra spool upstairs that she had not yet unwrapped from her last visit to the haberdashery. She placed her sewing in the work basket and made her way to her room. In a moment of spontaneous playfulness, she skipped over the noisy board by the bottom step and flew lightly up the stairs. As she passed her parents' room, she turned to ask her mother if she needed help finding her book. Instead, Verity saw her standing in the middle of the floor, her eyes transfixed upon an unfolded letter in her hand.

The letter. She had quite forgotten about it. That accursed thing—plotting her future without her say-so, Verity was sure.

She stepped into the room, trying to suppress the flush of agitation that surged to her cheeks.

"The light here is not nearly as good as in the sitting room," Verity said. "Would you like me to read it for you?"

Mrs. Lockhart jumped at the sudden interruption.

"Uh… No, I… Um… I am managing quite nicely, thank you."

"Not bad news, I hope?"

"No, quite the opposite."

"That is a relief. What is it?"

"What is what?"

"The news. You said it was good news."

"Oh. Er… It is just your sister, telling me how well the children are doing."

"May I read it after you? It would be lovely to hear what Hope is getting up to. Her life seems quite full compared to mine."

"No! I mean, no… It is rather a personal letter. Between mother and daughter. You understand."

"Of course, Mama. I understand completely."

All avenue of further investigation now closed to her, Verity withdrew from the room and continued on to her own. She sat upon the edge of her bed, musing over the facts, few as they were. What secrets were being concocted between Hope and their mother? Was it even Hope's letter?

She decided it must have been. Her mother might be a schemer, devising some means to secure Verity a husband, but she was not a liar. So, it must be someone her sister knew, but whose acquaintance was too new to facilitate introductions. Someone in Munro, else their mother would not have needed Hope's help.

Verity threw herself backward onto her eiderdown. It was all very vexing.

The soft heat of the eiderdown caused her eyelids to droop. She curled up into its nest-like protection and released a martyred breath. One of these days, she was going to have to put her foot down. One of these days…

Her breathing deepened. Her thoughts began to drift. One of these days…

But for now, she was content to sleep.

CHAPTER TEN

Munro, January 1815

"I SAY, THERE'S a good fellow. Would you hold these a moment?"

"Certainly, sir." William held out his arms. They were filled at once with a bundle of long, leafy twigs. His nose twitched at the scent of laurel so close to his face.

The previous bearer of the boughs reached down and snipped several strands of ivy from the nearest tree. Collecting them by their severed ends, he curled them up into a wreath-like coil and hailed another gentleman.

"You there. Collins. Give these to her ladyship at the house. Tell them we will bring the holly next." He turned his neat form to William. "I don't suppose you have a knife on you? It would go so much faster if there were more of us cutting the greenery. We are behind schedule as it is. And I see you have good, thick gloves. You could manage the holly quite nicely."

"No, sir. Sorry, sir," William replied. "I haven't a knife with me. But I could take these to the house and ask for one. I will come straight back and assist you."

"Good man."

William did not linger. When Captain Larson finished talking, it was time to get moving. A month of training had taught him that. He crunched through the icy shrubbery and headed for the kitchen rather than the front door. He did not imagine Lady

Penrose would care for any infantrymen stomping about her house with snow all over their boots, even if all the officers were there at her invitation.

At the door, he leaned carefully so as not to dislodge his awkwardly balanced bundle. The lever shifted and the door creaked open, light and heat streaming out into the darkening afternoon. Inside, the maids looked up, saw who it was, and a general titivation erupted. A hand went to the hair, another was wiped clean on an apron. The young women preened and blushed. And William still stood, holding the greenery.

"Oh, for goodness's sake!" cried Cook, wiping her hands on her already flour-dusted apron. "Betsy, go and fetch those to her ladyship. And the rest of you, stop gawking. One would think you'd never seen a man before."

"I don't suppose I could borrow a knife?" inquired William, once young Betsy had relieved him of his leafy burden, scurrying on short legs and with a deep blush on her cheeks to deliver the laurel boughs to her mistress. "The captain wants me to help collect the holly. We're slowing down the ladies who are putting up the decorations. If I can help, it will go twice as fast."

"If it means you'll be done sooner with your traipsing through my kitchen, you are welcome to it," replied Cook, passing him a large knife, handle first. "I can't get my baking done if my kitchen is a constant thoroughfare."

"Sorry. We shouldn't be much longer. Thirty minutes at the most. It will be dark then, so we won't have a choice but to come inside."

"Hmph. I wouldn't put it past your captain to have you collect foliage by lamplight. He's a hard taskmaster, that one."

William grinned. Several of the kitchen maids had pulled faces behind her back. Cook's reputation was very like the captain's.

"Well, don't stand there like an eager schoolboy. Off with you. I've got my hands full with this lot." She waved vaguely at a large table packed with bowls and ingredients. "And you," she cried, pointing her spoon accusingly at the giggling maids, "you're more trouble than help. Get back to work!"

William exited the house, leaving one beloved demi-tyrant to rejoin another. Captain Larson did not suffer fools, but he was a fair man. His men respected him. William thought himself fortunate to be under such fine leadership.

Military life was turning out to be everything he could have hoped for, even if his only experience thus far had been to undergo training. His quarters were comfortable enough. The men were stout souls, ready for action both on the battlefield and off. Days were busy and purposeful, and the nights brought companionship and laughter.

It wasn't all sporting fun, though. Training in winter had its downfalls. Even a good coat and gloves did not entirely ward off the bite of wind and damp of snow that filtered down the back of one's neck. But tonight, no thought would be given to any of that. Baron and Baroness Penrose hosted legendary parties, and Twelfth Night was the envy of them all.

Each year, on the sixth of January, Lord Penrose included his household regiment in the family festivities. A barrel of fine Scottish whiskey was delivered to the local tavern for the enlisted men, while the officers and their kin joined his lordship at the main house. Kin included daughters. And Twelfth Night promised games and mischief. The rules of decorum were relaxed. And there would be mistletoe.

Captain Larson had already cut a generous sample from the cluster of mistletoe on the hawthorn tree. "Good lad," he said as William approached. "I'm going to check on the others. Collins is in the kitchen garden, collecting rosemary. The rest are bringing in firewood. As soon as you have enough holly for four wreaths, join us inside." Without waiting for an answer, he gathered up the mistletoe and strode down the hill behind the house, carrying the most sought-after object for the evening in his hands.

William worked quickly. The light was fading, and the cold air sank its teeth into his skin. He gathered fistfuls of the twigs, working against time as his fingers grew numb. At last, he straightened, giving his back a good stretch.

His gaze fell on the hawthorn, dotted about with mistletoe. William's eyes glinted with inspiration. He reached out and clipped a tiny sprig, shoving it into his trouser pocket. Gathering up the prickly holly, he set off, back to the kitchen, past the stern supervision of Cook, and into the cheery, yellow drawing room where the rest of the company—both military and domestic— were gathered. Miss Frances Penrose, his lordship's eldest daughter—a flighty, rather silly creature—was in charge of ornamentation and sat, scissors in hand, cutting gold paper stars. Beside her lay a mound of white silk bows she had finished earlier.

"Oh, Lieutenant Cole," called Lady Penrose, "you can put those on the table. We're almost ready to add the holly." She lifted the wreath she had been working on to show him.

"A fine job, if I may say so, your ladyship," William said with a gallant bow.

"You may indeed, sir," she replied with a gracious tip of her head. William found it hard to fathom how such an elegant woman—one who had maintained her beauty and grace despite her years—had produced such an unsophisticated daughter. Even in her humor, she carried herself with dignity, pursing her lips playfully now and adding, "Perhaps you could find a suitable spot to hang the mistletoe."

A snort erupted from her husband. "Ha! You have certainly chosen the right man for the task, my dear."

Lady Penrose resumed her work on the wreath, commenting as she tucked an errant bow back in place amongst the inter- twined greenery. "Oh, I don't doubt that. The ladies will be hovering near the mistletoe all evening, awaiting their chance for a stolen kiss. I shan't imagine the berries will last long at all."

"The berries, Mama?" inquired the lovely Miss Penrose, her green eyes lifting from their task, her blonde ringlets bouncing slightly.

Lady Penrose ceased her activity and cast a doting look upon her daughter. "I had quite forgot this is your first experience. Last Christmastide, you were not out yet. But I imagine you are no stranger to the talk of Twelfth Night and all its tomfoolery. Still, there are rules, even in silly antics. With each kiss that is claimed under the mistletoe, a berry must be plucked. Once the bough is picked clean, no more kisses may be had except between husband and wife."

"Oh!" Miss Penrose cried in dismay. "Then one might well miss a chance for a kiss from the one you most desire? That hardly seems fair."

Lady Penrose stared at her daughter down the length of her nose. "All games must have rules, Frances. It is so with all aspects of life. Even when we are at play, there must be boundaries that are well understood."

Frances Penrose tilted her head toward William. "It is a pity one cannot have something like a dance card for the kissing bough. Then one could write one's name and that of one's preferred partner and stake one's claim, so to speak."

Her mother shook her head. "You do have some odd notions, Frances. Half the fun is in the chase. For the gentlemen, at least. If you planned the moment, it would not be nearly as exhilarating when it arrived."

"It's all those novels you read, Frances," her father complained, tucking his thumbs into his waistcoat, which spanned his stout chest. "They stuff your head full of nonsense. A kiss under the mistletoe means nothing. Good matches are based on more suitable criteria than chance encounters."

Miss Penrose pouted at her father but said nothing. Instead, her eyes spoke volumes to William, especially when she added a flutter of the lashes. He winked. Color rushed to her cheeks.

William had played these games many a time before. Doing so had become second nature to him. She would have her kiss, if she wished. But it was not the only encounter he intended to enjoy this night.

Next to Miss Penrose sat the quiet Miss Fairchild. She was, undeniably, the greatest beauty of all the ladies present. Her lush, dark hair piled upon her perfectly shaped head. Her lips were of the exact fullness to make them most desirable. Her lashes were long and seductive. But she was untouchable. Her father was a brigadier. Any man who thought to take liberties with his daughter could find himself posted to Australia.

Miss Fairchild was therefore quite safe from being surprised under the mistletoe—the *very public* kissing bough. But there were other options. William patted the tiny sprig in his pocket. It held just one berry. He only needed one.

"I wonder what the halls of Munro House look like tonight?" Lady Penrose mused. "It is the new viscountess's first opportunity to add her touch to what has been, I believe, a rather somber affair for some years. When the dowager left to live with her married daughter, the young viscount did not host parties or pay attention to frivolities like decoration. Lord Howell was never much for idle amusement. Do you think his bride will have changed him? I understand you have met her, Lieutenant Cole. Would she be the sort to influence a man so set in his ways?"

All heads swiveled toward William, curiosity clearly piqued. He froze. The mention of Ellena had been wholly unexpected and he was not prepared. Speaking of her was still quite impossible for him. The mere thought of her was only just becoming bearable. Three months had passed. But the image of her in the garden— denouncing him—was burned into his soul as if it had just occurred.

"I… I…" he stuttered. "I'm afraid I barely knew her," he lied. "I happened to visit my sister while Elle—I mean, Miss Trenton was staying as a guest before her nuptials. I did not even attend the wedding."

"But you must have formed some impression of her. Even a superficial one. What did you make of her? *We* thought she was rather an oddity. So many rumors…" Lady Penrose collected herself. "Of course, now she is everything a viscountess should be. Munro is lucky to have her."

The words that William had struggled to say now came rushing all at once to his lips. "I assure you, when I knew her as Miss Trenton, she was a model of perfection. I cannot imagine that has changed just because she married…" He restrained himself with difficulty. "Him."

"Goodness," cried Lady Penrose. "The model of perfection, you say. That is fine praise indeed. Well, then, I think it is safe to say that festivities will abound at the great house tonight. Perhaps she will even persuade Lord Howell to host a ball in the spring. That would be a wonderful opportunity for us all to celebrate their happiness." She glanced at her daughter. "And it wouldn't hurt to have Munro's finest gathered under one roof."

Miss Penrose's face lit up. "Oh, Mama! Do you think they might? Really? A ball at Munro House!" She clapped her hands in delight. "I would need a new dress," she decided promptly.

"Hmph, one would think you had enough dresses to clothe half of England," her father grumbled.

"Papa, you *are* funny." Miss Penrose laughed. "I can't go to a ball at Munro House in any of those old things." She fluffed her skirts and smiled coyly at William with her cat-like green eyes. Then they widened, and she asked with some excitement, "Would the officers be invited too? Surely, Lord Howell would want to shake their hands for their service to king and country."

William suppressed the urge to pull a sour face. He certainly had no desire to shake the hand of the rival who had won. Nor would the viscount want to make pleasant conversation with the man he had chased from Munro only a few months ago.

"If he did, it would only be the field officers," her father explained. "Sorry, Larson. Not that you aren't deserving."

Captain Larson gave a stiff bow with his head. "No need to explain, my lord. Everything has its time and place."

"Yes. Quite right." Lord Penrose puffed out his chest.

Good, thought William. *Awkward reunion averted.*

"I think you are getting ahead of yourself a little, Frances,"

Lady Penrose warned. "Nothing of the matter is decided. But I shall make inquiries. Perhaps even a suggestion or two to the right people." She sniffed. "I am sure someone as young as Lady Howell—and so inexperienced in the ways of the nobility—would welcome advice from the more established members of the class."

William needed fresh air. He couldn't listen to any more of this pomp and pretense masquerading as genteelness. They didn't know Ellena at all. She was nothing like them, and thank goodness for that! If she were here, she would have put that snooty baroness in her place. No one could step on her and get away with it. It got her into trouble sometimes, but at least she stood her ground. Watching them imagine themselves superior to her just because they'd been born into position made his blood boil.

He edged his way around the room until he reached the door to the hallway. When he was sure no one was looking, he slipped out and headed down the corridor to the library, a room he might have an excuse to be in if caught. It was dimly lit but empty. William sank into a chair and rubbed a hand roughly across his forehead and hair.

He had to stop getting so worked up whenever Ellena was mentioned As long as he was stationed in Munro, Lady Howell would be a popular topic. He would have to get used to it.

At least no one was harassing him about matters in Fernbridge. A small mercy. He imagined Miss Verity Lockhart was just as happy to be free of their once-expected alliance as he was. Although she *did* have an annoying habit of creeping into his thoughts. Like now. Why, when he smarted at the memory of Ellena—whom he'd loved passionately and lost—did his mind always lead him back to the vicar's daughter? She couldn't possibly compare. She was so... so...

Fascinating. She was fascinating. A challenge. A mystery. She wasn't as feisty as Ellena, but she had a quiet strength. Being around her had grounded him, albeit briefly. Long enough to focus his mind and choose his own path forward. For that, he owed her much.

What would now become of poor Miss Lockhart? Would her parents find her a better match? Or would she be a spinster, with her nose ever in a book, muttering about butterflies and beetles to anyone who'd listen? It seemed wrong for those piercing-blue eyes not to light up as they had at the pond. She should be outdoors, her pale hair shimmering in the sunlight, net in hand, sketchbook waiting. Would she, instead, be condemned to a parlor, serving tea to her husband's guests? Or hidden in a cramped space in a boarding house, left behind as her much older siblings gradually were lost to her?

William didn't like these thoughts at all. He shook himself mentally to cast them off. He was not responsible for Miss Lockhart. And, just down the corridor, sat Miss Fairchild, with lips that begged to be kissed. *She* couldn't hurt him. And he owed her nothing. It would only be a moment of bliss, a tender memory. She would blush whenever she saw him again. A secret shared. That was all he needed now.

If he said it often enough, he could convince himself of it.

William got up from his chair. He still needed to hang the mistletoe. The evening was full of promise. The past should stay in the past.

He made his way back to the bright space of the yellow drawing room. Seizing the branch of mistletoe, he looked about for a suitable spot to place it. All at once, Miss Penrose launched from her seat with what could only be described as a squeal of delight.

"Oh, Lieutenant Cole, you are standing under the mistletoe, and so am I!"

William looked at the bough in his hand. "Well, strictly speaking, I am not quite under it. Not yet, anyway."

"That is easily remedied," she purred. "You merely have to lift your arm, and I am yours."

"Frances!" Lady Penrose's voice was thick with shock. "This is *not* how ladies of good breeding conduct themselves! Sit down at once!"

"But, Mama, I might not have another chance if…"

"That is quite enough," Lady Penrose hissed. "Sit. Down."

Frances Penrose sat down sulkily, all grace and decorum quite forgotten.

Her mother looked up rather helplessly at William.

"I apologize for my daughter, Lieutenant. She is a little over-zealous, what with this being her first experience of Twelfth Night. She is not aware that we wait until after dinner before the more, shall we say, *frivolous* events of the evening."

William grinned at the glowering face of Frances Penrose. "Then may I be so bold as to say, I hope dinner may be brief."

The effect was immediate. Miss Penrose settled at once, all traces of sour mood gone as quickly as it had come. Her fingers lifted to her neck, which she arched coyly at him.

Saints above, she is such a minx!

"Um, I will probably need a ladder to hang the mistletoe," William said to no one in particular.

Lord Penrose turned to a footman. "Fetch the lieutenant a ladder and hold it for him." While he waited for his instructions to be carried out, he inquired of William, "Where were you thinking of, Cole? The chandelier?"

"Oh, goodness no!" Lady Penrose exclaimed. That is in the center of the room. People will be constantly coming and going beneath it and there will be far too rapid a depletion of the berries. No, I think a quiet corner somewhere. What catches your eye, Lieutenant?"

"What about above the mantelpiece?" William ventured. "A toasty spot to soothe the nerves of whichever maiden hopes to claim a kiss."

"Ha!" came the gruff laugh of their host. "You do not think it will be the menfolk, then, who do the stalking tonight? Well, I daresay you're right. These are modern times. Women are far more brazen now than they were in my youth."

As if to lend gravity to his statement, a heavy knock at the great doors echoed into the room. Moments later, the sound of footsteps preceded the appearance of the sinewy butler at the doorway to the drawing room. "Brigadier Fairchild, your lordship," he announced.

Fairchild marched into the room. He was a burly chap with a ferocious moustache and a booming voice to match.

"Sorry I'm late, Penrose!" the brigadier all but shouted. "The meeting ran long. Nice crowd you've got here. All the better to celebrate the news, what ho!"

"If you're referring to the treaty with America," said the baron, "that is hardly news anymore. It was ratified a week ago. All of England has been apprised of the fact."

"My dear!" Lady Penrose chastened her husband. "Whether it is a few days in the past, surely the end of a war is worth celebrating? Especially with so many of our officers here who have now been spared battle."

"You are right, of course," said the baron. "Fetch the brandy!" he called to the footman. "We shall toast to peace and the fine men who may stay in England to enjoy it."

William wasn't so sure it was something he wanted to drink a toast to. It was all well and good. War was a messy thing. He hadn't particularly looked forward to it. Not at all, to be honest. But the absence of war made for a military that served little purpose. How was he to earn a higher commission without a battleground on which to prove himself? Certainly, flaunting his uniformed good looks in front of the ladies was a pleasant pastime. Evenings with his comrades-in-arms were enjoyable. But they had their limits.

William had other dreams. He never talked about them to anyone. He wasn't sure people would believe him if he did. He had played the role of a Don Juan so long and so well that he had almost become persuaded it was his true self. Until he had met Ellena. She had stirred up a forgotten desire within him. Not carnal as such, but deeply passionate. He had wanted—more than anything—to woo her properly, to be worthy of her. She would have been the great love of his life. For her, he would have been a better man, a good man. Everything else had turned on the axis that was Ellena.

When she had cut him out of her life, his had lost all meaning. If he could not wake up in her arms, be teased by her eyes, cautioned by her wisdom, he was an empty husk of a man. The dream stayed buried in a heart that was too wounded to give it wings again.

His parents would be confounded by the truth—that he wished to be just like them. Like his brother, his sister. All happily ensconced in marriage to someone they adored. Sadly, no ladies of his acquaintance ever promised the romantic fulfilment he craved. Oh, they giggled and promenaded and tilted their fans *just so*. They circled him like bees round a honeypot. Empty-headed, buzzing things. So he became the honeypot they wanted. In time, he forgot he wanted to be anything else.

Ellena had ignored the honey completely. She had demanded more. And he had found himself listening to a voice he'd thought he had lost. The one that spoke of a home and children and growing old together.

But she would be growing old with Lord Howell.

And William, well, he had tried to find meaning in something smaller. The military. Something to keep him busy while he mended a broken heart. An occupation where he could establish himself. So that one day, if, by some miracle, he met another Ellena, he could offer her everything she deserved. And he could have the one thing that seemed to constantly escape him: his one great love.

A glass of brandy was pushed into his hand.

William blinked. He lifted the glass automatically to join the toast. In his other hand, he still gripped the bough of mistletoe. He glanced toward the fireplace. The footman, having seen to the brandy, now stood waiting patiently next to a stepladder. William pushed through the small crowd until he was face-to-face with the fellow.

"Let's get the job done, shall we? Is there a nail to hook it on?"

The attentive footman turned his head toward the wallpaper above the mantelpiece. An ornate hook was cleverly disguised in the pattern of the paper's design.

"Jolly good." William set his foot upon the ladder. The servant at once took hold of the frame to offer stability. In a trice, William had reached up and over and snagged the kissing bough onto the hook. It was the perfect height. Just about anyone could reach the berries. And the more diminutive ladies would no doubt be assisted by eager gentlemen.

As soon as William was back on the ground, the footman spirited away the stepladder. He looked up at his handiwork, such as it was. It gave him no pleasure. The waxy, white berries mocked him. So many mouths waited for his, waited for him to seek them out, hungry for the touch of the most charming man in the room. Oh, the conquest! Empty, bitter conquest.

He would put on a brave face. He would laugh and flirt. It was expected.

He shoved his hands deep into his pockets, as if they could seek sanctuary there. But what was this? He drew out the slightly bruised sprig of mistletoe, its single berry clinging steadfastly to the stem. He stared at it. What had possessed him? Revulsion rose within and he flung the object into the fire.

He must not be that man. Small wonder Ellena had abandoned him. If he was ever to be worthy of someone like her, he would have to do better.

A tingle in his spine told him he was being watched. He swiveled to the right and was met with a coquettish smile from Frances Penrose.

He was standing under the mistletoe.

Mercifully, it was not yet dinner and Miss Penrose was heeding her mother's reprimand. He was safe. For now. At some point later in the evening, he would have to satisfy her relentless pursuit. He had all but promised. He must play the role of *gallant* a little longer.

He forced what he hoped was a grin upon his face. It appeared to have the desired effect. The young lady lowered her lashes, touching the tips of her fingers to the low, embellished neckline of her dress.

Mercy! He had had his fill of such ardent women during his summer in Steeples. It was no surprise he hadn't found a suitable bride. At least Miss Lockhart had not thrown herself at him with such fervor. Or any fervor, for that matter. It had been a refreshing change. Perhaps he had misjudged her. Just a little.

He sighed. Peace in England was going to make military life more dull than he imagined. What on earth was he to do with himself, month after month? At least he could look in on his sister. She was the one woman he could always count on to be sensible. Even if her husband did try one's patience. She might even steer him toward a better class of young lady.

Of course, Charlotte always tended to see the best in others. A most unfortunate habit. Who knew what terrible flaws she might fail to spot in the ladies she recommended? Then again, James would be quick to point out any faults his wife had missed. William could always trust his brother-in-law to offer a barrier of mean-spirited discernment. It was only Charlotte who could bring James gently to heel. Even in their marriage of opposites, there was tenderness.

William swallowed down the rest of his brandy. It hit his throat like a glowing coal, flaming its way down to his stomach. What he needed now was dinner. And bed. And a chance to forget all his life's disappointments.

If he could get through an evening in the company of Miss Frances Penrose, everything would look better in the morning.

CHAPTER ELEVEN

Munro, March 1815

VERITY KNEW SOMETHING was wrong the moment she'd entered the room. For one thing, her father was hovering, instead of hidden behind a book in his favorite chair.

She froze mid-step. "What's the matter?" Her gaze flitted from her father to her mother and back. Her mother was pale and quiet. It was her father who answered.

"Napoleon has returned to France. He is amassing an army as we speak. I'm afraid war is imminent."

Ice trickled down Verity's spine. Her thoughts flew at once to Mr. Cole. His training would be done soon. He would be sent abroad—William Cole, and thousands of young men just like him. It felt like yesterday when the war with America had ended and her heart had sagged with relief. Now it clamped tight like a fist as peace was undone once more.

She clasped her hands and drew them to her lips. "How can this be? Napoleon abdicated! It hasn't even be a year since he was banished to Elba. How can we be at war again?"

Her mother shook her head, her eyes sad. "It seems we are to be forever sacrificing our sons on the altar of some tyrant's cause."

Her husband placed a protective arm about her. "Hush now, dearest. They are but serving their king."

Dorothy Lockhart pulled away from his embrace. Her eyes

flashed defiantly. "Would you say that if our own Joseph were in uniform? And what's to stop them from press-ganging him into naval service?"

"He is in the employ of Sir Walter. They will not touch him."

"And all the other simple folk whom we have served and befriended here in Fernbridge? What of their husbands, brothers, sons? You would think it merely their duty to step into the breach?"

"It is a blessing to live in times of peace. But a man knows to answer his country's call in times of danger." He nodded his head with the cadence of his words as though he were delivering a sermon from his Sunday pulpit.

"So it's that simple, is it?"

"Yes, my dear." He closed his eyes and opened them again as one who must see the truth even though it pained him. "But that does not mean it is not hard to bear."

Verity watched silently as her mother leaned against her father, hiding her face and her fears in his warm shirt. *She* had no one upon whom to lean like that. Verity stood alone, with only her worried thoughts to cling to.

Perhaps Mr. Cole had made a match in Munro. Even now, he might be comforting some maiden as the terrible news spread across England. She truly hoped there *was* someone for him. Someone for him to come back to. She smiled wryly. If there was a woman in his life, he would be able to strut about, showing her his brave colors. If he had a special lady, he would put on a front of fearlessness to ease her concerns—and his own. Reality was too much for playful Mr. Cole. He needed a disguise, a role to play. He was not at home with stark truths.

For the briefest of moments, she wished *she* could be that person for him. It was but a fleeting thought, quickly discarded. No, she had made her decision. And his absence from their home told her he had made his.

Still, she wished they had at least parted as friends. If he was to… She gulped down the horrific image that surfaced. Mr. Cole was so vibrant, so very much *alive*. Such an image must not be allowed to fester in her mind. But the thought lingered. If William Cole was lost in battle, and they had not made their peace, it would haunt her forever.

"Why, Verity, you look quite ill!" Her mother moved quickly to her side. "How these dreadful tidings have affected you!" Her mouth widened suddenly into a bright smile, which gave Verity more pause than reassurance. "It is well that we have further news for you. It will take your mind off such melancholy thoughts at once."

Verity's doubts must have shown on her face because her mother cocked her head and said, "See how she scowls, Mr. Lockhart. But we shall soon fix that. There will be no more skulking about the house, or lonely days with paint and easel."

"I am not lonely," Verity protested.

Her mother's expression clouded. "I know you try to make the best of things. But a mother sees what you would not have her see. You are afraid to take a chance. You have convinced yourself being alone is safer than the risk of an imperfect match. But that does not mean you like being alone."

When Verity did not answer, her mother turned to her husband and he nodded for her to continue. "Your father and I understand that the gentlemen of our acquaintance lack the qualities you seek to draw you from your solitude. So, we have decided it is time to cast the net wider." She threw up a hand to stem the outcry that was already in Verity's throat. "It is done. We have arranged for you to visit with your sister in Munro. There, you will have a better introduction into society. You can visit the theater and museums, attend dances, and meet the families in Hope's social circle. The opportunity for finding a match more suitable to your tastes is multiplied tenfold in Munro. Our country town can offer little in comparison to such a great city. Besides, your nephews and nieces adore you and miss you. They have said as much to their mother. And Hope is eager for your company."

So, her mother's *brilliant idea* was finally revealed. And it carried her father's approval. There was no way to wriggle out of it.

"When do I leave?"

"As soon as you are packed. Let us say, two days? Your father and I will accompany you by coach and return the next day. As long as he is home in time to deliver the homily on Sunday, we can go at any time."

"I see."

"*Really*, Verity, one would think you might show a modicum of excitement." Her mother threw out an open palm. "It is a wonderful opportunity. You should not be stuck at home with just your aging parents for company."

"I have never complained."

Her mother sighed. "No, you do not complain. But you do not thrive, either. Oh, Mr. Lockhart, do talk some sense into her!"

Verity stared equally helplessly at her father. To her surprise, he reached out his hands and cupped her face in them, his eyes warm and soft.

"Your mother and I have had a good and happy life together. And our children have been blessed to follow suit. All but you. The time has come for you to find your own happy future, my child. It is time you stepped out from beneath our shadow and shone forth your own light." He tucked a wisp of her hair behind her ear and smiled wistfully. "Shine forth just like the starlight in your hair."

It was a term he had not used since she'd been a little girl. Verity remembered the years when she had been free of care and infused with the wonder of life. As the years had passed, her world had shrunk, layers of rules and expectations winding tighter and tighter about her. Her dreams had become suffocated by the weight of reality. Not *her* reality, she corrected herself silently, but the one that had been foisted upon her.

Would Munro offer anything new? Her parents' optimism in this regard was endearing. They truly wanted her to find happiness in a match that did not compromise her hopes. Or at least, not compromise them *too* much. But Verity was skeptical. What if Munro was just a larger version of Fernbridge? A greater variety of gentlemen did not guarantee a greater range in their thinking. When all was said and done, regardless of their interests and idiosyncrasies, didn't all men want a wife who fell in with her husband's wants and needs?

At least, in Fernbridge, she knew everyone, knew their strengths and flaws. Munro would lay open a bountiful array of choice—all strangers—whose chaperones would suggest they could be trusted. But was that enough? How often would she have to open her heart and hopes before she found someone who did not disappoint? Because they always did. Oh, they would be charming at first. But sooner or later, her own desires would be discovered and discarded. That had been her experience during conversations with their many neighbors and fellow church attendees. Now that she was out in society, it would be worse. Her oddness would not simply entice a bemused smile. No, there would be outright rejection. She would be labeled unsuitable. Mothers would keep their sons from her. Friends would whisper warnings in the ears of keen suitors. She would be *that* woman. The one they whispered about behind fans. The one their eyes followed knowingly, eliciting a sad tutting from mothers who pitied hers.

Verity released a deep sigh. "I suppose I should begin packing. Could Nellie fetch me the trunk from the attic?"

Her mother, who had been wearing a worried frown while she waited for Verity's response, now lit up with inspiration. "Oh, I had quite forgot! Hope says you shall have your very own lady's maid when you are with them in Munro. And she has convinced her dear Daniel to provide funds for you to have a new wardrobe. No more country clothes for you. You will be a proper lady of Munro. Isn't it exciting?"

Verity pictured her own frequently muddy hemlines, re-minders of her happiest hours. The last thing she wanted was to primp and preen in unnecessary finery. It would be a lie. Such garb would draw exactly the wrong sort of interest. Who would accept her as she was if she did not dress as herself?

Ugh! It was yet another battle she would have to fight against good intentions.

As always, though, Verity forced herself to smile and say, "That is very generous of them. I will thank them in person."

"Indeed," her mother replied, "Hope is fortunate to have made such an excellent match. Daniel is a good father and a man of means. And he is kind. She could scarcely have done better."

It is easy when you are not considered odd, Verity grumbled to herself. Frankly, she would be happy as the wife of a farmer if he would let her wander about the countryside, sketching, and gave her leave to study her books on science. Then again, she had to admit, he would likely struggle to afford the paper.

Verity hated that her mother was right. She would need a husband with a decent income or allowance. The practical considerations could not be ignored. And Munro had a far broader selection of such prospects. Might one of them also care for her as she was? She only needed one...

Trying not to ponder how elusive that one man might be, Verity trudged off to her room. The floorboard at the landing groaned its familiar greeting. How many times had she skipped over it, shoes and stockings in hand, portfolio tucked under her arm? It was unlikely she would be able to manage similar escapades at her sister's home. Hope was not judgmental, but Daniel would likely disapprove of such a poor example for his children. Their Aunt Verity would have to behave herself. It would need to be portraits and landscapes if she were to paint at all.

In the sanctuary of her room, Verity began the painstaking task of collecting her insect art from the walls. If she was not to create new paintings, she could at least find comfort in those already in her possession. She paused with each, recalling the occasion of its creation, before lovingly laying it in a growing pile upon her bed.

The tansy beetle was next. Verity beheld it with a small degree of dissatisfaction. Its iridescent jewel tones had been hard to capture on paper. It might have worked better with oil paints than watercolors. But that had not been possible. Oils were expensive.

Maybe she could try again in the summer, when the beetle was easy to find. Verity wondered if she would still be in Munro then. If she had not found a husband in the next three months, would she be allowed to return to the vicarage and resume her quiet life? Or would she become an unofficial companion for the Sinclair children, a means to compensate for the burden her presence created upon their father's purse? She shuddered. No more pond. No more hidden books beneath her bed. No more barefoot escapades.

Her mind's gaze cast back to the day she had sketched the beetle, its discovery a wonderful surprise, just like the red admiral on Mr. Cole's hat the week before. Both times he had been present when nature had offered her a late-season wonderment. He had been patient with her as she'd marveled, even a co-conspirator as she'd sketched. And he had kept her secret safe. He had revealed a tender side that day, despite his attempts to hide it with playfulness. And if that had been the end of it, they would certainly have been friends.

Verity clenched her jaw. That accursed butterfly! She shook her head in frustration. The gift, a failed attempt at thoughtfulness, was lying in the very trunk Verity had asked Nellie to bring. She really must rid herself of it.

There was a simple solution. She would take it with her to Munro. She could deposit it—and a letter—with Mr. Cole's older sister, Charlotte, now Mrs. James Trenton. He would certainly visit with her and be able to reclaim the item. It didn't matter now whether returning it brought up hurts from the past. He clearly wanted nothing to do with her, anyway. And, being in Munro, he may well be able to sell it back to the Entomological

Society. Or give it as a gift to a less-demanding woman. Mrs. Trenton might like it, now that Verity thought on it. She was wonderfully easy to please. Verity had always liked her, even though their age difference had made a childhood friendship impossible.

More importantly, Verity thought, she must make peace with Mr. Cole. She would not presume a meeting, but a letter would offer some means of reconciliation. If nothing else, she needed him to understand that *he* had not been rejected. He had misjudged, certainly, and she had reacted with shock and dismay, but she believed that a frank conversation could have mended it. And he was the one person with whom she knew she could have such a frank conversation.

She might not want to marry him, but he deserved to know that she valued him nevertheless. She suspected this was something he had not been told often enough.

The tansy beetle was, at last, added to the pile of watercolors upon her bed. Her fingers lingered a moment upon the page. With all her heart, Verity prayed that the next sketch would be with someone who accepted her as Mr. Cole had done that day. A man who understood what it was to be different and gave her the space to voice it.

Until then, Verity would continue in silence. And, preferably, alone.

CHAPTER TWELVE

VERITY TRIED TO resist scratching her arm. The lace ruffles on the short, puffy sleeves of her new dress itched something awful. She missed her simple muslin garments. They had moved easily with her without announcing their presence. This decorative addition to her wardrobe rustled and tugged, and she was constantly longing to strip down to her shift and just *breathe*.

What made matters worse was the choice of color her sister had decided on. The dress was a very pale pink. Verity's skin and hair were already so white, they were almost transparent. She needed something a little bolder. Even lilac would have worked. Instead, she looked as if she had been drained of all life.

But she had allowed it. She had let Hope have her way because her sister had been so excited on Verity's behalf. And because she knew that Hope might then be less insistent on influencing her next choice. This was how Verity had managed to select a deep-blue silk, a charming peach with an embroidered hem, and an olive ballgown with a sheer golden overlay. She had to admit, the ballgown was exquisite. Though she was not used to such finery and would typically even avoid it, the olive-gold dress gave her an extra dose of confidence. It was elegant and unpretentious. It would help her fit in where she felt most ill at ease, without being overstated.

And then Hope had gotten *that look* on her face, the one their mother displayed when she had one of her *brilliant ideas*. It really was the only time she looked anything like their mother. Hope had inherited the light-brown hair and amicable nature of their father. But she had their mother's quick mind.

Hope had waited until they'd been home from the dressmaker, disappeared into her room, and returned almost immediately with a wide smile and something cocooned in her hand. She cupped her palms open and revealed... a butterfly! It was a brooch made of gold, with two tiny emerald eyes. She beamed as she tipped it gently into Verity's hands.

"There!" Hope's eyes sparkled. "It is a perfect match for your dress. Now you are ready for your first ball of the season."

Verity hesitated. "Surely, Daniel would not like you to give your jewels away." But her heart longed to have it. Already, it grew warm in her cradled hand.

"Ah, but we are keeping it in the family. And he will see the joy it brings. That is just the sort of thing he would want his gifts to do. Besides, I have ample other lovely pieces to choose from. The poor, little brooch was being quite neglected. You shall give it a chance to shine once again."

"Well, if you're sure..." Verity fought to keep her eagerness from showing.

Hope folded her fingers around her sister's, enclosing the butterfly in Verity's hands. "It's yours. Perhaps it will go some way to make up for the absence of your pond."

Verity felt her cheeks turn a warm pink, likely a deeper tone than her dress. "Is it that obvious?"

"Mother said not to encourage you." Hope's tone was gentle. "But I know what your little adventures meant to you."

Meant. Past tense. As if coming to Munro had ended not only her studies of nature, but also her desire for them.

"Thank you," was all she said. As so often before, silence now saved her from a frustrating conversation.

She wanted to speak plainly, as she had done that day with Mr. Cole. Perhaps, if he had given her a brooch instead of the mounted butterfly, things would have been different. But he would have known a gift of jewelry would never do. Not unless they'd been courting. And she had already made up her mind he could not be enough for her.

Had she been too hasty? Doubt pressed upon her for a moment before certainty returned. No, it would not have been wise for her to marry Mr. Cole. He was struggling, just like her. Struggling to learn how to be himself and yet satisfy the demands imposed upon him. They would have been two broken halves trying to make one whole, each missing critical elements to bond the fragments soundly.

Verity scratched her arm again. This terrible pink dress would be relegated to the back of her wardrobe as soon as the other gowns arrived. They had needed some alterations. As Verity's luck would have it, the pale-pink one had fitted perfectly.

The clock in the hallway gonged a somber round of chimes. Eleven in all.

"Oh, look at the time!" Hope cried. "Our guests will be along any minute. Quickly, Verity, put your brooch away and come through to the drawing room. The ladies will be very happy to meet you." She put a hand upon her hip. "Now, don't give me that look. This is why you have come to Munro, after all. To find a suitor. And, to meet the men, you must meet the mothers, the sisters, the aunts. If you make a good impression, they will recommend you."

"What if I don't like *them*?" Verity grumbled. "Can I ask them to make no recommendation at all?"

Hope sighed the longsuffering sigh of mothers and older sisters everywhere. "You will behave, won't you? No one is asking you to marry outside of your free will. But civility costs you nothing. And your actions reflect on us. I don't wish to sound so very old and prim, but that is how things are, as you well know."

"I will try my best." Verity caught her sister's wary eye. "My *very* best. I shall refrain from discussing the sciences. I shan't mention my love for things with wings and antennae. But if, then, I am quiet, it is only because I am myself. There are few things beyond these interests upon which I have meaningful thoughts."

"You don't need to have *meaningful thoughts*." Hope sighed again. "Compliment their fashion. Ask after their families. Then let them talk. And try not to roll your eyes. Not even inwardly. Your face really is an open book, you know."

The bell for the front door rang out. A footman hurried to open it and the butler followed on his heels.

"Shoo!" Hope all but pushed Verity down the corridor. "And hurry back! I will send for tea in the meantime."

Verity did as she was told. She tucked the butterfly brooch into a drawer, checked that her hair was still in place—it was, thanks to the skilled work of her new lady's maid—and hastened to the drawing room with as much decorum as she could muster.

Seated upon the brocaded chairs and settees were five ladies of various ages and description. They appeared to have divided themselves into two distinct camps, and a chill hung in the air between them.

Hope, who had just finished instructing the maidservant regarding refreshments, stepped forward and proceeded with introductions, seemingly oblivious of the tension in the room. "Lady Penrose," she began, addressing the senior member of the two-party camp, "may I introduce my sister, Miss Verity Lockhart, recently arrived from Fernbridge? Verity, this is Baroness Penrose and her daughter, Miss Frances Penrose. Miss Penrose, like yourself, has just come out in society. Lady Penrose hoped that you would be dependable company for her daughter this season. A vicar's daughter can usually be trusted to know how to comport herself in company."

The irony was not lost on Verity, and Hope's stern gaze told her this was no time to prove Lady Penrose wrong.

Verity bobbed a curtsey and dipped her head, determined to please both Lady Penrose and Hope. Lady Penrose scarcely moved in her tight, long-sleeved dress but lowered her eyes in acknowledgement. Miss Frances Penrose, however, did not concern herself with the greeting. Despite the visit barely having started, she already looked bored. She fiddled with her reticule, allowed her eyes to examine every inch of the room, and frequently threw a longing look toward the exit. She had clearly not been involved in choosing Verity as a potential companion. Most likely, she had plans for her season, and a vicar's daughter did not fit into them.

Oh, good, thought Verity wryly, *I have not spoken a word and already, I am unpopular.*

Next, Hope turned to what Verity could not help but consider the rival party. Like the Penrose duo, the unknown trio was led by a matriarch.

"Mrs. Sangford, Miss Sangford, Miss Amelia, this is my sister, Miss Verity Lockhart. Verity, this is Mrs. Albert Sangford, Miss Irene Sangford, and Miss Amelia Sangford." Hope gestured at each with an open palm. Despite the absence of titles, the three ladies sat with a pride bordering on haughtiness, their backs as straight as posts, their eyes looking down their almost-too-long noses. They did not even deign to offer a slow blink as Lady Penrose had done.

My face is an open book. My face is an open book. Verity repeated the reminder to herself and shoved her feelings down and out of sight. Or so she hoped.

"Very pleased to meet you all," she said. Although it was a terrible lie, Verity guessed they would all assume she *should* delight in their company and would not question her sincerity. She sat down next to Hope, who had indicated for her to do so. It seemed the safest place in the room.

Before her rose a tide of self-satisfaction from their guests. It poured forth in waves. Verity had never experienced anything like it. What—besides a title—did Lady Penrose have to recommend her? And what—if anything—did the Sangford ladies claim as their motive for superiority? And what if—Lord help her—they had eligible brothers who were just like them?

"Do you play the pianoforte, Miss Lockhart?" Mrs. Sangford wanted to know.

"I do, at my mother's insistence. But I would not go so far as to say I play it well," Verity answered.

"My girls have had the very best tutors." A definite flash of side-eye at Lady Penrose, and Mrs. Sangford continued. "Our Amelia is sought after at gatherings. There is nothing she cannot play."

Her Amelia was an obvious golden child. She had shiny, red-blonde curls that cascaded from a loose pile upon her head. Her chin was perfect. Her eyes green, like a cat's. Her mouth pouted naturally in the way that gentlemen were so fond of. In short, she was a younger version of her mother.

Miss Sangford, on the other hand, must have taken after her father. She was taller. Everything about her was elongated. A sharper chin. A longer neck. Her hair was dark brown, almost black, as were her eyes. There was an elegance to her, which made up for the fact that her youth had begun to fade. She was clearly not the favorite. Perhaps that was why her mouth had an unhappy turn to its corners.

And perhaps that was why, despite her mother's accolades, Miss Sangford picked their opponent's side. Her voice came out as a slow drawl, as if she were in no rush to have her say. "Amelia is rather like Miss Penrose, don't you think, Mama? I would say they are equally talented. And Amelia has definitely missed the note on her Mozart more than once."

"'Rondo alla Turca' is a notoriously difficult piece!" her sister cried. "I should like to see *you* try to play it half as well!"

"It is not *I* whom Mama has spoken so highly of." Miss Sangford spoke with a barely disguised bitterness.

Miss Penrose began to smile and quickly hid her mouth behind her hand. She pretended to yawn. "My, but it is warm in here. Unusual for early spring."

Ah, thought Verity, *we are retreating to the safety of platitudes about the weather.* "It certainly is warm," she replied. "I find it even more so, being from Fernbridge, which is farther north. Our spring remains chilly through the middle of May."

"Ah, yes." Miss Sangford chimed in, though "chime" was possibly not the best description for her languid speech. "Your family is acquainted with the Fernbridge Coles, are they not? The married sister, Mrs. Trenton, lives here in Munro, not far from our uncle."

Verity cast a nervous glance at Hope. How much of recent events was common knowledge? Hope shook her head almost imperceptibly, and Verity exhaled relief. "I have not seen Charlotte… I mean, Mrs. Trenton, since we were children. But I hold her in the highest regard. She has always been a good friend to Hope. More than that, I cannot tell you."

Miss Sangford leaned forward—a little hungrily, if her gleaming eyes were any indication. "Perhaps you are more recently reunited with Mr. William Cole, her younger brother? He returned home rather abruptly last year. We wondered what took him from us so suddenly. We heard he had gone to claim a bride. And yet he has returned to Munro an unmarried officer. Can you cast any light upon the matter?"

"Oh!" Verity's stomach clenched. "Er… I hardly saw him at all. He came to tea a few times but did not mention his plans for marriage as such."

My face is an open book! Verity squealed silently, praying that her discomfort would not be conspicuous enough to create suspicion. She felt quite naked under Miss Sangford's searching eyes.

"I saw him at our Twelfth Night celebration," said Miss Penrose proudly. "He kissed me under the mistletoe." She brought her fingertips to her lips. "My first kiss. And I shall never have another like it." She sighed dreamily.

Of course he had, thought Verity. So, he had returned to his rakish ways. How disappointing. Or was Miss Penrose now the focus of his attention? If so, it was equally disappointing. She had hoped for better judgment on his part. Miss Penrose lacked any of the qualities that would help make a real man of him.

"I'm surprised, Lady Penrose, that you thought it wise to include your daughter in such frivolous games," tutted Mrs. Sangford. "Many a fine gentleman looking for a wife would prefer to be the one who claimed her first kiss. And I cannot imagine you consider Lieutenant Cole among those you would consider for Miss Penrose."

"Oh, no, not him, certainly!" cried Miss Amelia Sangford. "I'm sure he kissed a great many young ladies that night." She sniffed. "Men like him take every advantage of naive, young women, and mistletoe is a ready excuse."

Miss Penrose scowled. "I don't know what you mean by 'men like him.' He was the perfect gentleman. And he kissed none but me." She preened a little, touching her hair at the base of her neck and lowering her lashes coyly.

Her mother cut in sternly. "I don't think these ladies"—Lady Penrose paused, as if the term "ladies" could not be applied to all present—"wish to hear an account of a young woman's first Twelfth Night. After all, since it is not the first season for most here"—she was met by a glare from both Miss Sangfords—"they have no doubt had similar experiences without feeling a need to share the personal details. Really, Frances, have I taught you nothing?"

"Why, Mama!" The brazen Miss Penrose continued. "I don't think Miss Lockhart would have been permitted such a worldly encounter, being the daughter of a country vicar." She smiled with pity at Verity. "And the elder Miss Sangford has been saving her attentions for a man of rank. Is that not so?" She offered an innocent cock of the head to the opposing party.

"Well, it is only natural!" Mrs. Sangford protested. "Should we demand anything less than suitors of nobility, since we are distant cousins to the queen?"

"How distant, exactly?" Lady Penrose replied, her face a mask of sweetness.

"Ah, tea!" Hope almost shouted with relief as the footman

entered with a tray. "Shall I pour? Two sugars, I believe, Lady Penrose?"

As Hope served the guests in a very particular order, a careful dance of hierarchy ensued, in which the Sangfords were obliged to concede that their relation to the queen—such as it was—ranked lower than an actual title. With everyone's place confirmed, the conversation proceeded rather more sedately, and Verity found herself the focus of their now-undivided attention.

"Which will be the first ball your sister attends, Mrs. Sinclair?" Lady Penrose wanted to know.

"I believe it to be hosted by the Macraes," Hope replied. They always draw a lovely crowd, and Verity will be able to meet a wide range of Munro's inhabitants."

"Yes," Lady Penrose agreed, but without the same enthusiasm. "They are rather modern in that way. But what can one expect from descendants of Jacobites? They may be loyal to the Crown now, but their thinking has always been a little... different."

Verity's ears pricked up. Different? Bless Hope's heart! The Macraes sounded *exactly* like the sort of people Verity would get along with. And everyone attending would feel the same way. How wonderful! Even better, it meant that the backstabbing, two-faced Penroses and Sangfords and their ilk would avoid the gathering at all costs. How positively heavenly!

"Of course," Lady Penrose continued, "*we* will be at Munro House for the viscount and viscountess's ball. The event will be for gentry only. Rather different than the Macraes, who throw their home open to just about anyone."

"I believe Lord and Lady Howell intend to grace the Macraes with their presence," Hope said in a measured tone. "And several other estate balls besides. The new viscountess is apparently a total delight. I imagine his lordship cannot wait to show off his new wife. They have been married but a six-month, and yet all who encounter them say the change in the viscount is marked. He has quite shed his previously taciturn nature. How lucky we are when we find someone who brings out the best in us!"

"I shall see that with my own eyes before I believe it," Mrs. Sangford mumbled. All heads—bar those of the Misses Sangford—turned to her in surprise. She shifted in her chair.

"Why, my *dear* Mrs. Sangford," Lady Penrose retorted, "how can you speak thus of our finest citizen? He has done nothing but good for our fair city."

"Cities don't have feelings," Mrs. Sangford answered bitterly.

Lady Penrose's head jerked up. Her eyes narrowed. "I'm sure I don't understand your meaning. Would you be so good as to explain?"

Mrs. Sangford glared at the baroness. She did not answer immediately. If Lady Penrose had meant to humiliate her, she was unwilling to take the bait.

She glanced at her daughters. They sat in equally uncomfortable silence. At the sight of her unhappy children, Mrs. Sangford was at once transformed. She lifted her head and sat taller, her mouth tightening, eyes blazing, as the mother tigress within rushed to the surface.

"Both my daughters have been slighted by that man." She growled. "Some viscount he is. He has the manners of a peasant!" She almost spat the words. "*No wonder* he married a commoner. And a merchant's daughter, at that! What can she offer the people of Munro but country manners to match those of her boorish husband?" Her hand waved in unison with her disdain. "*Of course* they are a good match! He would never have found a suitable wife among the *ton* of our fine city."

Mrs. Sangford breathed heavily, her tirade paused but threatening to resume at the slightest provocation.

Verity, who had never met either the viscount or his "country" wife, felt at once that she must like them very much if they drew such ire from Mrs. Sangford. How wonderful that Lord Howell had found happiness. He must have, else the Sangfords would certainly have reveled in his misery. She could only respect a man who had the wisdom to look farther afield when the

Munro *ton* seemed to offer such a meager supply of worthy women.

"Perhaps," Lady Penrose said smoothly, "if he had waited one more season until my Frances was out in society, things would have been different. A young woman of good breeding might have offered him a better outcome."

"Oh, *no*, Mama!" Miss Penrose cried. "I could *never* marry someone so high in the instep and always in the dudgeon. I would far rather have a simple officer like Lieutenant Cole, who is charming and kind."

Lady Penrose was unamused. "You can rid yourself of such thoughts immediately, Frances. Perhaps Miss Lockhart would find a young officer enticing, but he is not for you. Your father would disown you at once."

Miss Penrose considered Verity. Envy lay shallow in her hooded eyes and scorn twisted her pouting lips. Verity could only imagine the extent of the young lady's rage if she should discover that this very vicar's daughter had been the bride for whom Mr. Cole had returned to Fernbridge. And, worse still, that she had written him off as husband material! The urge to scratch her itching arm returned and it was all Verity could manage to restrain herself under the hawkish gaze of Miss Penrose.

By some merciful stroke of good fortune, the hallway clock began to steadily announce the noon hour.

"Ah," said Lady Penrose upon the first gong.

"Mama," chimed in Miss Penrose along with the timepiece. "Did you not say…?"

"Yes, indeed," her mother answered upon the third strike.

All the visitors rose and began their polite goodbyes.

"Well, this has been lovely," Mrs. Sangford said to no one in particular.

"Yes, just lovely," Miss Amelia echoed with a smile that shone like her Venetian-blonde locks. Her mother beamed at her. The dark and broody Miss Sangford remained silent.

"Such a pity we must leave so soon," Lady Penrose insisted,

shooing her daughter out before her. "So many other commitments. You understand."

"Of course," Hope assured them, walking with them toward the door.

A footman returned wraps and coats to each in turn. Hope waved the guests into their carriages from the steps. The front door closed. She breathed out a sigh of relief.

Verity could stand it no longer. "If that is what Munro has to offer, I want none of it," she declared firmly. "You and Mother can think of me what you will, but there is no universe in which the Penroses or Sangfords and I could ever form an alliance."

"Well, that is good to know," Hope answered pleasantly. "You would have greatly fallen in my esteem if it were otherwise."

Verity stared at her sister. "I don't understand. If they are not suitable companions, why did you introduce us?"

"You were so very reticent about what Munro has to offer," Hope explained. "I thought it best to show you the worst at your earliest introduction. Then all that followed would be less daunting. Even enjoyable, given half a chance. Our fair city has its share of disagreeable, gossiping, uncharitable persons. But there are also families worthy of your acquaintance. You will meet several such individuals at the Macraes' ball. And now that you have survived the worst of us, you can relax and enjoy the best of us."

Verity folded her arms. "I suppose you think you are very clever to manipulate circumstances thus."

"Oh, yes, indeed!" Hope grinned. Then she slipped her arm into Verity's. "Come on, let's put you back into one of your old dresses. This one's color does nothing for you. I don't know what I was thinking."

At the thought of the imminent release from the loathsome gown, Verity was instantly cheered and willing to forgive Hope just about anything. She no longer feared an enforced friendship with the girlish Miss Penrose, nor did she dread further probing questions by Miss Sangford. She did, however, still have a letter to write to Mr. Cole's sister. Once the butterfly had been returned to him and an explanation offered, all that was immediately problematic in her life would be dealt with.

Perhaps, after all, Munro was the fresh start her mother had hoped it would be. For the first time, Verity felt a rush of optimism toward the future. Really, she should give it a fair chance. In fact, she pondered, as she slipped the familiar soft muslin over her hips once more, she had already survived the worst. Hope was right. Better things awaited her.

Such pleasant anticipation did not fit as comfortably as her well-worn dress, but she was willing to let it linger. After all, what did she have to lose? If the Sangfords and Penroses of the world could be so easily discarded, she was free to risk without danger. And that was something she might just be brave enough to do.

CHAPTER THIRTEEN

C HARLOTTE TRENTON THREW open her arms to welcome her younger brother.

"William! How wonderful to see you!" She twisted her head to the side. "James, William has come!"

A surly voice floated up from behind a newspaper. "Don't shout, woman. You'll give me a headache."

The newspaper lowered in a crumpling fold, and the red curls and pale face of William's brother-in-law appeared with an all-too-familiar scowl. It soon evaporated, however, and James jumped to his feet, extending his hand as he did so.

"William! This is an excellent surprise. Why didn't you say it was William, Charlotte?"

Charlotte and her brother exchanged knowing smiles that were quite lost on James Trenton. He grabbed William by the arm and pulled him into a hearty embrace with a slap on the back.

"Always good to see you," James told his brother-in-law. "Especially now that Charlotte has been neglecting me."

"Oh, hush, Husband," Charlotte teased. "You have nothing to complain about. You are the most beloved of all men in Munro."

"That may have been true once." James pouted, though a smile had begun to break through the corners of his mouth. "Now, however, I am but third in your heart."

"Ah, yes." William pretended to scold his sister. "I have seen how you dote upon your children. How could poor James ever compete for your affection?"

"He does not need to." Charlotte slipped her arms about her husband's waist and hugged him, her blonde locks—so similar to Lawrence's—falling upon his shoulder. "There is room in my heart for all three of you. And you, too, of course, William," she added hastily.

"And for our brother, Lawrence," William reminded her. "And Mother and Father." He began to count them off on his fingers. "And don't forget the milkman and the butcher and the farmer in his fields. Charlotte has room in her heart for all of mankind."

"Oh, you!" Charlotte laughed. "I am not nearly the gracious soul you make me out to be."

"No, my dear. William is right." James was suddenly solemn. "You are the best of us. I am a lucky man."

"Well!" Charlotte blushed. "As usual, William, it has taken you but a minute to bring joy to our home." She lowered her lashes at her husband. "And you, dearest James, still know how to bring out the girlish flush in my cheeks."

"You do brighten our household, dear boy," said James. "Which is why I cannot understand that it has taken you this long to visit us. You've been stationed in Munro since December, I understand. Why have you waited more than two months to come and see us?"

"And scarcely a letter in six months, either," complained Charlotte. "I've had all my news of you from Mother and Lawrence, neither of whom tells the whole story, I'll wager. Lawrence is too correct and Mother is too protective. But I know you. To leave as suddenly as you did last year. And then to return just as suddenly, *sans* bride, and in uniform..."

"Do you like it?" William interrupted. He opened his arms to show off his red coat and brass buttons.

"I don't care about your attire," his sister replied. "I care about you. And poor Miss Lockhart. Did you have to break her heart? She is such a harmless thing. Not at all your usual type. Why would you rush off to claim her, only to give up on her completely?"

"Hmph, she doesn't have a heart to break," William said rather uncharitably. "She only loves the creatures of the meadows and streams, not men of flesh and blood. I could no more marry her than a tree stump."

Charlotte's eyes darkened. "That is unkind, William. I remember her being a quiet girl, but not without feeling. She was particularly gentle with frogs and beetles, I recall. And who can blame her when no one else gave her the time of day? We were always off on adventures too rough for her to join in. And when she *was* old enough, we were away to university or had families of our own. Given the opportunity, I believe all that affection and kindness she showed the little creatures could have been heaped upon a man willing to show it to her in equal measure."

William gritted his teeth. "I *did* try. I even gave her a gift. At some expense, I may add. She all but threw it back in my face. I did not see much of that kindness and affection you speak of."

"Ah. The butterfly." Charlotte's mouth drooped. "I know all about that. You gave up very easily, if you don't mind my saying it. If you are going to take marriage seriously, William dear, you will have to rise above such misunderstandings and pave the way to reconciliation."

"'Misunder…'" William spluttered. "'*Misunderstandings*'? Who told you this? There was no misunderstanding. It was simple. There was a gift, and an outright rejection of the gift. She is too full of sensitivities and delicate feelings. What is there to understand in a gift but thoughtfulness? Yet I received no gratitude, no appreciation of my efforts. I was effectively dismissed. So I withdrew my suit."

Charlotte said nothing for a moment. Then she turned and walked toward a sideboard in the drawing room, opened one of its inlaid doors, and withdrew a small package. William recognized the suede cloth wrapping at once.

"What is that doing here?" he demanded. "Has Miss Lockhart been to see you? Has she been telling exaggerations about me?"

"No, William," Charlotte answered calmly. "She sent this for me to give to you whenever you should make your way to our home. And there was a letter with it…"

"For me?"

"Don't be silly. That would be improper. She wrote to *me*. Though the contents were effectively for your attention. Here. I think you should read it before you say any further unchivalrous things about her." She folded back the first layer of the butterfly's wrapping and revealed an opened letter. "Go on. Take your time. Meanwhile, I will send for tea, and James can finish his paper." She firmly led her husband back to his chair and returned his newspaper to him amid the usual brief grumbling before he submitted to her soft insistence. Then she reached for the bell pull.

William saw nothing further. He lowered himself into the nearest seat, placing the discredited gift down on the table. Miss Lockhart must really have loathed it to make a point of bringing it all the way to Munro to return it. It shouldn't have surprised him. She had made no secret of her disgust with it.

And yet, he *was* surprised. Despite his earlier bluster, he knew he was not blameless. He had departed the vicarage in no better form than that with which Miss Lockhart had received his gift. She likely wanted no reminder of it *or* him. And yet…

She was not malicious by nature. Or resentful. She had taken his half-hearted attempt to woo her in her stride, even offering empathy and the beginnings of friendship. She had not encouraged him, but she had never been silly or cruel. Which was why her excessive response at their last meeting had caught him completely off guard. It was not like her to rub salt in the wound by going to such lengths to return the butterfly. If anything, she was probably as keen to forget the whole ordeal as he was.

Then why was he staring at that same discarded gift now,

here in his sister's home in Munro?

The letter!

William quickly peeled away the outer covering of the parcel and lifted the pages to his gaze. They were already partly unfolded. He straightened them further and began to read.

There were the usual greetings. A little catching up on family news. Congratulations to Charlotte and James on the birth of their daughter.

Ah, here it was…

I come now to a matter that is, unfortunately, less conversational. It has been weighing heavily on my mind. I regret having to burden you with the task of messenger, but it would be wholly inappropriate for me to contact your brother directly, as you understand all too well, I'm sure.

I shall come straight to the point. During one of his visits to the vicarage, Mr. Cole very kindly brought me a gift. No doubt he put a great deal of thought into it, which was a gift in and of itself. He had also been careful that it not be construed as a romantic gesture, since I had been clear on my feelings regarding marriage.

William stopped reading.

Miss Lockhart could have assumed he would be given the opportunity to read the letter eventually. But she was not only addressing him. His sister was the intended recipient of the letter. Its contents could thus be shared with whomever Charlotte saw fit. And Charlotte would want to share anything that benefitted her family.

In these few sentences, worded with such care, Miss Lockhart had gone to some lengths to protect his reputation. As a failed suitor. As a gift-giver. As a man. She was answering any doubts his family might have had regarding his behavior toward her. She had not apologized, though he sensed she was working her way up toward the very thing. But she was doing something even more important. She was defending his character.

William was numb with shock. No one had ever done that for him. Oh, he had been admired aplenty. But that was for his charm and wit and good looks. He had never before had his character praised. To the contrary. Indeed, the worst blow had come from Ellena, for whom he would have been the best man it was in his power to be. She had called his judgment into question, denouncing him as selfish, when all he had done was try to protect her.

Yet here was Miss Lockhart—whom he had all but discounted as a woman unworthy of his attention—trying to make amends for something in which he shared the blame. He knew she had seen something in him, something she valued deeply, even if only as a friend. And he had missed it completely. That was why the gift had been a disaster. He had quite misread her and her interest in little, winged creatures.

She hadn't even been angry. No, not angry. Devastated. She had appeared quite broken, as if a sacred trust had been trampled upon.

Despite her profound hurt and disappointment, Miss Verity Lockhart had come to sense *his* hurt and disappointment. She must have been quite haunted by the thought of it for her to reach out after all this time. William could not fathom such uncommon decency on his behalf. It made him more than a little ashamed of the way he had deserted her without so much as a goodbye. And he had allowed his recollection of her to remain tainted by his own conceit ever since.

He returned to the letter, humbled and contrite and amazed at her good nature.

> *Mama has tried her best to make me into someone she can present to society with confidence. I remain, however, somewhat of a disappointment.*

Her words stuck in his throat, as if it were he who had spoken them. In essence, Miss Lockhart and he were the same. An enigma to their parents. Playing a role they did not wish to sustain.

My strangeness is no secret in Fernbridge, where everyone has seen my sketches of insects or come across me at the pond or along a stream, seeking my next subject to study and then release with envy at its freedom.

William remembered how she always set her little models free. And how she had spoken of them with… What was it? Yes… With love. While her sketches might have been scientific, there was something else she had been trying to capture. Something—she had said it now—that she had envied. And her chasing after this had cast her as a figure most strange.

It was this very strangeness that had given them a connection. She had not been afraid to question his motives, to confront his disguise, perhaps because she saw someone else who was hiding from themselves.

Suddenly, everything Miss Lockhart had to say was precious, urgent, vital. She understood him. Now he wanted to understand her. To see her, as she had truly seen him.

Mr. Cole had not thought me strange. He had seen a woman of science who received no encouragement and he had tried to offer me a measure of it in his own way.

So she *had* grasped his motive!

Dear Mrs. Trenton, how can I explain my reaction without seeming spoiled and ungrateful? You are a woman of quality. I am not formed or polished to the same caliber. Everything I desire seems contrary to the norms of society. Your brother was wise to sever his association with me. I am an odd country-woman who yearns for the freedom of fields, while my mind is filled with detailed observations that would bore guests who must suffer my company.

All I could see in Mr. Cole's carefully chosen gift was a rare and wonderful creature that was trapped, pinned on display forever—a rare being that was to be owned without being understood. I'm afraid I rather saw myself in this butterfly,

though I would not go so far as to call myself a wonderful crea-
ture. But Mr. Cole is certainly not to blame for being unable to
read my mind.

William could read no more. His breathing grew tight as he
fully grasped Miss Lockhart's pain. He knew it all too well. Except
he had escaped some of the loathsome constraints merely by
being a man. He could follow his own will. And if he so desired,
he could choose a wife who must grant him his leave as he
wished it, to have a drink with the lads, to ride his horse, to leave
his family and go to war. It would not be the sort of wife he
wanted, but it was possible to marry and resume his individual
interests.

What he *did* want, he now realized with great surprise, was
someone like Miss Verity Lockhart. A woman who was true to
herself even if it drew judgment from others. A partner who
would accept him as he was, who would fight on his behalf.

But she didn't want him, did she? He had been childish, petty,
selfish. How could he expect to have a great love—one for the
ages—if he didn't pay better attention to what his lady truly
needed? That was exactly how he had lost Ellena. He hadn't
understood until this very moment. And he had made the same
mistake with Miss Lockhart.

At least, he told his mortified conscience, he had not betrayed
Miss Lockhart as fully as he had done Ellena. Fool that he was, he
had not seen his actions as treachery then. Oh, no, he had
convinced himself of his noble intent. It would have been
laughable if it weren't so humiliatingly dishonest. Small wonder
she had been aghast at his declaration of love. He could see it so
clearly now. It filled him with a deep sense of disgrace.

He was almost too afraid to read further. Afraid of the shame
he would feel as Miss Lockhart apologized for overreacting. If he
had spent more time really listening, he wouldn't have put her in
that position in the first place. They could have remained friends.
They might have become more.

He *must* read on. Learn the full lesson. Never make that mistake again.

His gaze returned to the letter. There were but a few lines remaining.

My humble request is for you to return this rare butterfly to your brother, that he might gift it to someone more worthy, or, at the very least, sell it to a collector and regain a measure of the funds he so willingly spent. And, if you will allow it, let him read these words that I may unburden myself of the sorrow I feel at having hurt him. I behaved badly. And I regret it deeply. Having lost his friendship was a high price to pay for a moment's folly.

Yours in good faith,
Verity Lockhart

There it was. The olive branch. A reason to hope. An opportunity to recapture a fledgling friendship. William could think of nothing he wanted more in the world. He had missed out on making her his wife, but to have her as a friend would be the next best thing. Like his sister, Miss Lockhart would brook no nonsense from him. But, just like Charlotte, she would also accept him as he was. In exchange, he wanted to be her champion. He could lend his worldly knowledge to her debut season, guiding her through the pitfalls of Munro society. With the necessary chaperoning, of course. He would not have her reputation tarnished.

William felt a surge of purpose. But he would not forget the lesson learned. Action, yes, but listening also. A lot more listening. And maybe his next venture into romance would be the stuff of legends, the lifelong passion that he so craved.

"You are smiling." Charlotte's voice broke through his thoughts. "I am amazed. I did not think there was much humor in the letter."

"No, not humor," William answered. "Truth."

"And the truth makes you smile?"

"It does. There is pain, and regret, but also a new goal."

Charlotte cocked her head to one side. "May I ask the nature of this goal?"

"To be a better friend, if Miss Lockhart will allow it."

Charlotte clapped her hands in delight. "I *knew* you would do the right thing!"

"Did you?" William's brow furrowed, his eyebrows drawn together in confusion. "How could you know it with such certainty when I have but come to that conclusion myself this very minute?"

His sister's eyes sparkled. "Because I know *you*, William. You like to play the scoundrel, but you are a good soul, dear brother. And if you are going to put your youthful energy to good use, I am all for it. In fact, I know exactly when and where you and Miss Lockhart may rekindle your friendship."

"You do?" William's eyebrows rose and his lips quirked into a pout.

"I do. The Macraes are having a ball in a few weeks. And I happen to know that Miss Lockhart and her sister will be in attendance. Her first ball of the season, I believe. You could use the occasion to accept her apology. And offer one of your own, perhaps?"

William felt oddly nervous at the prospect. He did not want this one chance to go awry. "Will you be there?" he asked, his forehead pleated with uncertainty.

"She doesn't want to leave the children," James piped up. "We've hardly been to a single gathering since our daughter was born. And I will not go without her. I did tell you I was being sorely neglected."

"We-ell." Charlotte hesitated. "I suppose if it's for a good cause…"

"Hmph," grumbled James. "It is clear my happiness has not been cause enough."

Charlotte half-turned in his direction. "Oh, do stop complaining, James dear. It is not as though you were deprived of my company. Only the company of others. And I did say we should have friends to dinner, here, in our home. I simply am not ready to abandon my little cherub to the nurse completely, coming home in the early hours and too exhausted the next day to give our children any attention."

James remained silent and sullen.

Charlotte slipped across the room and hunched down by his chair. "Mr. Trenton," she said softly, "will you do me the honor of escorting me to the Macraes' ball? I would be so happy if you did. I have not been out in ages and it would do me good to dance upon your arm."

William watched as James fought to stay welded to his mood.

"What about the children? You will spend the night fretting about their wellbeing."

"I shall endeavor not to," came the reasonable reply. "You will be the perfect distraction."

Warmth returned to her husband's eyes.

"Well, I suppose it is the least I could do."

"Thank you." Charlotte rose again, lightness returning to her movements. "What shall I wear, do you think?"

"It matters not," James answered, his eyes tracking her silhouette. "You will outshine them all."

Charlotte lowered her eyes. The air in the room grew close. William cleared his throat.

"Ahem. If you will both be there, I think I might be brave enough to face Miss Lockhart and try to make amends."

"Oh, and Lawrence will be there too!" Charlotte recalled. "I had invited him here for the end of April to celebrate your coming of age. He would not want to miss a dance at the Macraes', since he will be here already. They always throw such cheerful parties."

William was about to say that he had quite forgot about his twenty-first birthday, and that Lawrence really needn't bother to come at all, when Charlotte added, "*And* the ball will be graced by the company of Lord Howell and his new viscountess. You remember James's cousin, don't you, William? You flirted with her something terrible. We were fortunate that she did not take umbrage at your forward manner. Though I do suggest that, as a married woman, she would take exception now."

William grew solemn at the mention of Ellena. That had been a job badly done indeed. That friendship could never be salvaged. If he so much as looked at her, let alone approached her to try to make amends, her husband would likely have him by the throat.

A strange new sensation accompanied these thoughts. It took William a minute to identify it. It wasn't quite peace. Nor was it the absence of regret. It was… He had it on the tip of his tongue… His heart lurched as the word came to him. Acceptance! How curious. For the first time, William did not bewail the loss of Ellena. Nor did he feel rage against the man she had chosen instead. Did this mean he could finally leave it all in the past? He must, if he were to move forward. He could not open his heart to another while it was still filled with ghosts.

"So, will you be staying for dinner?" Charlotte asked. "We have so much catching up to do."

"If you will have me, prodigal brother that I am," William replied.

"Even better, why do you not stay with us a while?" James suggested. "It seems a waste to pay for officer's quarters when you could have rooms here with family. I'll wager the food is better, too. Although we offer no carousing, such as you're used to."

"Perhaps less of that would do me good," William pondered aloud.

"Why, William." Charlotte winked. "Don't tell me you are growing up."

William waggled a finger at her, though his smile was broad. "How can you suggest such a thing? I have a reputation to uphold, you know."

Charlotte's smile remained, but her voice grew soft and serious. "You might benefit from an altered reputation, William dearest. Not that we would change one whit about you. It's just, well, you don't seem to let anyone see the real you. The William they think they know doesn't really exist, does he? Not in the true sense of the word. He is something of a phantom, a guise, if you will. It is such a pity. It attracts all the wrong sorts of women, you know."

"Oh, leave the poor boy be, woman," cried James. "You will drive him away with your sermon when I would persuade him to linger here a month or two at least."

"Ah, fear not," William answered. "It would be a privilege to make my home with you while I can. Especially since we will no doubt be called to Europe before you have had a chance to tire of me. Our field marshal, His Grace the Duke of Wellington, has already left for Brussels. I expect the remaining officers and troops will be called to follow shortly. In fact, I would count myself lucky if I were still in Munro for the Macraes' ball. If I am, it will certainly be a high point before my departure to more somber activities."

The room grew quiet.

How odd, thought William. *I have wished for nothing but a life in the military. The seductiveness of the uniform. The glamor of the sword. The camaraderie of my peers. Yet a time is coming for blood to be upon it all.*

He shivered slightly.

"No, no, no," Charlotte scolded, grabbing William by the hand and patting it with some vigor. "We shall not think of such things while you are in Munro. There is time enough for worry when you are abroad." She wrapped William's hand in hers and sat down beside him. "Tea will be served shortly. And you will stay for dinner. I insist. And tomorrow, you will bring your things from your lodgings and settle here with us. In no time at all, our threshold will be quite worn out with young ladies and their chaperones calling on us."

The shadow receded from William's thoughts. "Good," he

said. "Then I shall have opportunities aplenty to practice being less charming and more solemn."

A peal of laughter escaped Charlotte's throat. "I should like to see you try. You cannot help but be a gentleman of great allure."

"Thank you. But I must, in all earnestness, strive to be more than that."

"And so you shall. I have every faith in you."

"Ah," said James as a maid entered the room with a tray. She placed it neatly upon the small, square table before quickly tucking an errant strand of hair back under her cap. "Our tea has come. And not a moment too soon. William was in grave danger of becoming quite dull. And we can't have that. I rely on you, dear boy, to lift me from my own doldrums. Perhaps we shall go riding later this week?"

William nodded. "I look forward to it."

Indeed, it occurred to William as he lifted the cup of sweet tea to his lips, that he now had a great many things to look forward to. But the time to enjoy them was growing sparse. With his coming-of-age mere weeks away, he should make earnest work of becoming a worthy man. Maybe then, at last, he would be able to find—and keep—a worthy woman.

CHAPTER FOURTEEN

Munro, April 1815

VERITY STEPPED GINGERLY from the Sinclair carriage, the olive-gold folds of her skirt clutched in her nervous fingers. The home of the Macraes was bathed in the soft glow of moonlight, while the light of hundreds of candles shone forth from every window and doorway.

The sheer expense of it was hard for Verity to fathom. In the vicarage, they went to bed early rather than waste such a precious commodity as candles. Even the dress she was wearing equaled the cost of her entire wardrobe in Fernbridge, not counting shoes or hats, of course. Thanks to the quality of the material and its sophisticated style, she felt less self-conscious entering such a grand home. Still, there was the matter of all the strangers. And the dancing.

Hope had done her best. But Verity had not taken to dancing. She had discovered that, unlike her fingers, which were skilled in fine artistry, her feet were rather ungainly. Or perhaps they were merely feet that would rather wade through a pond than follow the confusing patterns of a cotillion. She had more than once nearly knocked Hope's cap from her head when she had raised her arms and turned left instead of right. Or was it right instead of left? Whatever the case may have been, she fully intended to be mysteriously unavailable when they danced the cotillion.

At least she would be spared the waltz. Her father had strong opinions about the intimate contact this shockingly modern dance allowed and would not have his unmarried daughter perform it. Thanks be for her old-fashioned papa!

"Now, don't be worried," Hope whispered as they stepped inside the warm foyer of the Macrae home. "There will be plenty of country reels where you will spend much of the time standing in conversation while you wait your turn to dance down the center with your partner."

"Oh, good," Verity replied weakly. She knew Hope was trying to lessen her fears, but conversation was little better than dancing, especially when it was with a stranger. She was sure to speak too freely. Or, in holding her tongue for her mother's sake, say too little. It really wasn't much of a choice—to be branded as odd or viewed as painfully shy.

"Are you sighing already?" Hope asked. "Don't look at me so woefully! Come on, you are here to have fun. And meet people."

And find a husband, Verity grumbled to herself. She had no illusions as to the real purpose of these balls. They were the ultimate convenience for the unwed—a crowd of potential matches, dressed to display beauty and wealth, such as they had. Every conversation, every dance, every tilt of the fan was a step toward achieving one goal: to procure an engagement. Everyone else who attended was really just a chaperone.

Perhaps that was why Hope looked forward to the night ahead. She had found an excellent match in Daniel Sinclair. Whether or not they danced and exchanged scintillating dialogue, they would return to their home satisfied and happy.

Verity, on the other hand, had no such assurance. The best she could hope for was to not make a fool of herself. But she had promised her mother she would try. And Hope was so excited on her behalf. At the very least, she should bear it bravely.

Verity resisted the urge to find a quiet corner behind some potted foliage. Instead, she clutched her fan and reticule tightly and followed Hope and her husband around the edge of the large ballroom toward a slightly less crowded spot.

"Mr. and Mrs. Sinclair!" called a friendly voice. "How lovely to see you here!"

"Mrs. Trenton!" Hope turned to Verity. "I scarce need to introduce you, as you have known each other since childhood. Perhaps, though, you do not recognize each other, as it has been some years since your acquaintance. Mrs. Trenton, this is my sister, Miss Verity Lockhart. Verity, this lovely woman is Mrs. James Trenton. You knew her as Miss Cole."

William's sister.

Charlotte Trenton had been kind enough to send a note, acknowledging receipt of the butterfly and accompanying letter, and offering the assurance that William would be informed of both when next he visited. He must have done so by now. Verity searched Mrs. Trenton's face for any clue as to how he may have reacted.

"My dear Miss Lockhart." The lady smiled warmly, reaching out and taking Verity's hand in hers. "How you have bloomed! It amazes me that the gentlemen are not already lining up to ask for a dance. But then again, there seems to be no accounting for the whims of men."

Was she making friendly chatter, or did a message lie hidden deeper among her words? No doubt Mrs. Trenton was aware of the courtship that had stuttered to a halt before it had quite begun. Was she offering a measure of understanding, even an apology of sorts for the fact that her brother had abandoned his effort so abruptly? If so, Verity must set her straight at once. After all, the lack of romantic progress between Mr. Cole and herself had been as much her own choice as his.

"I am only too grateful to be left to myself," Verity hinted. "Gentlemen cannot be blamed for offering me a wide berth when I make no effort to be sought out."

Mrs. Trenton cocked her head to the side. "I am of the humble opinion that a bud will open spontaneously to the warmth of the sun. No true gardener expects to pry open her heart. He would rather provide the environment in which she would offer it willingly."

Perhaps Verity's letter had said enough, for it seemed she and Mrs. Trenton understood each other. It was a great relief. Not only was Hope's friendship with Mrs. Trenton intact, but the lady seemed to comprehend Verity's position as well. For the first time since she'd stepped from the carriage, Verity was buoyed by optimism. Perhaps there were others like Mrs. Trenton. The evening had only just begun, and already, Verity had an ally. In the form of Mr. Cole's sister, no less!

Verity squeezed the hand that held hers. "You have not changed at all. Even though I was too young to mix often in your company, I always remember your kindness. It is good to know you again."

"Certainly, Mrs. Sinclair must bring you to tea, and soon," Mrs. Trenton replied. "My maternal cares prevent me from leaving the house as often as I'd like. Some company to look in on us would be very welcome."

"You are the most dedicated of mothers," said a voice behind them. Verity whipped around to find a gentleman of very average proportions smiling pleasantly at Mrs. Trenton. He looked about ten years older than Verity, the very first wrinkles appearing about the corners of his eyes. He was neither tall nor particularly short. His medium-brown hair appeared undecided as to whether it was straight or wavy. Though ample in supply, it lay subdued upon his scalp while the ends twisted haphazardly at the nape of his neck. His face did not boast refined cheekbones. Nor did it lack structure. He was entirely mediocre in appearance, except for the sincerity of his smile, which lit up his features and gave them a sweetness that was very welcoming.

"Dr. Westbridge!" Mrs. Trenton cried with delight. She pulled lightly on Verity's hand, which she had not yet released, and guided her to more fully face the gentleman. "Miss Lockhart, may I introduce Dr. Arthur Westbridge? He is our physician and was present at the births of Clarence, our firstborn, and Jane, our daughter. Dr. Westbridge, Miss Verity Lockhart of Fernbridge, a childhood friend. This is her first ball."

Dr. Westbridge dipped his head to Verity, his smile widening to include his eyes, which twinkled cheerfully. "What a pleasure, Miss Lockhart," he said. "You have chosen the best possible ball with which to begin your venture into society. The Macraes are a very good sort indeed. And their guests likewise." His eye caught something and his speech hitched. "Yes, ahem, well, with the possible exception of one or two personages who will insist upon attending without knowing how to behave."

Verity tried to catch sight of whoever had caused him to alter his endorsement of the event, but the crowd was too dense to pick out the individuals.

"Nevertheless," Dr. Westbridge continued, "I am confident your chaperone will know whom to keep from you." He paused, as if pondering a private thought, then added, "Perhaps I may be considered worthy of a dance? One of the country dances, if you like. I am not proficient enough to offer you the cotillion. Your first experience of that dance should not be with a clumsy oaf like myself. But I can offer you a fair reel and some not-too-terrible discourse. Is this acceptable?"

Verity looked at her sister. Hope looked positively exultant. "I see no reason why you should not dance with *Dr.* Westbridge," she said, raising her fan and giving an exaggerated wink behind it. "That is, after all, why you have come… To *dance.*"

Verity looked away before Hope could wink surreptitiously at her again. Honestly! Her sister was practically planning their nuptials already!

"I'm afraid," Verity said to the gentleman, "my own contribution to the dance will be inferior."

"Nonsense!" said Hope. "You are just nervous. Daniel and I shall take our places next to you and you may follow our steps when you falter. There are plenty of unmarried gentlemen here tonight, so I may be forgiven for stealing my own husband for a dance instead of lending him to the unmarried ladies."

Dr. Westbridge shrugged. "It is not for me to push Miss

Lockhart toward an activity that alarms her. Perhaps," he said, addressing Verity, "when we next meet at a ball, you will feel more inclined."

"Oh, I…" Verity faltered. He was being very reasonable. She was not used to being accommodated so readily. His company would not be loathsome. And he seemed the sort of man who might forgive her stepping on his toes. If she could get through a dance with him, it might give her courage for the next. One step at a time.

She lowered her lashes. "Thank you, sir. I would be honored to have my first dance with you, if you are certain it will not be a disappointment."

His eyes widened. "Your 'first' dance? No one else has asked you yet? How can that be? To be sure, I shall have to check the eyesight of every man in this room."

Verity felt the color rush into her cheeks. With the help of her borrowed lady's maid, she *had* made an effort to look her best. Her hair had been curled and the top half twisted into a loose knot at the back of her neck. The rest of her white-blonde locks cascaded down her back. Hope's butterfly brooch added a touch of class. And yet, Verity had never considered herself a beauty. Certainly not in the traditional sense. Her looks had never really mattered. Certainly not to frogs and grasshoppers and beetles. Hearing a gentleman decry the fact that he was alone in admiring her came as something of a surprise.

"You are very kind," she murmured. "But I assure you, I do not thrive on the attentions of men. The absence thereof consequently does not disturb me."

"I think you'll find, Miss Lockhart," said Dr. Westbridge, "that the current situation will not last. Expect to quite wear your shoes out tonight, for your dance card shall soon fill up." Before Verity could protest, he held out his hand and asked, "Shall we? I see the dancers are lining up."

Verity placed her gloved fingers onto his palm. She looked to Hope to make sure she was coming too, as promised.

Daniel Sinclair took his wife's hand lightly, as if for the first time. Hope fanned herself with the other hand like a flattered young maiden, gave a deep curtsey, and followed him to the center of the room. Verity and Arthur Westbridge took their positions beside them.

"Well, here we are at last." Dr. Westbridge grinned. "We have made it to the dance floor without tripping over our feet. I think this is a most encouraging development, wouldn't you say, Miss Lockhart?"

Verity stifled a giggle. "And we continue to stand without falling over," she added, joining in the game.

"Hurrah! It bodes well for us. Do you think the other couples dare to feel such confidence as ours?"

Verity laughed aloud. She quickly threw open her fan to hide her embarrassment at doing so. She caught Hope's eye and saw her nod almost imperceptibly.

Approval. Never before had Verity's impropriety received approval. Yet she knew what Hope was thinking—that her little sister had relaxed in the company of this gentleman. And that was a very good sign indeed.

It was true. Dr. Westbridge was an easy sort of fellow. He might not have been as handsome as Mr. Cole, but she would rather give up looks than kindness when it came to a potential match. Besides, he wasn't unappealing. His features might have been uninspiring on the whole, but his mouth was full and gentle and his eyes sparkled with good humor.

Verity lowered her fan as the chamber ensemble started to play their first notes. She began to count the rhythm, imagining her first step. It would be some time before it was their turn. Her nerves began to twitch once more.

But Dr. Westbridge had not abandoned her to her building apprehension. He had nodded to his neighbors to the left and right of him and then returned his focus squarely to Verity. A moment later, he squinted at her bosom and remarked, "Is that a butterfly?"

Verity reached for the brooch instinctively. "Er, yes. It was a gift from my sister."

"It is a very curious design. The artist has chosen to bend the antennae toward the wing. Perhaps the fully extended filament was too fragile."

"Yes!" Verity cried. "I noticed that too. And the wings have no pattern at all. Even the very plain wood whites have fine speckles. Perhaps the artist did not study his model closely enough or lacked the skill to emulate its design."

Dr. Westbridge's head drew back and his mouth opened. "Why, Miss Lockhart, you are very knowledgeable on the topic! That *is* refreshing. I had quite expected you to change the subject or comment on the bejeweled eyes instead. It is rare to meet a young woman who shares my interest in the natural sciences. My compliments to your tutor."

It took Verity several seconds to find her tongue again. She had expected Dr. Westbridge would have a detailed understanding of human anatomy, certainly, as well as a dedicated interest in the sciences. But the fact that this extended to the study of nature was a startling discovery. Moreover, he did not denounce her own desire to discuss such matters.

Could this be a sign?

Don't jump to conclusions, Verity. He believes you to have studied in a formal manner, not with your skirts hitched up to your knees. Still, he had received her answer with excitement. There had not been the usual frown or condescending air. Verity tentatively ventured deeper into the previously forbidden discourse. "I confess my tutor to have been myself, much to my mother's dismay. As you can imagine, the study of insects is not the usual fare for young ladies. She would be mortified that I have mentioned it at all."

"How delightful!" Dr. Westbridge clapped his hands together, then, just as quickly, held up his palms. "My apologies. I did not mean that your mother's disapproval was delightful. I was merely celebrating the exception that you are, Miss Lockhart. Insects, no less! That is my particular fascination also. In fact, I am a member in good standing with the Entomological Society here in Munro."

Now *that* was a sign Verity could not ignore. There was just one more test to pass before Dr. Westbridge had her full approval.

"An acquaintance of mine recently obtained a mounted butterfly for display from the Entomological Society," she said. "A *Maculinea arion*. Or 'large blue,' as it is commonly called. Do you know it?"

"Ah," he replied, "a rare species. And a privilege to see one in the wild. Not, if you'll forgive my bluntness, to be pinned to a board, but rather to observe in its natural habitat. But there are many who would consider it a valuable addition to their collection. No offense to your acquaintance, but they seemed to have missed the point of the lovely creatures."

With those words, Verity was undone. How could she resist a man who so utterly understood her? Not once had he judged her unfit for her views, nor did he share the colonial approach of nature as possession. This was a man to whom she might safely lose her heart. She felt warm and safe and understood.

And then, all at once, it was their turn to dance. Arthur Westbridge reached his hands across the space between them and stepped forward on his toes. He was not especially nimble, but then neither was she. They joined hands and skipped lightly in a circle or, at least, as lightly as their mutual dance impediment would allow. *Skip to the left. Skip to the right.* Verity called out the steps to herself.

Dr. Westbridge was not encumbered by the same need to recite the pattern of movement, possibly because he had danced such figures many times before. Instead, he smiled encouragement, even calling out, "Well done, Miss Lockhart!" when she corrected herself on a misstep, recovering in time to pick up the rhythm once more.

Soon Verity had built up a similar confidence to his, the constant repetition imbedding the progression of the dance into her mind. The conversation, such as it was between the pointing of toes and much bouncing about, flowed comfortably, and time passed all too quickly. A half hour later, they finally took their leave of the dance floor—exhilarated and rather out of breath—and made their way back to Mrs. Trenton. Hope, perhaps seeing that Verity was tended by a chaperone in the form of their mutual friend, left on her husband's arm to greet a family of their acquaintance on the other side of the room.

"That was very prettily done, Miss Lockhart," Mrs. Trenton said.

"Dr. Westbridge is a most accommodating partner," Verity replied. "I must thank him for an enjoyable initiation to the country dance."

The good doctor shook his head emphatically. "I had nothing to do with it. Miss Lockhart is fearless. She threw herself into the movements with great gusto."

"Ha!" Verity laughed. "Certainly more gusto than talent, but I thank you for the kind words nevertheless."

He opened his lips to respond, when a pale gentleman with noticeably fiery curls approached, bearing two cups of punch. "Ah, *Mr.* Trenton," said Dr. Westbridge. "I wondered where you were this evening. I assumed you must be unwell, for you have never been known to miss a good party."

"Dr. Westbridge." The red-haired man nodded, handing his wife her drink. "I must have just missed you earlier. Sadly, even at events such as these, I run into acquaintances who wish to discuss matters of business instead of sampling the music and excellent fare."

"It is good to see Mrs. Trenton out and about," commented Dr. Westbridge. "She has recovered well from your daughter's birth."

Mr. Trenton grimaced. "I would see her venturing out more often, but she is determined to stay home with the children. I don't know why we bother employing a nurse."

At that, a voice, deep and sensual, spoke up behind Verity. She froze at the hauntingly familiar sound of Mr. William Cole.

"My sister may be an angel among women," said Mr. Cole, the usual teasing tones present in his speech, "but she is stubborn in matters of family. Best leave her to it, James. She will not thank you for depriving her of even an hour with those little cherubs of yours."

Verity didn't move. Mr. Cole hadn't recognized her. She could hardly blame him. She was not ensconced in the cozy parlor of the little vicarage, embroidering a beetle, much to her mother's annoyance. Nor was she ankle-deep in the pond, waving a net about, her hair coming undone about her face. Other than the color of her hair, there was nothing by which Mr. Cole could identify her from behind. She was grateful for the temporary anonymity. It gave her a chance to catch her breath and order her thoughts. She quietly raised her fan to cover her face, keeping her back to Mr. Cole.

James Trenton had meanwhile shifted his attention to a different guest. "Do you see Lord Howell is here? And clearly enjoying himself, to boot. My cousin Ellena has had a remarkable effect on him. He was seldom seen at such gatherings before. I have never found him to be much of a talker, but he has been in animated conversation with her all evening."

"That is true love, James dearest," his wife replied. "Lord Howell is a changed man. And she has become every inch the viscountess." Mrs. Trenton tilted her head and smiled up at her husband. "Look how fine her garments are. She is always the best-dressed woman in Munro. Even now that she is with child, she is as elegant as ever."

"'With child'?" Mr. Cole shot back in reply.

"Yes," answered his sister. "Four months, I think. She is just beginning to show." Mrs. Trenton crossed her hands to her heart. "It brings such happiness for me to know our Clarence and Jane will have a little cousin before the year is out."

From behind the safety of her fan, Verity looked across the room. She knew who the Howells must be. There had been enough whispered comments in their direction and people often did not take care to keep their whispers low enough not to be heard. The viscount and viscountess were a handsome couple. And not at all haughty. Even now, they did not stand apart with their noble peers, but remained the focal point of an ever-changing arc of people seeking their company. Verity recalled the rivalry and animosity between Lady Penrose and Mrs. Sangford at the tea that Hope had hosted. Lady Penrose was only a baroness, yet she and that supercilious Mrs. Sangford—and her equally unbearable daughters—had put on more airs then than the viscount and viscountess did now. Mercifully, the Sangfords and Penroses had thought it beneath them to attend tonight's event.

William had not spoken for a while. From the corner of her eye, Verity could see him staring across at Lord and Lady Howell, seemingly lost in thought. Suddenly, he asked, "Who is the blonde woman?"

For a frightful moment, Verity thought he meant her and prepared to reveal herself. But his gaze had not shifted, still resting upon the viscount and viscountess and the company around them.

"Do you mean the one standing beside my cousin?" asked Mr. Trenton. "That is Miss Jillian Kinsey. I would say she is exactly your type—lacking boundaries, and prone to bursts of laughter—but she is not for you, old boy. She is a guest of the Howell household and a particularly close friend of the viscountess, my cousin. That can only mean trouble. Ellena would encourage an unhealthy degree of independence in her companion, such as she has shown in her own character. No man wants to deal with that sort of nonsense." Mrs. Trenton lifted her fan quite suddenly, but not before Verity spotted the beginnings of a knowing smile.

"Besides," continued Mr. Trenton, evidently entirely unaware of his wife's secret opinion, "it would appear Miss Kinsey has her eye on Mr. Lewis Bradford, a friend to the viscount. A rather overreaching act on her part, if you ask me, what with her being a groundskeeper's daughter and him being a barrister and a baron's son. But Ellena has no doubt emboldened Miss Kinsey in this regard. She never did understand the rules of society. No, William, what you need is a wife who will know her place, and many of these country folk do not. In that regard, my Charlotte is a rare find."

"Er, James…" Charlotte Trenton touched his arm urgently. "Perhaps such remarks are best kept from present company?" She indicated with her head toward Verity.

James, never having met Verity, seemed to have no idea why his chatter should offend. "We have not been introduced," he remarked. "Perhaps my wife could rectify that."

She could, and did so at once. "Miss Lockhart, may I introduce my husband, Mr. James Trenton? James, this is Miss Verity Lockhart. You know, *of Fernbridge?*"

Mr. Cole sucked in his breath.

Verity reluctantly lowered her fan. "Mr. Trenton," she said, acknowledging the introduction with reservation. The gentleman had not made a good first impression and she could hardly say she was pleased to meet him. But she was willing to tolerate him awhile to enjoy the company of his wife. He did not seem to notice or care that he had not found favor. Instead, he offered a quizzical raise of the brow to Mr. Cole. It gave Verity no small gratification, for his look seemed to say, *"This* is the woman of whom you spoke? The vicar's awkward daughter? This fair maiden is her?" Of course, Mr. Trenton had never seen Verity traipsing mud into Cook's kitchen with skirts dripping and tucking errant strands of hair behind her ears.

Mr. Cole, meanwhile, had found his tongue, if only barely. "Miss Lockhart," he murmured, "I confess I did not recognize you."

Verity turned to face him squarely and was rewarded with even greater surprise in his eyes and mouth, both opening more fully at the entire sight of her. She silently blessed Hope for the sophistication of her dress and the nimble hands of her lady's maid, who had managed her hair. She knew she looked her absolute best. She had seen herself in the mirror before she'd left home this evening and recognized the look of amazement that was currently fixed upon Mr. Cole's face, for she had borne it too.

"Good evening, Mr. Cole," she said with a confidence granted her by her style of dress and hair alike. "Or should I call you 'Lieutenant Cole'?"

"Mr. Cole will do, thank you."

"Of course. Mr. Cole. I am…"

What *was* she? Relieved to see him, to have a chance to heal wounds? Happy, even, to be in his company? Hopeful for a rekindling of a friendship that had scarcely begun? Which of these, if any, could she say aloud?

"…happy to see you again," she decided. "It seems a world away from the simple life of our little village." She cast a pointed look at Mr. Trenton. "And," she added quickly, "we are both wearing entirely different feathers." She smiled down at her skirt, which she displayed by pulling it to the side with one hand.

Mr. Cole hesitated but a moment, then appeared to take her cue. "Why, yes, Miss Lockhart," he answered, brandishing his uniformed arms in an open "T. "We both display well indeed. Do you like my dress sword?" He put his hand upon the hilt and struck a pose.

Verity tapped the lacy tip of her closed fan to her mouth and pretended to give the question serious consideration. "I am in two minds as to how I should answer," she said after some thought. "If I speak true and say that you are particularly well suited to the uniform, I am sure to be seen as flirting with you. And you know I do not encourage this type of thinking. However, if I say you are but a man dressed for dancing and deserve no further compliment, I will have done the truth of the matter an injustice. So you see, sir, it is better I say nothing."

Charlotte Trenton clapped her hands. "Ah, William, Miss Lockhart has you well in hand, I see! Take her dancing, dear brother, for she knows no one else here but Mr. Sinclair and Dr. Westbridge, and the latter has already had the privilege."

Dr. Westbridge made a small bow. "It was a privilege indeed,

Mrs. Trenton. Do not allow the opportunity to pass, Mr. Cole. The lady is a fine dancer."

Verity felt her cheeks grow flushed. "I am really only able to attempt a country dance. Also, I cannot converse well while dancing, as I must concentrate on the figures they have called. And my stepping is labored at best. It is only fair that you should know my limitations before you make the invitation."

"It is well we are honest in this way," agreed Mr. Cole, furrowing his brow into a frown that was contradicted by the mischievous twist to his lips. "For example, I am not permitted to wear my sword while dancing. Alas, the thrill of dancing with me must therefore be somewhat reduced. However, my appearance, being thus diminished, will provide less distraction from the minutiae of counting to which you are bound. So you see, we are a disappointing pair and would be better suited to dance together than burden any other with our company."

"I accept!" Verity laughed. "As always, Mr. Cole, you lack neither eloquence nor wit. At least while we stand and talk—and do not dance—we shall have a commendably good time of it."

Oh, it felt so good to banter with him again! Mr. Cole, while not a good match pragmatically, brought out a side of her she revealed with no other. Although, now that she thought on it, Dr. Westbridge had managed to perform similar magic earlier. Granted, he had a milder form of humor. More... appropriate. Safer. He had managed to distract her from her insecurities with a gentler wit, one that would not appear unseemly. Mr. Cole, on the other hand, was a shameless Don Juan. She would have to be cautious not to give the impression she was encouraging him. Perhaps she had already erred in this way. She would need to take greater care. There was little wisdom in denouncing his informal suit before, while welcoming his flirtation now. That was not the sort of reputation she wanted. She would rather be known as a strange, quiet sort of character, misunderstood and possibly avoided, than a woman who appeared trivial in her mores.

With her thoughts settled thus into a clearer path forward,

she joined Mr. Cole on the dance floor in a rather more subdued fashion than she had done with the good doctor.

Verity noticed far more eyes upon her now than there had been when she'd danced with a more innocuous partner. Mr. Cole, no doubt, had already made his mark with the ladies of Munro, and they must have been wondering at his connection to Verity. Was she competition for his attention? Was she the sort to invite it?

"You can feel it, can't you?" Mr. Cole asked suddenly.

"Pardon?"

"The stares that are hidden behind fans and the whispers cupped behind gloved hands."

"Yes," Verity answered truthfully. "It is very discomfiting."

"As it should be."

Verity looked at Mr. Cole pointedly. "I would think you were used to it. In many ways, you choose a behavior that provokes it."

An arched eyebrow was followed by a slow, spreading smile. "Ah, Miss Lockhart, I have missed your candor."

"Perhaps," she said, venturing toward the topic she had long hoped to broach with him, "I was *too* candid at our last meeting."

His face clouded but less than she'd thought it might have. "I'll admit," he replied, "your response to my gift was... surprising. But I have had time to reason further. I understand now where I went wrong. Your letter made it clear."

Pain shot through Verity's heart, so strong, it must surely have shown upon her face. "That was not my intention! I was trying to apologize, not attribute blame."

"And so you did, Miss Lockhart, to my shame. That you should apologize when it is I who hurt you is not something I can be proud of."

"But you meant well. And I was terribly ungracious in my reaction." Verity shook her head slowly, her heart pinched with remorse. "You must have been hurt too. I had fully intended to explain myself at your next visit." She grew quiet. "But... there wasn't one."

Mr. Cole's expression softened. "I am sorry. It was badly done." He raised his eyes to hers. "Would it help you to know I've done a little growing up since then?" He grinned. "Why, I've even come of age!"

"Oh, congratulations! And, may I say, further felicitations on your military commission. I know how much the opportunity means to you." Verity paused, uncertain whether she should utter *all* her thoughts. She had so often regretted the loss of Mr. Cole's company, and the way they might have conversed openly as they had at the pond. It seemed that now, given the chance to talk to him again, it was better to do so unreservedly. After all, was he not the *one* man to whom she had spoken with ease? Had she not wished for more time spent with him?

Verity pulled up short in her thoughts. She must amend them. Mr. Cole was the *first* man with whom she had experienced such comfort. Dr. Arthur Westbridge had managed an admirable result also. He might not be as glamorous a specimen as Mr. Cole, but he was nevertheless someone of whom she thought warmly. Verity tucked this realization away in the back of her mind to ponder again at her leisure.

Mr. Cole, unaware that her thoughts had taken this detour, continued with the conversation they had begun. "Thank you, Miss Lockhart," he said in reply to her previous good wishes. "You must know that you have played a role in my happy outcome."

"I did?"

He nodded. "You are a good influence on me. You call me out on my empty talk, the type I fall back onto when I feel I can't be myself. It was your straightforward manner that gave me the courage to speak to my father more forcefully about what I truly wanted."

Verity did not know how to respond. She was deeply moved that he thought of her in such a positive light. And yet...

"I do not consider myself a revolutionary, Mr. Cole."

"But you *are*, Miss Lockhart," he insisted. "Not all revolutions are won with cannon and bloodshed. Some happen so quietly, yet insistently, that change is achieved without fanfare. Think of your visits to the pond. Your mother does not approve of them. Yet you may keep your paints at the ready and are left unguarded, as it were, when she knows you will slip away and seek out your little subjects for study. You have stood up for yourself without so much as a whisper. Only determined action. And you do so every moment of every day because you would rather be true to yourself than enjoy the acceptance of those who would ask you not to be."

Blood pounded in Verity's head. *This* was what she had wanted. *This* was the gift he should have given all those months ago. Not that pinned butterfly. This. He could see her. See her as she really was—and not turn from her. Her entire body buzzed with electricity. If he had spoken to her like this all those months ago, maybe…

It was too late. He would be leaving soon for war and…

"I wish you didn't have to go!" she blurted out. She had wanted to say this earlier but had held back. Now the emotion rushed to the surface, furious in its intensity, wholly unstoppable. "I should never have encouraged you to choose this path! It's all very well to promenade in your smart, red coat with its brass buttons, but it's another thing entirely to wear it into battle. You could… You might…" The words choked in her throat. She was very aware of the gangly gentleman beside them staring at them and then glancing away as she caught his eye. "I'm sorry," she said to Mr. Cole, her head lowering with her voice. "I don't know what came over me."

Mr. Cole matched her more solemn tones. "Don't apologize, Miss Lockhart. I am touched that you feel this way. War is, shall we say, the less attractive side of military life. But many of us live to boast of our exploits." He offered a small, wry smile. "You do not think the universe would deny me my little pleasures, do you?"

Verity supposed he'd said this to lighten the mood, but Mr. Cole did so without his usual twinkle. She wanted very much to reply with a light and teasing comment, but she could not bring herself to jest while the thought of Mr. Cole being killed by the French dominated her thoughts.

"You know," he said, the casual tone still overlaying a serious mood, "you only helped me with *one* of my difficulties."

"What do you mean?" Verity was intrigued in spite of herself.

"I am still without a wife." And there it was. The playful grin. It almost reached his eyes.

"Oh," replied Verity, at a loss for how to answer.

"Do not look so alarmed, Miss Lockhart," said Mr. Cole, his eyes creasing at last with mirth. "I shall not burden *you* with my hapless suit again."

Disappointment planted its heavy boot on Verity's heart.

"However," Mr. Cole continued, "you could assist me in my future endeavor. I trust your judgment implicitly. Do you see anyone here with whom I might make a good match?"

"No."

Mr. Cole huffed a short laugh. "You didn't even turn your head!"

Verity tried to shed the sudden sulkiness that had infiltrated her heart. "I don't know anyone here except your sister and mine. And they are both married."

"Ah. Perhaps a few introductions are in order. When I spot a promising lass, I shall make sure the two of you meet. Then you shall give your insight as to her character and whether it might be a match for mine."

Verity loathed the idea out of hand. Why should she, by Mr. Cole's own admission, have guided him toward change and not benefit from it? It was decidedly unfair. But what could she do? Announce that, after all, he might be worthy of her consideration? That she, who was demanding in her requirements, unorthodox in her expectations, would now be all *he* wanted?

Verity sighed long. This was what friends did for each other, was it not? This had been what she'd wanted: his acceptance, his trust, his companionship. And if, as her friend, Mr. Cole was willing to do better for someone new than he had done for her, should she not be happy that he was willing to change? Only... if he was going to grow, become a man worthy of another, should *she* not be given a chance to consider him?

"I see you hesitate, Miss Cole. That is good. It means you take the matter seriously. Perhaps I may sweeten the pot and offer you a similar service in return. I have spent much time in Munro over the years. I know many of the families. We could assist each other. You may gauge the worth of the daughters while I get the measure of the sons. We can be allies, you and I. And they will be our chaperones, while *we* talk of what really matters, like the qualities of great passion and... er... tansy beetles."

"Tansy beetles," Verity corrected him automatically.

"That is what I said."

"Oh." Verity stuttered to a halt in her thoughts. "So you did."

At last, the dance had reached them. Mr. Cole rose up on his toes. He was naturally elegant, and his dancing no less so. Verity scrambled to get her thoughts shuffled back in order. What were the steps again? She moved forward hastily to meet him in the space between the lines, almost stumbling as she returned to her original position.

"To the right," Mr. Cole called, just loud enough for her to hear. She circled the gentleman diagonally to her right, the one who had heard her earlier cry of dismay and tried politely to hide having heard it. Verity blushed as they capered around each other, but the lanky gentleman merely completed the figure and returned to his place. Back she went to Mr. Cole, hands united briefly, then pulling apart again.

Verity couldn't help but regard these motions as an echo of her relationship with Mr. Cole, such as it was. Together, apart, together, apart. And all of it a formal display. Nothing was real. If it had been real, she would be holding a net instead of a fan. Her feet would be wet and bare. And Mr. Cole would be holding the reins of his horse, telling her of his dream of being an officer. There would be no pretty steps upon a ballroom floor, hoping—in one or two dances at a time—to discover the partner with whom you would spend the rest of your life.

What if she had found that partner already, only to have him believe that her previous disinterest was permanent?

Down the line, they skipped. Down and down, until they drew to a halt and faced each other once again, cheeks flushed with exertion.

More couples pranced past them. The line shifted. Together. Apart. Circle the gentleman to the right. Together. Apart.

And when Verity thought she could bear the dance no longer, for the echo of loss would break her heart, the dance ended. And she could touch Mr. Cole's hand no more.

CHAPTER FIFTEEN

WILLIAM LED MISS Lockhart from the center of the room and reluctantly released her hand. He would gladly have danced another set with her. But he would not have her reputation tarnished. The last thing she would want was a rumor that they were engaged. The question was, would *he* mind all that much?

What a dolt he had been! Pining after Ellena as if she were the only woman in the world. Showing gross misjudgment in his conduct to secure her hand. Hindsight was a brutal teacher.

He looked across the room to where she stood in animated conversation with her husband. They were a good match after all. He was amazed to find himself happy for her. These were the only feelings that remained for her. That, and the lingering shame of his actions toward her.

Whenever he was around Miss Lockhart, it was as if a mist cleared from his mind. She spoke boldly, as Ellena—Lady Howell—had done, but it was matched with a clear sense of self. If he had known Lady Howell's mind as well as he thought he now understood Miss Lockhart's, he would never have… Well, it was all in the past now.

To think he might have made a sensible match with the vicar's daughter. But he had not given the possibility a fair chance. His thoughts had turned constantly to Lady Howell and his motives had all been selfish. He could see now the potential in a future with Miss Lockhart. Except... he could not think what he had to offer. Yes, he had apologized. And yes, he had felt a change within himself. Or at least, the first steps toward it. But he had no business seeking her affections until he could be sure he deserved her.

William contemplated the crowded room. Before the night was done, Miss Lockhart would be a favorite. He had already lost his chance. There would not be time for another. Help her find a match, indeed! What had he been thinking?

Hmm, he knew exactly what he'd been thinking. Any excuse to spend more time with her. Perhaps he might even steer her away from other candidates...

No! He must not follow this way of thinking! That was the sort of madness that had quite run away with him before.

This great love he wanted—it must be a thing of wonder. Not tainted with manipulation and raw desire. It should burn a lifetime, slow and steady, not burst into unmanageable flames.

A smile formed despite his self-chastisement. Even a slow and steady fire could grow hot. And Miss Lockhart ignited just such vigor within him. For her rare blend of blunt honesty and devoted passion, he would give the world. And, in turn, receive it.

"I say, Cole, you don't mind if I join you?"

Captain Larson came striding up to the small gathering where William stood. They all lifted their eyes to the newcomer, whose bearing was every inch that of a meticulously disciplined officer. William could see no harm in an introduction. The captain was an honorable man. A career officer, like himself—or, at least, as William hoped to be. And a gentleman in every sense.

"It seems," explained Larson, "I have found myself without a dance partner for this round and could use some intelligent conversation to while away the next half hour."

"I'm grateful you think I might have it to offer, sir." William turned to the rest of the group. "Mr. and Mrs. Sinclair, James and

Charlotte, Miss Lockhart, may I introduce Captain Larson? He is the officer to whom I report, and gladly. Captain Larson, this is Mr. and Mrs. Daniel Sinclair; her sister, Miss Verity Lockhart; and Mr. and Mrs. James Trenton. The latter is my sister."

Captain Larson made a stiff bow when introduced, smartly clicking his heels together. He followed with a nod as each of the rest of the party was named. But before the captain could say a word to any of them, he was jostled roughly from behind.

"Sorry there, Cap'n, old boy," slurred the uniformed fellow. "Didn't see you there. Was just making my way to a game of Vingt-et-un with the lads, but I seem to have stumbled over someone's skirt." He looked back at the offending article. "'Don't how the lady hopes to dance in it if it's draped all over the floor. Oh, hello, Cole." These last three words were added with decidedly less joviality, though the man quickly recovered his mood when he saw Miss Lockhart. "I say, aren't you going to introduce us?"

William looked the tall, lean, scruffy-haired fellow up and down. "I hardly think the lady would welcome an introduction from someone in your condition, Foyle."

"My 'condition'?" Foyle scowled in a rather cross-eyed manner. "My *condition* is that I am a lieutenant in His Majesty's army and a baron's son. You would do well to remember that, Cole."

"Nevertheless, Lieutenant Foyle," Captain Larson added sternly, "you do not represent either of those roles in particularly good light at present. Perhaps, if you ate something substantial to balance the drink, your common sense would return to you. An introduction may be made when you could do it justice."

Lieutenant Foyle ignored them both and turned a rather unfocused eye to Miss Lockhart. "I, madam," he began, his hand to his breast, his knees attempting to hold him upright, "am Lieutenant Richard Foyle, at your service. Whom do I have the pleasure of addressing?"

Miss Lockhart, quite understandably, looked horrified. She had drawn back into herself as though attempting to create distance between this foul man and her person. Even her face was tilted away and her eyes roved up and down in clear disbelief that such a fellow was allowed to persist in his behavior. She turned to her sister, who, in turn, appealed to her husband. Mr. Sinclair stepped forward. In all the years William had known him, Sinclair had not been a man who often raised his voice, nor did he do so now. Instead, he leaned in so that the inebriated fellow could hear him say quietly, "You will address no one but me. I am Daniel Sinclair, and you, sir, are not welcome in the presence of these ladies, nor any lady, for that matter. Now, move on, before I report your scandalous behavior to our host."

Foyle glared at him, shifting his disdain to each of the men in turn. "My father will hear of this," he sneered, pointing a finger at the end of an unstably-waving arm. "You are just a bunch of nobodies. I"—he poked Mr. Sinclair in the chest—"am the son of a lord."

"Then behave like one, damn you, Foyle," snapped Larson.

"I do not think you would like your father to hear of this as much as you say you do, Lieutenant Foyle." James smiled grimly. "But, as cousin to the Viscountess Howell, I could ensure that he does." The smile stayed. The threat hung in the air.

Foyle flung his arm harmlessly to his side. "I was just off to play a game of cards anyway. Don't need you lot to get in my way." He stopped and gave Miss Lockhart a lecherous grin. "I'll get your name yet. So don't you forget mine." Then he stumbled on toward the card room, bumping into guests and swearing under his breath.

A stunned silence hung in the air.

"I can only apologize unreservedly for Lieutenant Foyle's shameful behavior," said Captain Larson. "He was assigned to our company just two weeks ago. I have not had enough time to whip him into shape. And his father has the unfortunate habit of whitewashing his actions with his name and money. It is most regrettable."

"You are not to blame, sir," Mr. Sinclair countered. "While

you may not have been long exposed to Foyle's particular brand of debauchery, Munro's society has known it for too many years. Since the lad was old enough to drink, gamble, and philander, he has done so. I am not entirely certain his father even disapproves. They are of the feudalistic nobility who believe they are *entitled* rather than merely *titled*. I'm afraid you will have your hands full with that one."

"While he is wearing the uniform, I am his superior officer," Captain Larson insisted. "It makes no difference who his father is."

Mr. Sinclair shook his head sadly. "Ah, I wish it were as simple as that. However, you have our full support here this evening, sir." His mouth pressed into a thin line. "As for the battlefield, I would not trust him to have your back. Do have a care, Captain Larson. The man has no scruples."

William did not care about battles and scruples. He had seen the fear in Miss Lockhart's eyes when Foyle had aimed his parting shot at her. She had stood, silent and motionless, her rigid limbs and frozen gaze the only clue that she was terrified beyond reason. Now that the perpetrator had left, she was trembling, her grip on her fan fierce, her gaze still locked before her.

"Are you all right, Miss Lockhart?" he asked, for what else could he say? He had no claim on her by right of family or marriage. He could not take her in his arms and comfort her with his presence, whispering reassurances into her ear until she leaned against him and released her fears to him. "Perhaps you should sit down. I could bring you something to drink."

"That's a good idea, Lieutenant Cole," said Mrs. Sinclair. "Something strong, if you don't mind. I think she's had rather a shock." She guided her sister to a nearby chair, the small group forming a protective half-circle before her.

William pushed through the crowded ball room, muttering apologies as he went. Fortunately, a dance was in progress, and the edges of the venue were not as densely littered with guests, many of them having joined the line. He entered a side room where tables had been arranged around the perimeter and filled with all manner of refreshment. Footmen stood waiting to replenish the food and drink as needed.

William hastened to fetch a glass and two fingers of brandy. With his mission complete, he returned, clearing the space before him with cries of "Pardon me! Coming through!" until he reached Miss Lockhart and proffered the glass to her.

"Down it quickly now," urged Mrs. Sinclair, "for it will burn your throat. But you will feel the calming effects soon after."

Miss Lockhart did as bidden, gasping as she finished and coughing at the sudden heat in her chest.

"That is very strong liquor, sir," she said, her voice hoarse. "But I do believe it has done the trick."

"Does someone need smelling salts?" came the familiar, friendly sound of Dr. Westbridge. "I saw Miss Lockhart take a seat rather suddenly and thought perhaps she had overdone the dancing somewhat. The room is dreadfully warm, too. She wouldn't be the first young lady to swoon at her debut ball."

Miss Lockhart still had her hand to her chest, though the color was returning to her cheeks. "I am quite all right, thank you, Dr. Westbridge. I just had a sudden turn. But I have recovered. You are very kind to come to my aid, but I shall not require a physician."

The doctor turned to James. "Does Miss Lockhart have an ailment that would bring on such a sudden faint?"

"Not that I am aware," James replied. "Unless you consider Richard Foyle a physical disease rather than merely a blight on society."

Dr. Westbridge pressed his lips together. His stony countenance suggested he was all too familiar with the "gentleman" in question. "Did he...? Are you...safe?" the doctor asked Verity.

"He did not touch her," William said firmly. "He wouldn't dare. Not while we are here to protect her."

"He was most uncouth in his speech," Charlotte said softly, her eyes gentle upon Miss Lockhart. "I am surprised someone with his indecorous manner was allowed to attend. The Macraes are good people. They would be heartbroken that a young lady was harassed by one of their guests."

"I believe his father accompanied him to the event in previous years," Mr. Sinclair explained. "No doubt his presence had maintained some form of restraint upon young Foyle. It is a pity he was not in attendance tonight."

"I shall report the incident to my superiors," said Captain Larson. "Though what good it will do, I cannot say."

Miss Lockhart stood up quite suddenly. "Please, everyone, don't fuss on my account. I'd rather just forget everything that happened, if you don't mind." She gave a residual shiver.

"You need a distraction," advised Dr. Westbridge. "I would ask you to dance." He pulled his lips into a lopsided smile. "The comic effect of my steps should lighten your mood in a trice. However, it would be unseemly of me to request more than my allotted pair of dances with you."

"Alas, Cole," said Captain Larson, "you have also had your turn dancing with Miss Lockhart. Perhaps, then, my lady, if I may be so bold, could I offer you that very distraction Dr. Westbridge recommends?

"I am not a very good dancer," said Miss Lockhart, repeating her former claim.

"But we dance to amuse ourselves with happier thoughts," answered Captain Larson. "There is no need for fine steps or perfect coordination."

"I suppose, if you're sure."

"I am. As soon as this line is done, I shall join you in a new one."

"Ah," said Dr. Westbridge, lifting his finger as if the thought had sprung up through it, "I may have another suggestion to cheer you up further. The Entomological Society is hosting a talk this week on the *coleoptera* of Egypt. Do you have a chaperone, Miss Lockhart? If so, I would consider it an honor for you to attend. If you are interested, that is. Or perhaps I have overestimated your fascination with the subject."

William watched Miss Lockhart's face light up. Confound the doctor! He was thoughtful, intelligent, and he shared her love of creeping, flying things. William was going to witness Miss Lockhart losing her heart to Dr. Westbridge right in front of his eyes. He was helpless to prevent it. And why should he? Did she not deserve someone exactly like the good doctor?

Miss Lockhart turned with eagerness toward her sister. "May I go? Please say *yes*. Mama would not mind me going if it was an invitation. Dr. Westbridge is not offended by my passion for insects."

"Goodness, no!" cried the gentleman. "Quite the opposite. I have only ever bored young ladies with my talk of habitats and species, not to mention the displeasure I evoke if I should speak of—heaven forfend—larvae!"

Miss Lockhart laughed. It was a beautiful sight. Her pale-blue eyes glistened like melting ice in the spring. Her nose wrinkled as she abandoned decorum for pure joy. In that moment, William knew…

He loved her.

It was a terrible, crushing sensation, wholly unlike the expectations he had fostered for years. Love was meant to be a soaring flight of the heart. A realization that this person, and this person only, would fulfill his waking dreams. It should bring peace and exhilaration, all at once.

It did none of that.

For this love, his love, was not to be.

Miss Lockhart would laugh with Arthur Westbridge. Pore over scientific studies with him. Dance upon his arm. Sleep within his embrace.

He really was the perfect man for her. And now she waited, with the innocent zeal of a child, for her sister to allow them that one critical step closer.

"On what day is this talk to be given?" Mrs. Sinclair asked.

"It is on Wednesday. Four days hence," the doctor replied.

"Oh, dear." Mrs. Sinclair seemed genuinely regretful. Her brows tugged downward. The edges of her mouth did likewise. "We promised the children a picnic on Wednesday. We have already given their tutor the day off."

"I could accompany her," Charlotte offered. "As long as we sit near the back, far from any"—she shivered—"specimens."

Confound his thoughtful sister! If not for her, the doctor's offer to Miss Lockhart would come to nothing. Did she not see the danger of bringing them together?

"Oh, *would* you?" Miss Lockhart seemed ready to throw her arms around Charlotte. She lifted folded hands to her sister, as if pleading, which was exactly what she did. "There can be no faulting Mrs. Trenton as my chaperone, surely? She is as sensible as she is kind. And I shall be on my very best behavior, I promise. Oh, do say *yes*, Hope. Please?"

Mrs. Sinclair looked at her sister, then considered Dr. Westbridge. No doubt she saw what William had seen. That this was a man who would make a fine husband for her little sister. He was a true gentleman. He earned a good living and would not discourage his wife in her most earnest pastime. It was, therefore, no surprise at all when she nodded.

"I can see no reason why Mrs. Trenton should not accompany you, if she is willing. That she *is* willing is proof yet again of her goodness. It is well we have a picnic planned. At worst, we may come across some ants, perhaps some bees, or, if we are very unlucky, a wasp. All of these are still better than a room full of beetles. I admire your fortitude, Mrs. Trenton, for even the farthest seat at the back of the room would not entice me."

"Oh, do not describe it so!" Charlotte cried, screwing her face up as if she had bit into a lemon. "I am not as brave as you think. But, having offered, I do not wish to disappoint Miss Lockhart. Let us turn to other subjects. It is best I do not dwell on the topic of insects until I am standing in the rooms of the Entomological Society."

"Why do you not join us for the next dance?" suggested Captain Larson. "The new line is forming, and I see Nathaniel Macrae heads the top this time. He always calls the most elaborate figures. Miss Lockhart could use your support, as she appears to doubt herself in this. And it is a matter utterly devoid of beetles." Despite his usually formal manner, Captain Larson let the smallest of smiles slip across his lips. It contrasted so starkly with his dignified bearing that it made him look almost playful, which had likely been his intention.

"Do take me dancing, James," Charlotte said, hugging her husband's arm. "We have spent near half the night in chatter. While I do enjoy the company of our friends and relations, they can always come to tea. We cannot always dance. It won't be many years before we are considered too old to join in."

"With pleasure, my dear." James strode at once toward the center of the room, his wife waving her fingers over her shoulder as she departed their company.

"Miss Lockhart." Captain Larson bowed, then offered his arm.

William watched as she placed her gloved hand upon his, watched Larson grasp the tips of her fingers and lead her toward the line. He watched with envy and regret. If he had taken his chance with her, they would be married now, or at least engaged. And every dance with her would be his to claim.

He saw her stand shyly opposite the captain. Larson did not make easy conversation. She did not laugh but cast nervous glances at Charlotte.

Nathaniel Macrae—blond, athletic, undeniably charming, and mercifully too much of a Don Juan to appeal to Miss Lockhart—waited until the last straggling pairs had joined, then began to explain and demonstrate the figures he had in mind. They were complex, sophisticated, and he performed them with grace and ease. But Miss Lockhart gripped her fan and chewed her lip. Larson did not seem to notice.

The dance began and the first couple proceeded to exhibit their skill. Captain Larson watched them as if they were soldiers completing a drill, focused on their precision, nodding his approval almost imperceptibly.

Charlotte chatted merrily to both James and Miss Lockhart. She called across to Captain Larson, breaking his attention that had been locked on to Macrae and his lead partner. The captain answered, the slightest bit of color creeping into his cheeks. His gaze shifted to Miss Lockhart.

There it was. William had been waiting for it. The admiration. The awe. Larson was now as focused on Miss Lockhart as he had been on Macrae. Idle conversation would not be easy for him, but, by gum, he would try!

William sighed. The rest of the night would be filled with more of this. Every gentleman who danced with her would have the same reaction. They would marvel at the starlight in her white-blonde tresses, the gem-like quality of her ice-blue eyes. One by one, they would note the way she minimized her own qualities, wrongly assuming she was docile and willing to submit her own worth at their feet.

She deserved better. William wished it for her. But was he the man to offer it?

Not yet. He must be sure he had left his old self behind. He needed more time with Miss Lockhart to make certain he understood her needs and that he could meet them.

But he wouldn't have the time. Tonight, the gentlemen of Munro would be planning their courtships of her. And William? Well, he would soon be off to war.

Perhaps, then, friendship was all they could have. If only th—

"Found you at last!"

Lawrence clapped his hand on his brother's shoulder. "Sorry I'm late. Our father had me attend a meeting on his behalf. It was an interminable to-and-fro, but I believe our interests have been upheld. Good evening, Mr. and Mrs. Sinclair."

Before the couple could respond beyond mere civilities, Lawrence gestured to William. "Walk with me, Little Brother."

William hated when Lawrence called him that. Yes, William

was younger by several years, but he was a full grown man now, and of age. Being called "little" only reminded William that he was inferior to Lawrence in many ways. No wife. No children. No true income. And, most importantly, no reputation for being "a good sort." While William had flirted and caroused, Lawrence had worked at the bank with their father, emulating Marcus Cole in his role as provider and all round decent fellow. And, like their father, Lawrence enjoyed giving a well-intentioned scolding.

"Why are you not dancing?" Lawrence began.

This was not a typical starting point, and William was, for the moment, caught off guard. "You think I should be dancing? Is it not more your usual fare to chastise me for having *too much* fun?"

"Come now, William, we both know enjoyment is not the real purpose of a dance."

"It isn't?"

"Do you think these ladies' families spend their money on dresses and shoes simply for their daughters to amuse themselves of an evening?"

"Oh." William's voice flattened. "That."

"Yes, *that*, William. Why are you here if not to further your prospects through marriage?"

William bit his tongue. He had any number of honest answers. He had come to see Miss Lockhart and make amends. He was enjoying the company of others, without being expected to play the role of a charming rogue. He wanted to dance and laugh before he was shot apart by cannon fire. Which one would his brother like to hear?

"You wouldn't understand," he said instead.

"No," said Lawrence with a slow, longsuffering sigh, "I probably wouldn't."

"But you can tell Father you did your best."

"Hmph. I would rather tell him you are doing yours."

"Tell him what you like."

Lawrence grew quiet. Then, as if he had made up his mind about something, he took his brother by the elbow and steered him through a nearby doorway leading, as it happened, to the card room. A few heads looked up, but the two gentlemen were soon forgotten. No doubt the card players had high stakes at play.

"I thought you were done with Miss Lockhart," Lawrence said in a low voice.

"I am. I was. I…"

"Well, from where I stood earlier, you could not take your eyes from her."

William felt his neck grow hot. "Were you spying on me?"

"No, I was looking for you. And when I saw you, I also noticed you barely moved, considering the way your gaze was riveted. Not to mention the range of emotions that flitted across your face."

"I was making sure she was all right."

"And why should she not have been?"

"She had an encounter with Lieutenant Foyle."

"That blackguard!" Lawrence ran his fingers through his sandy-blond hair. "What bad luck."

"Precisely," agreed William. "He had since let her be, supposedly off to play cards. I see he is over there." William gestured with his chin. "He is so thoroughly foxed, he can barely keep his head up."

"At least Miss Lockhart is well away from him."

"Yes."

Lawrence cocked an eye at his brother. "You care a great deal what becomes of her."

William shrugged. "No woman deserves to be singled out by that reprobate. Least of all a lady of our acquaintance."

The eye of suspicion remained. "Granted, but why is it you remain vigilant when the danger has passed?"

William squirmed a little. He did not like his brother circling the truth so closely, especially since William himself was uncertain what to make of his own feelings. "Well, she is… That is to say… There is no reason why… Oh, shut up, Lawrence!"

Lawrence lifted an eyebrow. Then a smile spread slowly and

annoyingly across his face, the wrinkles around his eyes radiating out toward his side-whiskers. "Your secret is safe with me, Little Brother."

He reached out his hand.

William ducked his head. "If you are going to ruffle my hair as if I were five years old, I shall knock you on your back, Lawrence!"

His brother laughed heartily. He had a beautiful, broad mouth designed for just such moments. It was one of the few things he and William had in common. "I was merely going to shake your hand to seal the deal, so to speak. My, but you are touchy, Little Brother."

"And stop calling me that," William grumbled. "I am as grown as you are."

Lawrence regarded his brother a moment. "Indeed, it seems you are, or at least well on your way to it. Won't our parents be pleased!" He tapped a finger to the side of his nose and winked. "Not that they will hear it from *my* lips."

"Well," said William, straightening his jacket, "I thank you for that."

"I take it you will dance with Miss Lockhart tonight?"

"I already have."

"Perhaps you should again."

"That would imply a relationship we do not have."

Lawrence cocked his head jauntily. "Perhaps that is what she wants. If she does not, she may simply refuse."

"If she does not seek my attention, she will consider my request very forward. I have only just persuaded her I am made of better stuff than that."

"Ah," replied Lawrence, "perhaps I should dance with Miss Lockhart and sweeten your case before her."

William stared at his brother. "You would do that?"

"Yes, of course, Littl… William. But with so many unmarried gentlemen here tonight, it would be improper for me to dance with an eligible lady in their stead."

William considered his brother with new affection. "I am not used to your support. It is a pleasant change, to say the least."

"Ah," said Lawrence, "but you have never delivered up a cause worthy of supporting before. It, too, is a pleasant change."

The shift in their relationship was oddly comforting to William. For the longest time, he had felt alone. Oh, his family loved him. Of that, there was no doubt. But they were each busy with satisfying lives. And he had always lived along the periphery of their world. His relationship with them had, to his mind, been bound by their expectations, something in which he was sure to be a disappointment. He had followed his own heart from the start. It had felt like rebellion. And so a rebel he must be.

Only, where had that gotten him? A strained bond with his father. A reputation for tomfoolery. He was a man who could not be taken seriously. Was that not how Charlotte often introduced him? *"Don't mind my brother. He is harmless in his flirtation."* Perhaps she was embarrassed by him. He had never considered how his choices affected others, except where it had pleased him.

But, all of them, to the last, liked Miss Lockhart. They believed she would be good for him. They supported his interest in her wholeheartedly—even if his sister had unintentionally helped the competition. And, suddenly, William felt part of a greater good, a collective united in purpose and dignity.

He was not ready to give Miss Lockhart up to another. With his siblings' encouragement, he would fight a fair fight for her hand. Not a selfish theatrical as he had with Lady Howell, one that might ruin her reputation. No, a suit that did justice to the character of his beloved, for she deserved nothing less.

The war was forgotten. The rogue, Richard Foyle, was forgotten. Larson and Westbridge and whosoever else danced with Miss Lockhart this night were forgotten. William would focus on her, and her alone. What she wanted. What she needed. What he had to give.

But where to start?

A single thought rammed into the forefront of his mind. It

jolted his thoughts into focus and spread a delicious glow of resolve throughout his body.

"Lawrence," he said. "Will you still be in Munro this week?"

"I will. Charlotte asked that I not rush home too soon. She is such a welcoming hostess, one cannot say *no*, even if it does mean enduring James's frequent surliness. Why do you ask?"

"I don't suppose you'd like to attend a lecture on Egyptian beetles with me…"

CHAPTER SIXTEEN

"Miss Lockhart?"

The voice of the butler stirred Verity from the book she had been reading. She looked up and saw him hovering by the entrance to the drawing room.

"The Trenton carriage is here, miss."

Verity laid the book down on the little table beside her. "Thank you. I am ready." She rose and followed him out to the foyer where a footman helped her with her wrap, then opened the front door for her.

At the bottom of the steps, one of the Trenton footmen stood waiting to help her up into the carriage. Verity's shoes tapped down the stairs and crunched across the gravel.

Immediately, Charlotte Trenton's head peeked out the carriage door. "Miss Lockhart! Do join us. I hope you don't mind, but my brothers have indicated their interest in today's lecture and are riding with us. Here, come and sit beside me."

Verity entered the gloom of the interior, her heart pounding in her chest. She had been looking forward to this outing for days, counting the hours to her first sanctioned study of the fascinating creatures she was normally expected to avoid.

Another part of her—though much smaller—was nervous to be seeing Dr. Westbridge again. He had been on her mind constantly. Not in the same way Mr. Cole had occupied her thoughts. But she had to admit, the doctor was a very promising candidate for her affection. He did not have the same giddying effect upon her that Mr. Cole did, but William Cole had lost interest, and it was pointless pining for him—even though her heart had not been cooperating with this practical wisdom.

With William Cole beyond her reach, she had to consider other possibilities. Perhaps today, after she had spent more time in Arthur Westbridge's company, the good doctor would awaken deeper feelings within her than mere appreciation. She would leave the door to her heart ajar and see if Dr. Westbridge was able to swing it open more fully.

At least, this had been her intention.

Except now, on the seat across from her, sat the two Messrs. Cole: Lawrence Cole, who was happily married and nodding his head politely at her, and William Cole, infuriatingly handsome and frustratingly unattached. And the beats of her heart stepped up several notches.

"Miss Lockhart," said Lawrence Cole, "please forgive us. We have made bold to insert ourselves into your day. You see, I am rarely able to spend time with my brother. When he mentioned this fine lecture on Egyptian *coleoptera* and told me that he planned to attend, I took it upon myself to tag along. I believe we will be blessed with your fine knowledge on the subject if we have questions afterward."

Verity was, to put a point to it, confused. Mr. Cole—that is to say, *William* Cole—had spoken of combining forces with her so that they might find each other good matches. Surely, he did not hope to find a bride among countless insect displays reeking of camphor? Or had he merely come to support her in her endeavor? That was more likely. He was no fool. He would have realized that Dr. Westbridge showed potential. It had just never occurred to her how devotedly Mr. Cole would champion her future. Nor did she wholly believe she wanted that. If he would show half as much interest in her for his own sake…

"I'm afraid I will not be of much use in that regard, sir," Verity answered Lawrence Cole. "I am well versed on our English countryside and its tiny inhabitants, but I know very little, if anything, about Egyptian beetles. However, Dr. Westbridge might have broader knowledge. If not, I imagine the gentleman giving the lecture will welcome interest in his specialty."

"Ah, Miss Lockhart." Mrs. Trenton sighed. "If only you had asked me to chaperone you to a tea house. I do love a good cake. And the conversation is more likely to be palatable, too."

William Cole, who had been unusually quiet, spoke at last. "Might we reward my sister for her sacrifice, Miss Lockhart? We could stop for tea after the lecture. Unless you are expected home at a particular time."

"I am not," Verity replied. "Although I would not linger too late for fear of making my sister worry."

"Oh, dear." Mrs. Trenton put her palm to her belly and pulled a face. "Let us see if I have a stomach for cake after the Entomological Society has filled my mind with images of crawling things."

Verity cast a thoughtful eye at William Cole. What was he up to? Tea with his siblings need not include herself. And he was unlikely to discuss his opinions on Dr. Westbridge's suitability in front of his brother. So why invite her along? Was he just being charitable?

An unlikely possibility entered her mind. If he was secretly trying to court her, that would explain his desire to spend more time with her. And she would gladly accept. But he was not. He had had the opportunity to indicate his intentions at the ball. Yet instead of seeking out her company for his own sake, he had asked for her help as merely a friend. Help, no less, in finding a different match for him altogether.

Because Verity knew that, her choice regarding tea was undecided. More time with the delectable Mr. Cole? An afternoon of laughter and great conversation? Yet also more time to forcibly resist his allure. To enjoy him from a distance, knowing that he was never to be hers. No, it was better to refuse.

"Shall we arrange a separate outing for the ladies instead?" Verity offered. "An hour or two devoted to fine English tea and excellent cake? No insects to speak of. You are right, Mr. Cole, Mrs. Trenton deserves just such a show of gratitude. And my sister would be thrilled to join us."

William Cole's face fell. He shuffled his expression back to its usual friendly arrangement almost immediately, but his eyes remained sad a moment longer. Even his brother glanced at him briefly, as if offering silent support.

Poor Mr. Cole. He was trying so hard to be a better man. Verity regretted robbing him of his generous attempt at chivalry. But she dared not allow him even an inch closer to her heart. He would simply have to find someone else upon whom to practice his improved nature.

Mercifully, he made no further appeal for Verity to join them. Instead, Mrs. Trenton said, "That is very kind, Miss Lockhart. Of course, there is also the community picnic planned for next week. No doubt, we shall all see each other there." She looked with particular kindness upon her younger brother as she said this. Verity could see that she, too, wanted him to find his true love. A casual gathering of that size would certainly present him with a wide array of ladies from which to choose.

"Will you be attending, Miss Lockhart?" asked Mrs. Trenton. All eyes turned to Verity. Was she mistaken, or was there a strong sense of anticipation in the carriage?

"If Hope and Daniel will be there, I will be too," Verity guessed.

"Ah, well," replied Mrs. Trenton, "we know the Sinclairs love a good picnic. Your family has a particular fondness for the outdoors, I have noticed. I shall remind your sister. It would be such a pity to miss it."

William Cole turned his attention to his shoes. There was nothing about them that Verity could see that should warrant such a keen eye. They were quite new and well-polished. Perhaps he was simply confirming that this was indeed so.

The motion of the carriage slowed as the driver pulled it to a halt. William Cole's head lifted and turned to the window.

"It seems we have arrived." He looked back down the way they had come. "The lane is quite busy. Better to send Ned home and have him fetch us later. Shall we say two hours? That should give us plenty of time to satisfy even Miss Lockhart's enthusiasm." He turned to Verity. "Or have I underestimated your need?"

"Goodness!" replied Verity. "I wouldn't dream of asking Mrs. Trenton to stay a minute longer than that. But thank you for your consideration, Mr. Cole."

"Right, then, ladies," said Lawrence Cole. "Let's be on our way. I will let Ned know of our plans."

They bundled out of the carriage and waited on the pavement for the elder Mr. Cole to instruct the driver.

"Oh, look!" cried Mrs. Trenton, indicating with her gloved hand at a splendid carriage waiting a hundred yards down the lane. It had a crest painted in blues and golds upon the door. "Lord and Lady Howell must be attending the same lecture. How marvelous! I'm so glad Ellena has convinced her husband to partake more in all that our fine city has to offer. I can't wait to introduce you, Miss Lockhart. And you..." She tapped her younger brother playfully on the chest with her fan. "You will have to mind your Ps and Qs. She is no longer a houseguest you can tease. She is the finest lady of our city."

If Verity didn't know better, she would have quite believed William Cole had seen a ghost. The blood drained from his face and he looked as if he were ready to run.

"Are you all right, Mr. Cole?" Verity asked quickly.

"I... Yes... Something from breakfast must have disagreed with me."

Verity was alarmed at the suddenness of his change in pallor. "Would you prefer to go home? The scent of so much camphor might not be the best thing for an unsettled constitution."

He stood, evidently undecided, casting his gaze from Verity

to the door of the Society building. His eyes came to rest again on Verity. He looked upon her with earnest concentration.

His sister came to stand by his elbow and touched his arm lightly. "If you do not feel well, take the carriage home. There will be other opportunities…" She left the sentence hanging in the air as if there were more to be understood that need not be said aloud.

Verity assumed Mrs. Trenton was referring to time spent with his brother. But William Cole did not glance in his direction even once. His eyes remained upon Verity, as if all rested upon what would become of her if he left. Perhaps he had shared their little pact with his sister. He might feel he was letting their guest down if he did not see the outing through. Had he not promised to help Verity sift only the best matches from the chaff that might distract her?

"I will stay," he said eventually. "But I will forego unnecessary conversations and confine my energy to our little crew."

"Very well," his sister replied. "But don't be surprised if Lady Howell comes to greet you. You haven't spoken since…" Mrs. Trenton stopped and pondered a moment. "I believe it was just before her wedding. I was amazed neither of you sought the other out at the ball. Especially when one thinks what fast friends you had become. It would be good of you to at least wish her well on her nuptials."

William Cole nodded, though his face remained grim. "If she wishes to speak with me, I will do so gladly," he said.

"Of course she would wish it!" Mrs. Trenton laughed. However, the sound carried no conviction. She looked at her brother with a small frown but said nothing further.

Up the stairs they went. William Cole managed them well enough. The color had returned to his face. In fact, it had returned in excess. Verity hoped he was not coming down with a fever. If he was exerting himself for her sake, she would never forgive herself. It was all very well for him to take his promise to her so seriously, but it wasn't worth the cost of his health.

Inside, the rooms were filled almost to capacity. People mulled around, perusing the various displays. Butterflies in one room, glass vivaria in another, and so on. Down a hallway was a larger assembly room, its chairs waiting to be claimed once the lecture was ready to begin.

"Perhaps you should rest here," Verity told the younger Mr. Cole. "We will stay with you. I can always browse afterward if you are feeling better."

This did not appear to comfort William Cole as it should have. He shook his head slowly. "I am well enough. And if I weren't, I would take myself home. Please, Miss Lockhart, take every advantage of your time here. I would be dismayed to rob you of even a moment of it."

"Well…" Verity looked uncertainly upon her friend. "If you are sure…"

Mr. Cole gathered himself, standing straight and determined. Verity had to admit, he did seem to have recovered a great deal. "I am fine," he said. "In fact, I might even offer you my arm. My sister can hover at your side so that my propinquity might not be misconstrued by others." He offered her a lopsided grin.

Verity breathed out a sigh of relief. "Ah, sir, I see you are indeed yourself again." She countered his mischievous smile with her own. "And because you are, I shall rely on myself for locomotion. To be on the arm of such a charming gentleman would discourage the attentions of the very suitors you have promised to help me find. After all, is this not the perfect place to find them?"

"What is this?" asked Lawrence Cole, his blond brows lifting at his brother. "Are you to play matchmaker for Miss Lockhart?" He turned to Verity and scoffed. "It seems you are taking advice from a gentleman who has not yet secured his own partner in life. If that is the case, Charlotte and I shall have to add our efforts to the cause. With your permission, of course."

The irony was not lost on Verity. The very family she had almost married into, the one she wished now could be her own, had—to a man—volunteered to help her find any other partner than she one she wanted. And how could she refuse?

Just look at them. Three pairs of eyes willing me to happiness. And one pair belonging to the man who could give it.

"Er… thank you." What else could she say? William Cole was never going to be hers. She might as well explore other avenues. And what better than the support of three people who were so sincerely invested in her well-being?

A crowd began to filter into the lecture hall. Among them, Dr. Westbridge. His eyes lit up the moment he recognized Verity and her companions, and he hurried over to where they were standing.

"Miss Lockhart! So glad you could come!" He acknowledged the rest, then turned his attention back to Verity. "Have you seen the mounted large blue in the butterfly room? It was donated to us anonymously this week. Isn't it funny that we just spoke about it at the ball? Do you think your friend has had a change of heart?"

Verity willed herself not to look at Mr. Cole. He certainly was full of surprises! "It would appear so," she answered. "What a generous gesture! Then again, it seems to be more and more the norm for that particular friend."

Charlotte Trenton, having also looked away from her brother for likely the same reason, now tapped Verity on the arm. "Look, there are Lord and Lady Howell. And they have Miss Kinsey with them. Let us make introductions before they are surrounded by entomologists hoping to fund a favorite project."

Mrs. Trenton walked toward the Howell party at once and Verity was obliged to follow. She was a little annoyed. She had not come to make conversation with strangers. When would she have a chance to browse the displays with Dr. Westbridge?

The Messrs. Cole did not join them, which Verity thought odd. William Cole seemed himself once more. There was no reason for him not to greet an old friend. Then again, it would have been rude for them to all abandon Dr. Westbridge just as he had arrived.

Verity decided to give it no further thought, focusing instead on the party they were approaching. A quick introduction, she hoped, would free her to admire the specimens she had specifically come to see.

Lord Howell cut a fine figure—tall and broad-shouldered, with dark hair curling into an alluring forelock. His wife was no less handsome, her intelligent eyes already tracking them from across the room.

"Lord and Lady Howell," said Mrs. Trenton, reaching out her hands to take the viscountess's and planting a fond kiss upon her cheek. "May I introduce Miss Verity Lockhart, a friend from my hometown? She is probably the only woman here who is genuinely interested in today's subject matter."

Lady Howell's perfect skin creased into a warm smile. "Miss Lockhart, a pleasure to meet you. This," she said, indicating to her left, "is my very dear friend, Miss Jillian Kinsey. We are country folk, like yourself—more familiar with the denizens of the meadow than our counterparts of the city would be. Though I doubt we will recognize any specimens from today's talk. Unless they have stag beetles in Egypt." She finished with a half-wink at Miss Kinsey.

The lovely Miss Kinsey, golden-haired and cheerful, took Verity's hand at once. "Miss Lockhart, how happy I am to make your acquaintance! Ellena assures me that Munro is not all pomp and pretense, but I have not met many folk who suggest otherwise, unless they are handpicked by the viscount to visit Munro House. He has impeccable taste in people's character, don't you, Lord Howell?"

Before the gentleman could answer, she had tripped merrily along in her conversation. "I hope I shan't be bored today. I am so easily bored in the city. It's a pity I can't ride. Never learned how, you see. And I must always have a maid running after me if I leave the house. It is very droll, you know. The theater is all right. And I do enjoy dancing. But Ellena is attempting to educate me, though I cannot say it has been a success. The greatest lesson I have learned is that a lady's life is altogether dull. Unless you have a lovely husband like the viscount. Then it's not so bad. Do you have a beau, Miss Lockhart?"

Miss Kinsey's monologue ended so abruptly that Verity was caught quite off guard. "Oh, I… er… no, not as yet."

"Well, good luck, say I. Chances are you won't find him here. The gentlemen are far too occupied with six-legged creatures to notice the two-legged ones." She laughed brightly, the sound echoing across the heads of the very many people she likely thought needed some laughter in their lives.

Lady Howell leaned to the side and said quietly, "Jilly, I think you might want to give Miss Lockhart a moment to assimilate all that you have said."

While Miss Kinsey obliged by taking a breath, Mrs. Trenton asked the viscountess, "Do you know who else is here today? I shall give you three guesses."

Lady Howell cast her eye across the room. Her smile faltered. She looked up at the viscount quickly, taking his arm as if to keep him close. "I see your brothers are both in Munro, Charlotte," she said. "It must be a special blessing to have the whole family together." Her voice was light and friendly, but her fingers were wrapped tightly about the solid muscle of her husband's upper arm. His eyes found what she had seen, and he also stiffened.

Verity twisted her body to catch sight of what had so visibly disturbed them, but all she could see was Dr. Westbridge and the Messrs. Cole, all three of whom were chatting in a pleasant manner, seemingly oblivious of the attention.

"You will come and say *hullo*, won't you?" Mrs. Trenton asked. "It has been more than a six-month since you and William have last spoken to each other. I know he will want to wish you well since he was not at the wedding to do so."

"Alas," came the formal tones of the viscount, "the lecture is about to begin, and we will be in a hurry to leave when it is done."

Mrs. Trenton blinked, the rest of her features momentarily

frozen. "It will take but a moment." She tried to reset her smile, but it wavered uncertainly.

"Perhaps another time," Lord Howell said firmly. "Come, ladies, let us take our seats." He stepped forward at once, his wife still on his arm.

"I'll join you in a minute," said Miss Kinsey to her friend. "I would like to talk to Miss Lockhart a little longer. Everyone else here is so stuffy and serious. But your little ensemble look like fun." Before Lady Howell could stop her, Miss Kinsey had headed in the opposite direction, with Mrs. Trenton and Verity trailing helplessly after her.

"She's something of a hurricane," breathed Mrs. Trenton as they hurried to catch up.

"A friendly one, thank goodness," replied Verity. "Look, she's actually starting introductions already! Lady Howell must be beside herself. Miss Kinsey is such an unlikely friend for a viscountess."

Mrs. Trenton answered in bursts as she puffed along, sucking in a breath where she could. "For many years… she was her only friend… Ellena… will therefore likely… forgive her anything. *Hallo again*, Miss Kinsey. My, but you walk quickly!"

"I am used to running across the fields at Trenton Grange," Miss Kinsey answered, her eyes sparkling as of one who is in their element. "What lovely brothers you have, Mrs. Trenton. I myself have three. Little mischief makers, every one of them, but I love them so. And Dr. Westbridge here reminds me of dear Papa, whom I miss with all my heart. I know it is a privilege to visit in Munro, but there is nothing quite like home, is there, Miss Lockhart?"

William Cole, who had recovered soonest from the onslaught that was Miss Kinsey, quickly replied, "I imagine Miss Lockhart misses her opportunities to paint the most. She has quite the talent for it."

"You paint, Miss Lockhart?" cried the delighted Miss Kinsey, her eyes crinkling as a broad smile lit up her face to a fullness of cheer. "Then you must visit us at Munro House. There is a lake on the grounds that offers the most beautiful views. It will be such fun. Better than sitting around and drinking tea yet again. The aristocracy could learn a thing or two about money not buying happiness."

"I...I..." stammered Verity, flustered by the raging energy that poured from Miss Kinsey. "I do not paint landscapes," she managed at last.

"You don't? Then what *do* you paint?"

Verity fumbled with the ribbon at her bosom. "Insects. I study them. I sketch and paint each one that I have observed as a kind of scientific record."

"You don't say!" Miss Kinsey clapped her hands together. "How absolutely marvelous! So *that* is why you are at this dull gathering. I had wondered. But one doesn't like to ask. Apparently, I give offense with my questions. But how else am to discover what I need to know?"

"Um, yes," Verity agreed before lapsing into silence again.

"Are you all as fond of insects as Miss Lockhart?" Miss Kinsey asked, surveying the group, who—except for William Cole— stood in mute awe of her.

"Goodness, no," replied Mrs. Trenton. "I have offered to play chaperone, as Miss Lockhart's sister was unable to attend. But I take no interest in the lecture for its own sake."

"I suspect," said Dr. Westbridge, "I am the only other enthusiast among the six of us, unless you count yourself, Miss Kinsey. It is I who extended the invitation, knowing how rare an opportunity this might be for a young lady with such an unusual pastime."

"And I am very grateful for it," Verity assured him. "I only wish I could have brought my sketchbook. But my sister was adamant I shouldn't."

"Well, then, Dr. Westbridge, your kindness should be repaid in full," said Miss Kinsey. "Why do you not join us at the lake? You and Miss Lockhart may regale me with stories of all the wildlife to be found at the water's edge, and I shall have a marvelous afternoon out of doors. In fact, why do you not all come? It shall be very merry indeed!"

Lawrence Cole was the first to shake his head. "Alas, I must return to Fernbridge. I have been several weeks away from my family, and our father has need of my assistance at the bank."

"And I cannot bear to be parted from my little ones for long," said Mrs. Trenton. "Jane is but five months old and Clarence has just turned three. His is a very precious age and I do not like to miss even an hour of it. But your invitation is very kind."

"What about you, sir?" Miss Kinsey asked of William Cole. "Will you be joining us?"

The strange discomfort seemed to seize Mr. Cole once more. His lips flattened their smile. His gaze was thrown to the floor. His breathing grew shallow.

"Mr. Cole?" Miss Kinsey prompted once more. "Do you have family commitments or"—her eyes rested a moment on his uniform—"military commitments that keep you from joining us?"

"I do not," he finally answered. "However, I have another prior arrangement to attend to."

"But I have not even mentioned a date!" said the astonished Miss Kinsey. "How will you know if you are available?"

"It is a personal matter. I do not know when it will be resolved."

"Well, you are certainly mysterious, sir," remarked Miss Kinsey, an opinion which Verity currently shared. "And now I wish more than ever that you would be joining us. But I shall console myself that I have two new friends to entertain. And you shall hear from them what larks we have had without you!"

William Cole bowed his head. "As you say, Miss Kinsey, the loss is mine entirely."

A polite voice that belonged to no one in the group coughed behind them. "Pardon me. Is there a Miss Kinsey here?"

All six heads turned to find a rather nervous young man pushing his spectacles higher up on the bridge of his nose.

"I am Miss Kinsey," said the young lady.

"Oh, mm, ah, Lord and Lady Howell ask that you take your seat with them." He paused, then added, "Ah, yes, indeed, it would be best for you all to do the same. Our speaker has arrived and is about to present his treatise."

Verity wanted to stamp her foot in frustration. All this chitter-chatter had taken up all her precious time in a building that she could only have dreamed of entering before. No conversation with Dr. Westbridge about why tansy beetles rarely flew, even though they had wings. No closer inspection of the minute differences in various types of flour beetles. And no opportunity to see if Arthur Westbridge might be the man with whom she could have a future.

"Oh, Miss Lockhart!" called Miss Kinsey as she swooped off to join her friend, "I will send the carriage to fetch you at two in the afternoon tomorrow. Don't forget your paints!"

Before Verity could answer, the blonde whirlwind had disappeared in the crowd.

"I would have offered to fetch you myself," said Dr. Westbridge, "but it seems your companion in lieu of a chaperone is to be Miss Kinsey. So, I will meet you at Munro House, if that suits."

"I can hardly say if it will, sir," Verity responded. "I have yet to find out if my sister approves this outing."

"Perhaps you would be so good as to send me a message with your sister's answer? It would not be seemly for me to attend upon Miss Kinsey on my own."

He was right, of course. Dr. Westbridge, Verity was realizing, did everything by the book. It should have been a reassuring fact. But right now, Verity was irritated. Unlike Dr. Westbridge, she did not want to be accommodating toward Miss Kinsey. And she wished he would show a measure of disgruntlement also. Should he not bewail that this woman had stolen their time together? It was so rare a gift to find a man who shared her passion, but he had not protected their precious connection. Since he could visit this establishment whenever he chose, did he not understand the value it held for her? He had *said* he did. But he had not fought for it when Miss Kinsey had entered the fray. Instead, Verity had to wait for the lecture to end, praying it did not take much more than an hour if she was to walk and talk with Dr. Westbridge, meandering past displays that both educated and enthralled her. It was all very vexing.

They took their seats. Charlotte Trenton sat on Verity's left, with Dr. Westbridge to the left of Mrs. Trenton. To Verity's right sat Lawrence Cole, his unwed brother to his right. All very proper and correct. Bother! Verity could neither consult with Dr. Westbridge on the facts of the talk, nor could she whisper her opinions of him against William Cole's shoulder. Double bother!

Verity sulked and fretted throughout the talk. The speaker droned on. He spoke of his travels to Egypt and Morocco, how very dangerous the Nile was, how very great the heat. He talked at length about his connection with great European naturalists and how they respected him.

Verity stifled a yawn. So far, not so much as a mention of a single beetle, Egyptian or otherwise. She cast her eye to the left. Mrs. Trenton was listening attentively, possibly because there *was* no mention of beetles. Dr. Westbridge was scribbling in a little notebook. She wondered what he had found worth writing down.

To her right, Lawrence Cole was muttering something to his brother. She couldn't be sure, but it sounded very much like, "Sit up. Why did you even come?"

Now *that* was a good question. William Cole was clearly as bored as she was. But that was likely the speaker's fault. If Mr. Cole had believed the subject matter to be uninspiring, he would not have wasted his time here. Verity could not believe he would have come merely to assess Dr. Westbridge. Not when their little pact had been agreed to in humor.

But why such a sudden interest in entomology? Verity pondered the possibilities. He might have wanted to see what she found so intriguing about insects. Chances were, he would have numerous teasing comments to make about them. But he definitely cared. No man attended a lecture simply to tease. No, William Cole would merely package his interest in banter. *"How many legs did you say an insect had, Miss Lockhart? Six? My, that seems a bit excessive!"* Or *"That cardinal beetle's antennae look exactly like Lord Penrose's moustache."* She began to smile and received a quizzical look from Mrs. Trenton. She swallowed it down in haste and tried to forget about the charming qualities of William Cole.

She wondered what he made of Dr. Westbridge. After all, he had spent more time in conversation with him today than Verity had. Had he discovered anything to suggest whether the doctor was a suitable match? She wished she could have found out for herself. Instead, she had been dragged off to meet the cream of society and their highly energetic friend, who was not, as one might say, as *creamy* as they were.

Had Mr. Cole known to avoid Miss Kinsey? Was that why he'd stayed with his brother and the doctor instead of greeting an old friend? No, it was not so. Verity remembered Mr. Trenton telling him about her for the first time at the ball. Unless, perhaps, Mr. Cole had ignored Mr. Trenton's advice and danced with Miss Kinsey after all, only to discover she was more than he had bargained for. No, she would have noticed if he had. Her eyes had been riveted to his movements all evening.

A thought that had been nagging at her now resurfaced. Lord and Lady Howell had seemed equally reluctant to greet Mr. Cole. In fact, now that she thought on it further, each time that Mr. Cole had flinched or felt ill or given a vague reply, it had been at the mention of meeting with the viscount and viscountess. The cogs in her mind began to turn. Why had he not attended their wedding if they were so fond of each other? Their last encounter had been just before the wedding, more than six months ago. That was around the time he had returned to Fernbridge. Why had he returned *before* the wedding and not after? Verity could recall no urgent matter that had brought him home.

At the time, she had just turned eighteen, and both sets of parents had hoped for a match between their children. But there had been no hurry. No rivals were rushing to take his place. So why had he hastened home?

Realization dawned like a lead weight. Mr. Cole and Lord and Lady Howell must have had a falling-out of some kind. Something so unforgivable that he had not only chosen to avoid their wedding, but had departed Munro altogether. Something so private that his sister knew nothing of it. And, despite the passing of time and the convenience of writing letters, they had not made amends. But who had offended whom?

"And so, this brings me—some might say, *at last*—to the scarab, the quintessential Egyptian beetle."

General laughter followed this statement by the lecturer. Verity sat up. Yes, at last indeed! She could wonder about Mr. Cole's fallen friendships later. Or not at all. It really had nothing to do with her. *She* was not on bad terms with him. Anyway, who knew what might upset the members of the *ton*? Lord Howell seemed a very stiff sort of chap. Perhaps Mr. Cole had erred with them, as he had with her butterfly... with good intentions. Or *they* had somehow offended *him*.

No matter. It was likely petty and best forgotten. Here and now, she could fill her mind to the brim with new knowledge, without her mother fretting, and with full approval of her peers. She might even be solidifying her connection with Dr. West-bridge in the process.

Verity shut away all thoughts of Mr. Cole. Well, almost all thoughts. She was still manifestly aware of his presence, and that *she* was his reason for being here. It was only in friendship, but it left her feeling warm inside. Very warm indeed.

The talk proceeded and Verity was, for the moment, en-grossed in it. But it was short-lived. Egypt, as it turned out, did not have a wealth of variety in the *coleoptera* family. Soon, they were applauding the lecture's end and rising from their chairs. To explore, Verity hoped. To better know Dr. Westbridge, she assumed.

But it was William Cole who pointed out the sacred scarab in the corner display and laughed when he discovered it was a kind of dung beetle. It was William Cole who asked questions and expressed his admiration at how many of them Verity could answer. It was he who graciously accepted that she did not mind these "dead things," for, as she explained, they had been collected for science and not for someone's personal satisfaction. Ah, yes, it was William Cole who seemed disappointed that the afternoon had come to an end.

And it was he whom Verity thought of for the rest of the day, into the night, and deep into her dreams. Not Dr. Westbridge, who had merely nodded while she'd perused the displays, as if he were a museum curator taking them on a tour. Not Dr. Westbridge, who had bowed politely when they'd parted and expressed his keenness at seeing Verity again on the morrow, without managing to sound particularly keen.

No, it was William Cole who haunted her thoughts. His low, seductive voice. His deep-blue eyes. The way he looked at her as if there were no one else in the room.

But that was just his way. She wasn't special. And she couldn't have him, though she wanted him so very, very much! For her, it would have to be a blander union. Someone like the doctor, who accepted her, liked her, respected her, shared her odd interests for longer than one afternoon.

Verity supposed she should have felt grateful. Wasn't Dr. Westbridge, in fact, everything she had wished for? Someone who didn't expect her to give up her passion? Someone with whom she could be herself?

And yet, Verity wasn't sure she *did* want him. Despite his qualities covering all those she had listed for herself. Oh, it was enough to make her want to pull her hair out! Her mother would say she was looking for excuses not to be happy. That she would never find love if she didn't give it a chance.

Only, it was dawning on Verity that she *had* found it. *Mr. Cole* gave her butterflies. Not the pinned and mounted kind. The sort that made her feel giddy. She wished *he* could come to Munro House with her. He would deflect Miss Kinsey's high energy with his own. Verity felt… safe with him.

She had rejected him once because he had seemed too child-ish, too preoccupied with selfish pursuits. Now he had shown a better side, but it was too late. He would offer this better self to someone else. Verity would love him, desire him, need him, to no avail.

She sighed. Best to make a life with Dr. Westbridge, if he would have her. He could give her stability without changing her. And that should be enough. She would keep telling herself that until she believed it. One day, she would.

But that day was not today.

CHAPTER SEVENTEEN

Munro, May 1815

SHILLINGTON'S GENTLEMEN'S CLUB could get a little rowdy of an evening. Nicknamed "The King's Shilling" because it was largely frequented by His Majesty's officers, it had its share of gentlemen who did not deserve the nomenclature. Unlike other gentlemen's clubs, Shillington's offered some leeway to its members, knowing these were men who served their country and might want to drink to forget about what they had seen or were about to endure. It was therefore the natural choice for people like Lieutenant Richard Foyle, who were overfond of their tipple.

William had learned to steer clear of the tables where such men played cards or dice. They were prone to drunken outbursts, accusing fellow players of cheating. And William was in no mood for a scene. He enjoyed the camaraderie at the club, especially now that his prospects in love were so uninspiring. But he did not wish to dwell upon it. That was exactly why he was at Shillington's.

He had spotted Foyle almost immediately upon entering and steered a wide berth around the game of hazards, which was Foyle's favorite. Instead, William sat himself down at a table of whist players, waiting for a chance to enter the game. He did not gamble much these days. His earnings were rather pitiful, and he still relied heavily upon his father's allowance.

Six months ago, this would not have bothered him. He would have been among the louder members of the club, if he had been in Munro then. And his father's money would have carelessly departed from his purse. Now, his youthful exuberance somewhat stilled by his maturing insights—not to mention the sobering thought of imminent war—William was simply happy for an evening of distraction sans the usual carousing for which he had been known.

Ah, but how much he would have rather had the distraction of Miss Lockhart's company!

At the Macraes' ball, she had violently expressed her dismay at the thought of him endangering himself in battle. The way she cared, without fear of speaking her truth, deeply moved him. Under her reserved exterior beat a passionate heart. She really was an excellent friend.

If she had been a man, they could have written each other. It would have given him great comfort when England's shores were far away and the smell of death and gunpowder hung in the air.

Yet, if she had been a man, he would not desire her so. He would not want to trace the curve of her chin with the back of his fingers, or lean in slowly, her eyes closing in anticipation, as he pressed his lips against the softness of hers. The mere thought prickled his skin into gooseflesh, the thrill of their imagined touch rushing through his blood.

"I'm done," said the gentleman in the seat next to William's. "You may take my place if you wish."

William cleared his throat. The sensation of Miss Lockhart's nearness, though not a reality, was hard to release. "Ahem, thank you. What is the starting bet?"

"A shilling, as always." The man rose to leave.

"Of course. Stupid of me," muttered William. It was tradition at Shillington's to place its namesake as the first bet. But William's mind had been on other things.

A strong note of liquor wafted over him as the seat to his right was filled with the pungent body of a newcomer. "Count me in," slurred the man, tossing a shilling onto the table.

William hardly needed to turn his head to know who it was. Richard Foyle bent over the dark-green cloth to retrieve the cards that had been dealt him. He eyed them suspiciously, his head bobbing forward and back as he tried to tried to focus on his hand. The man was deep into the bottle—that much was clear. William would have left at once, but he had already entered the round and it would have been bad form to quit before it was done.

At least Foyle was not his partner for the game. William felt sorry for the gentleman whose bad luck it was to risk his money with the lieutenant as his playing mate.

At first, the game proceeded quietly, Richard Foyle using much of his concentration to follow the pace of the play. It did not take long, however, for the soaked fellow to realize who was beside him and for a memory to bubble up from his addled brain.

"Cole," he said, "I've been looking for you." He paused, his thoughts likely taking their time to assemble. "You were at the Macraes'," he finally said.

"I was," William replied warily.

"There was that girl. Hair as pale as a woman's ti…"

"Watch your tongue." Cole cut him off. "That is no way to speak of a lady."

"She won't be such a lady when I'm through with her." The vulgar fellow laughed throatily.

William's hackles rose. "You are not to go anywhere near her," he snarled.

"Soft on her, are you? All doe-eyed for the little virgin." Foyle gave a lascivious smile that was more wolf than man.

"How I feel is none of your business." William spoke through gritted teeth. "And Miss Lockhart is not to be toyed with," he warned.

"Ah, yes, Miss Lockhart. That was the name." Richard Foyle sat back and pulled a cigar from his top pocket. "Thank you for reminding me. That was the very thing I wanted to ask." He leaned to the side and a footman stepped forward to light his tobacco. Foyle puffed a few times, then licked his lips. "It should be simple enough to inquire about Miss Lockhart's movements. And a servant can always be bribed to leave her alone for half an hour…"

"You disgust me!" William growled, standing up. "You have no right to be in a club for gentlemen. I could have you black-balled for such talk."

"Oh, do sit down, Cole. From what I've heard, you're no altar boy yourself."

William was revulsed to be compared to this wretched being. "We are nothing alike," he hissed. "I have never forced my attentions on anyone. Nor have I gone beyond a harmless flirtation. What you are suggesting is foul to even consider. I would not even have a paid wench treated thus."

"And what would you know of paid wenches, hey, Cole? There is nothing I want that money can't buy."

William pulled his chair back. "Your money cannot protect you from the law. You lay so much as a finger on Miss Lockhart, and I will see to it that you are strung up by your lecherous neck!"

"You witless sap." Foyle smiled with the patience of one who believes he has the advantage. "My father has the magistrate in his pocket, and I have carte blanche in Munro." He flicked cigar ash onto the floor.

By now, William was shaking with rage. If he didn't remove himself this instant, he was going to wring Foyle's neck himself. With his last ounce of self-control, he turned to the other whist players and bowed his head. "I apologize, gentlemen. I will have to take my leave at once. The air does not agree with me." With a final glare at Lieutenant Foyle, William strode from the room, through the foyer, and into the darkness of the street beyond. He stopped and sucked in lungsful of cool, night air until the buzzing in his brain began to subside.

"Cole, you blackguard!" came the slurring voice of Foyle from the top of the club's steps. "It's bad form to quit in the middle of a round! I had money on that game!"

"What are you talking about?" William called up to him. "We'd barely started. The stakes had not even been raised."

But Richard Foyle continued down the steps toward him, taking some two at a time as his feet fumbled beneath him. He came to a clownish stop before William, arms and legs flailing to right him. "I say!" he cried, seemingly startled at the suddenness of his descent. He stood a moment, swaying, then belched unabashedly. "That's better." He grinned. "Be a good fellow and help me back up those damnable stairs. Then you can buy me a drink. There's a good chap."

"I won't lift a finger for you until you apologize for your vile insinuations toward Miss Lockhart," William insisted.

"I didn't take you for a Puritan." Foyle scoffed. He fished about near his belt and pulled out a hip flask, removed the stopper, and prepared to take a swig.

The flask flew from his hand.

"What the devil…?"

"Not another drop until you apologize!" William demanded.

"What for?" sneered Foyle. "Because I want little Miss Lockhart the same way you do? Only, *I'm* man enough to say it."

"You *filth!*" cried William. He balled his hand into a fist and drew his arm back, ready to teach the cur a lesson.

"Lieutenant Cole, stand at ease, sir!" came the stern voice of Captain Larson.

Despite being in his evening dress, William obeyed instinctively.

"Let's not do anything ill-considered that I would have to report you for," Larson continued, though rather less gruffly.

"I'm sorry, sir. Thank you, sir." William *was* relieved. Another moment and he would have struck Foyle. Hard. Not that the man didn't deserve it, and more, but it would not have stopped his repulsive behavior in future. William, however, would have paid the price, anything from a reprimand or a flogging to his commission, even his freedom. It would all depend on how many friends Foyle's father had to influence the outcome.

"He was going to hit me!" complained Foyle. "You saw that. He should be punished!"

Captain Larson spun around on his heel and shoved a furious finger in Foyle's face. "No doubt you had it coming. Look at you. You're a disgrace!

"You can't speak to me that way! I'm not in uniform. My father shall hear of this."

"What an excellent idea," Captain Larson answered grimly. He lifted two fingers to his lips and whistled sharply. A young lad—his clothing a size too small for him, his eyes intelligent— materialized beside him. "Fetch Lieutenant Foyle's horse. He wants to go home and speak to his father about an urgent matter. On your way, collect the gentleman's hat and gloves. There'll be a sixpence in it for you."

"Yes, sir!" the boy answered brightly before disappearing as quickly as he had come.

Larson pinned Foyle with a look that brooked no argument. "Go home, Lieutenant Foyle. That's an order."

Foyle tried to focus his bloodshot eyes. "Shan't," he said petulantly.

Captain Larson stepped closer, his nose almost touching Foyle's, his fury turning his face as red as the wine-seeped nose of his opponent. "I. Said. Go. Home."

Foyle blinked a few times, as if trying to comprehend the instruction. Perhaps Captain Larson had triggered a memory of Foyle's father, the only man the drunkard seemed to fear, for his entire body relaxed into submission. "Well, why didn't you just say so?" He patted Larson on the shoulder. "Good man. Fetch me my horse, will you?"

"I have sent for it," Larson replied. "And when it comes, you are to take your miserable bones directly home. Have I made myself clear?"

"Like a crystal bell." Foyle hiccupped. "All tinkly."

Captain Larson sighed. "Heaven help us when we go to war.

Let us pray the enemy have several Richard Foyles in their battalion too."

"If that be so," William said in a low voice, "it will be my pleasure to shoot them."

The three men stood and waited for Foyle's horse to arrive, though for one of them, it was less standing and more of a gentle rocking. Fortunately, it did not take long for the boy to reappear, leading the horse with one hand and carrying Foyle's hat—with gloves stuffed inside—in the other. Getting the fellow up into the saddle was a far more time-consuming matter, as was the trick of having him stay in his seat.

"Get a grip on yourself, Foyle," Larson commanded. "The least you can do is not fall off while the animal finds its way home."

"I could walk with him, sir," the boy offered.

Captain Larson's face brightened. "Now there's a good lad. Here's another sixpence for your trouble. Mind you make sure he gets all the way home, not just to the street. And you tell the butler Captain Larson sent you."

"Yes, sir!" The youngster threw a salute to make a drill sergeant proud.

"Now there's a fine young man the army could use," said William. "How'd you like to sign up for a smart uniform and a bit of adventure?"

"Still too young, sir," the boy replied, his eyes cast down.

"Ah, well, maybe it's for the best," William replied.

"Good night, then, sir," said the lad, who began to lead the horse and its almost unconscious rider away. "Where to, sir?" he asked Foyle, leaning closer to hear the mumbled response, then waving to William and the captain as he walked on.

"That was more work than he was worth," Larson muttered. "What was he up to this time? I cannot imagine something trivial setting you off like that, Cole."

William's lips grew tight. "I'd rather not repeat what he said, sir. But I will say that he was expressing most dishonorable intentions toward Miss Lockhart, sir."

"Ghastly fellow! No woman should be prey to that man's foul thoughts, least of all an innocent like Miss Lockhart."

"Indeed, sir."

Captain Larson picked at the finger of his glove. "Er... Does she have an attachment? Someone who could defend her if it came to that?"

William wished he could say *yes*. Instead, he hesitated. There was something about the way the captain had asked. Did *he* hope to fulfill that role? Heavens, was there not a man in Munro who did *not* want to claim her?!

"Sadly, there is no one at present that I am aware of," William answered honestly. "The best we can do for her now is to haul Lieutenant Foyle off to Europe with us and hope to leave him there."

"Ha! Yes, certainly. Or..." There was that thoughtful pause again. "One might be bold enough to create such an attachment."

"You would be a fine candidate for the task, sir," said William, and he meant it, even if the thought of Miss Lockhart in the captain's arms sank its teeth into his heart.

Captain Larson dropped his jaw slightly. "Why, thank you, William. That is very good of you to say. Though I do wonder why you have not claimed the enviable task for yourself."

"Oh, I.... Well, the truth is..." William floundered. "The truth is..." He took a deep breath and exhaled it. "I missed my opportunity."

"That is a great pity." Larson shook his head. "And yet you do not strike me as the sort who would give up. What keeps you from trying again?"

"The lady has made her feelings clear."

"Pardon my blunt observation, but what was clear at the ball was that she very much enjoyed your company."

"We remain friends."

"And that is all?"

"That is all."

"Women have been known to change their minds."

William's brow drew into a frown. "I'm sorry. I don't understand. I was under the impression you might prefer Miss Lockhart and me to be just friends. Why do you now encourage me to pursue her once more?"

Captain Larson formed a wry smile. "I am a man of discipline, William. Discipline, order, and efficiency. It is not prudent to invest my efforts where they are likely to be wasted. If there remains a chance that Miss Lockhart has not fully closed her heart to you, I would prefer to support your endeavor rather than my own."

William scratched the back of his head. "Alas, sir, I have no desire to offend the lady by approaching her when I have already been rejected. We have become friends for the very reason that I no longer take her for granted."

"That's just it, Cole, don't you see? It is very unusual for a lady to welcome friendship with a gentleman after she has rejected his suit. If I may, she is not the only one who has noticed a change in you. You are a long way from the newly commissioned officer I met five months ago. That chap was all swagger and not much substance, if you'll forgive my bluntness. But women are a forgiving sort. If Miss Lockhart liked you then but wished there was more to you, she may be pleased with what she sees now. It would seem a terrible loss if she carried the same regret you do, and nothing comes of it. I certainly would not wish to proceed with my own efforts until I was sure her affections were not aimed elsewhere."

"Are you saying I should risk my newly formed friendship so that you can court her without fear? That hardly seems reasonable, sir."

"Come now, William. There are ways to establish where a woman's heart lies without so greatly offending her that your friendship is at risk. An honest conversation could do the trick, for one."

William drew a hand across the stubble of his jaw, his eyes

narrowing as he tried to decide the wisdom of the captain's words.

"You know, sir, you are much more the romantic than I would have credited you."

Larson looked down at his feet. "Let's just keep that between the two of us, hey? There's a good chap."

"I shall think upon what you have said."

The captain's head lifted briskly. "Good for you. And don't waste time. Life is short. It is often especially so for men who march with the king's colors." Larson looked wistfully into the distance, as if he saw his future there. Then he turned to William once again, his businesslike manner reestablished. "I believe there is a picnic next week in Munro Park. Everyone who is anyone will be there. And you should be too. It is a public place. The lady will not need a chaperone as long as you speak in view of others. Yes, I believe that will do nicely."

William folded his hands across his chest. "And if it is a charming, little disaster, I can let you know I am officially out of the race, I suppose?"

"Just so. Though I suspect, given what you have told me, that I have already lost." Larson patted William on the back. "Don't fret, Lieutenant. You and I shall maintain our mutual respect, regardless of the outcome. Though, perhaps, the winner can buy the loser a drink. What say you?"

"I say you are putting the cart before the horse. I have yet to think further on it. But I promise that I shall."

"Good man. In the meantime, how about we enjoy our evening at Shillington's now that the riffraff has been removed?"

William grinned. "I'd say that is an excellent idea, sir."

They turned toward the entrance of the gentlemen's club, when the moonlight caught something gleaming on the ground. William picked it up. It was Foyle's hip flask.

Larson whistled a descending scale in admiration. "Looks to be pure silver, Cole. You're in luck."

William shook his head. "It's Foyle's, sir. I'll return it to him when he's sober."

Larson uttered a single, gruff laugh. "You may have to wait some time, then."

William stared at the flask, the earlier events rushing through his mind. "I want him to apologize first. He won't do that when's he's half-sprung."

"Just promise me you won't risk everything by laying a hand on him. He's not worth it."

"I promise."

"Right. Good. Now where were we? Ah, yes, onward and upward."

They marched smartly up the stairs and back into the warm rooms filled with the smell of good brandy and cigar smoke. The thick carpeting and hum of conversation swallowed the sound of their footfalls.

Soon William was seated once more at the whist table, his shilling on the dark-green cloth. All thoughts of Richard Foyle were forgotten. And a wonderful feeling of anticipation for a certain picnic grew full in his heart. Given enough time, it would galvanize him to action. Then he would know, once and for all, if Miss Lockhart might ever be his one great love.

CHAPTER EIGHTEEN

AN AVENUE OF trees lined the drive to Munro House, casting long shadows toward the carriage as Verity approached the Howell estate. The wheels rumbled across the pebbled surface, turned a corner, and slowed to a stop outside the vast home of the viscount and his wife. Soaring marble columns stretched the full height of the triple-storied building. Statues weathered by centuries of wind and rain stood atop these columns, gazing sightlessly across the expansive fields that surrounded the great house.

The butler descended the steps sedately, waiting for Verity to be helped out of the Howell carriage by the footman. "Miss Lockhart, I presume," he said once she had shaken the creases from her skirts.

"Yes," answered Verity. "I am she."

"You are expected. Please follow me."

He led her along a paved path that rounded the house and diverged onto a well-trimmed grassy route up and over a low rise to where the lake sparkled in the afternoon light. In the near distance, Verity could make out two easels facing the water. A table had also been carried out and supplied with a jug of something cold, as well as a variety of sandwiches and small cakes. Three chairs stood empty, a footman behind them waiting to serve as needed.

At the edge of the lake, Dr. Arthur Westbridge kneeled low to the ground, his attention focused in front of him. Miss Jillian Kinsey stood beside him, her cheerful, yellow dress blowing lightly in the soft breeze, her arms gesturing excitedly.

Verity and the butler approached unnoticed by all except the footman, who stepped forward to offer Verity a chair. She refused the seat, instead placing her sketching portfolio and small case of watercolor paints upon it before following the butler farther down the slope.

As they came up behind the two figures, the butler cleared his throat loudly. Both Dr. Westbridge and Miss Kinsey turned at the sound.

"Ah, Branson, I see you have brought me dear Miss Lockhart!" Miss Kinsey began before poor Branson could do his own announcement.

"Indeed, ma'am," he said stiffly. "Will there be anything else?"

"Yes, could you ask someone to bring me my shawl? I know you suggested it to me when we left the house, but I expected to be walking about much more and now the breeze has come up. I am not truly cold, but I feel I might become so if I am to only stand and observe as I have been doing. I see Miss Lockhart has been very clever and practical and brought hers. Such a lovely color too." She beamed at Verity. "It really suits your eyes. I never noticed just how clear and startlingly blue they were. Will you come and see what Dr. Westbridge has found? I'm sure you will know at once what it is, so I shall not spoil the surprise by telling you." She grabbed Verity by the hand and tugged her joyfully toward the lake.

Verity looked helplessly over her shoulder at Branson, whose unmoving features revealed nothing of his opinion, though Verity could imagine well enough. He turned smartly and retraced his steps to the house, no doubt grateful that he could do so.

Meanwhile, Verity and Miss Kinsey had reached the water's edge.

"Good afternoon, Miss Lockhart," said the doctor. "I was so pleased to receive your note saying you were able to join us after all." A brightness in his eyes underscored the truth of his words.

Verity was flattered. Dr. Westbridge had said he would not come if she did not. But joining her there meant suffering through hours of Miss Kinsey's special brand of liveliness. He must have been very keen indeed to see Verity if he was to endure the company of both ladies. Or he might simply be grateful that a companion for Verity allowed him to visit Munro House and its healthy supply of winged and crawling creatures.

"Good afternoon, Dr. Westbridge," she replied warmly to encourage him if he were, indeed, there for her. "I believe you have found something noteworthy. May I see?"

Dr. Westbridge gently parted the leaves of the wildflowers at his feet and smiled up at her. Below were two gem-green beetles, one larger and more bulbous, the other more compact. The smaller one hugged the larger from behind in a pose Verity recognized but would not name.

"They're mating!" Miss Kinsey declared with delight, making Verity blush. Like Miss Kinsey, she was all too familiar with the countryside and the animals who went about their various types of business. But she would never, never speak of it in such a gauche way. Especially not if a gentleman were present to judge her for it.

"Tansy beetles, I believe," she remarked instead. "I wonder if there are eggs or larvae hereabouts?"

"I was about to do a search," remarked Dr. Westbridge. "Perhaps, if we all look together, we will have greater luck finding any."

"I shall rather make a daisy chain for Miss Lockhart to wear." Miss Kinsey proceeded to gather said daisies from a patch nearby. The activity keeping her thus occupied, she was remarkably quiet, humming a tune instead of producing effusive speech.

In the ensuing almost-silence, Verity was able to enjoy the subtle sounds of the meadow. An invisible frog croaked a steady rhythm, while several buzzing things, well, buzzed. It was very peaceful. Verity stood for a moment, her face turned to the sun, drinking in the sensations of warm skin, scented plants, and the delicate song of nature.

"Have you spotted something?" asked Dr. Westbridge when she remained in this pose. "A butterfly? A dragonfly? A wasp?"

Her tranquil trance broken, Verity dropped her gaze shyly to the ground. "No, I was momentarily captivated by the serenity of this place. It is so different to the mood of the city with its busy streets, its noise, and relentless activity. Here I feel I can breathe more deeply."

"Why, Miss Lockhart," cried Miss Kinsey, "I couldn't have said it better myself! That is why I love to be outdoors. It reminds me of home, where I could run freely with my brothers and not fear getting mud on my skirts because no one would mind. Ellena—that is to say, Lady Howell—and I would often plait daisy crowns for each other. But she was learning to be a lady, and life here has not been such an adjustment for her. I, on the other hand, wish to kick off my shoes and scarper about barefoot. I hope I do not shock you!" She laughed gaily, the thought of shocking anyone clearly no real concern.

"Um," said Verity, wondering how frank to be in the presence of Dr. Westbridge. "No, I am not shocked. It may be that I have needed to dispose of shoes on occasion to capture a specimen I wished to study." She felt the heat rise in her cheeks. It was better this way. If Dr. Westbridge was the right man for her, he would not now exclaim against her. Was he not himself currently on his knees, scouring the underside of leaves for the same reason?

It was Miss Kinsey, unsurprisingly, who was the first to respond. "My, Dr. Westbridge, do you hear? The three of us are quite the set! Which of us would not rather be here, amongst the wild things, than cooped up in a drawing room making tiresome conversation over fine china?"

"Actually, Miss Kinsey," said the doctor, grunting slightly as he got up and dusted off his trousers, "while entomology is a fine hobby, my true passion lies in service. That is why I chose to become a physician. To be honest, I spend most of my free hours volunteering at the Royal Hospital for soldiers who are too old or incapacitated to serve their country any longer. There is another just like it in London, near Chelsea. But ours accommodates the retired men from the northern counties. Lord Howell donates generously toward the running of it, while I offer my skill and time instead."

"That is a very noble gift in and of itself," Verity replied. "And it does not surprise me in the slightest. When you took pity on me at the Macraes' ball, I could tell you were a man who thought of the wellbeing of others."

"Thank you for your kind words, Miss Lockhart." Dr. Westbridge shrugged. "However, I did what any gentleman of good character should have done."

Verity could not decide if the doctor was merely modest, or whether his actions at the ball had truly meant nothing. Likely, he would have done the same for any other young woman in need. He was that sort of gentleman. But did he feel something a little more than courtesy and the fascination of a shared interest toward her? She really could not tell. It was most frustrating!

Fortunately, she did not have to wonder long, for Miss Kinsey thought much the same and was not afraid to speak her mind.

"Oh, pooh, Dr. Westbridge! I did not take you for a man who withheld the truth. You and Miss Lockhart made a fine match at the ball, as you do here, among the insects that intrigue you both. I am surprised you have not called on her before now to express these very thoughts. You would not want another to snatch her away before your very eyes, would you? You are so well suited, it would be a terrible waste."

Dr. Westbridge, to his credit, neither blushed nor expressed the horror he must have felt to be addressed in this fashion. Instead, he calmly replied, "There were a great number of gentlemen at the ball of whom the same could be said. Mr. Cole, to name one, would qualify just as well as a suitor. I do not claim to be a better match than any of them. And if I were to have such hopes, my nature is not to rush these matters."

For the briefest of moments, he cast his eyes directly upon Verity, then looked away as if to confirm that he had no right to gaze upon her. Verity almost missed this minutest of signs because Miss Kinsey had reacted quite differently a few seconds before. At the mention of Mr. Cole, Miss Kinsey had stiffened, an action so opposite to her usual self that it drew Verity's attention at once.

Why should Miss Kinsey mind the idea of Mr. Cole as a suitor for Verity? Did she want him for herself? No, it couldn't be. Mr. Trenton had mentioned she had her eye on a friend of the viscount's, a Mr. Bradford, if Verity remembered correctly. Why, then, did the mention of Mr. Cole create such a strong response? Did it have anything to do with the seemingly ill blood between Mr. Cole and Lord and Lady Howell? Verity was determined to find out once and for all. The challenge was to create an opportunity for such a discussion to occur.

"I am flattered that you both think me worthy of such broad attention," she said. "However, there has been no such interest expressed by any gentleman since the ball. As for Mr. Cole, we are merely friends. Now, if you will permit, I shall attend to my painting. Dr. Westbridge, you will tell me if you find the tansy beetle's offspring?"

"Indeed, I shall," he replied, returning to his search among the reeds.

Verity made her way back up the gentle slope to retrieve her sketchbook and paints. As hoped, Miss Kinsey joined her, no doubt because a lady's company promised better conversation.

Verity had placed a sketch upon the easel and was readying her paints and brushes and a glass of water, when Miss Kinsey launched into her next unrestrained monologue, which, for once, was exactly what Verity wanted.

"I say, Miss Lockhart, I *am* glad you do not consider Mr. Cole among your potential suitors. Dr. Westbridge is so much more aligned to your needs. Certainly, Mr. Cole is very handsome and has charm enough to sway many a young woman's heart. I confess I may even have advised you to encourage his attentions if it weren't for a startling exchange with my friend the viscountess just yesterday."

Verity readied herself for the revelation of the secret as Miss Kinsey talked on with barely a pause.

"I informed Ellena that you would be coming to visit at my invitation, and, to my surprise, she appeared none too pleased. As you may imagine, this made as little sense to me as why the *ton* use so much cutlery when they have their meals."

Miss Kinsey rolled her eyes, took a quick breath and continued. "I hope you do not mind me saying so, but, when pressed, Ellena wondered at your connection to Mr. Cole and whether you were the right sort for me to keep company with. Now, I see your dismay, and I am sorry to be the cause of it. I was equally stunned and could find no reason why either of you should not make excellent friends, and I told her so."

Annoyance, impatience, confusion, and indignation vied for supremacy within Verity as Miss Kinsey raced along with her narration.

"Well, Miss Lockhart, you may be shocked to hear her reason, as I was. Indeed, it pained her to speak of it. I must therefore trust that you value the truth over your attachment to Mr. Cole, however deep it runs."

She stopped so abruptly that Verity was startled by the silence. Now that Miss Kinsey was willing to reveal all, Verity was no longer certain she wanted to hear it. This was not the simple spat she had predicted, but something far more sinister-sounding. And the blame seemed to rest squarely on Mr. Cole.

"You will not despise the messenger, will you, Miss Lockhart?" Miss Kinsey clasped her hands and hugged them to herself. "I should be devastated to lose your friendship. There are so few folk I like whom I may engage with. I miss the ease of our village, where everyone knows each other and the most important rule is to be kind."

Poor Miss Kinsey! Verity had not considered how lonely it must be for a groundskeeper's daughter to mix with the elite. If the Sangfords and Penroses were any indication, Miss Kinsey would have struggled to find a friend beyond the safety of Munro House.

"I assure you," she told the worried woman, "that I shall receive the news with fortitude. I shall not judge you for sharing what burdens you."

"Oh, Miss Lockhart, I had hoped it would be so! Let me tell you quickly, then, so that the injury might be brief, and we can paint and laugh again."

Verity sat down, Miss Kinsey joining her in the adjacent chair. She leaned forward and said, "I shall speak softly, for people forget the servants are there. I will not have this talked about beyond our confidence."

Verity cast a quick glance at the footman, who stood unmoving—likely bored—but near enough to hear their speech. "Excuse me," she said to him, "but could you see what has become of Miss Kinsey's shawl? She asked for it some time ago and it has not been brought to her."

The footman nodded and strode off briskly, no doubt happy to stretch his legs and possibly even catch a quick flirtation with a scullery maid as he entered through the kitchen.

Miss Kinsey made an "o" with her mouth and clapped her hands together. "Oh, you are clever! I wish I had thought of that." When Verity did not share in her delight, she grew serious at once, her smile slipping from her face. "To the heart of the matter, then…"

She looked over her shoulder to see if Dr. Westbridge was still occupied, then returned her attention to Verity. "I shall be as brief as possible."

Verity thought this a very fine idea, though she was not convinced brevity was Miss Kinsey's strong suit.

"When Ellena came to Munro last year for her wedding, she stayed with her cousin Mr. James Trenton." She rolled her eyes to the heavens. "Ugh! Horrid man! But we are not here to discuss his petty ways. His wife is quite the opposite. How they found each other and made such a fine match, I will never know. Anyway, Mrs. Trenton, as you know, is Mr. Cole's sister, and he happened to surprise her with a visit at the time Ellena stayed with them. So, they were houseguests together.

"You will agree, Mr. Cole is a terrible flirt. I would not have minded that if I did not know what I do now. And, certainly, Ellena did not mind, either. She thought it all rather harmless fun. She didn't have experience of men, you know. Her father kept her from them like a princess in a tower, only there was no tower, and she was not a princess, but you understand my meaning, I hope.

"Well, it turned out Mr. Cole was not so harmless after all. He got it into his head that Lord Howell was not a good match for her... although, in fairness, there had been some unpleasant- ness... but I digress.

"In fact, he thought himself a better choice and took certain steps to force an end to the engagement so that he might marry my friend instead."

Miss Kinsey's meandering speech came to the point so sud- denly, the truth thrown out so brutally, that Verity gasped aloud.

"I see I have shocked you. Truly, I am grateful to see it, for it means you did not know. I told Ellena as much. I said that you did not seem the sort to befriend a man whom you believed lacked morals. It is a relief to see I was right."

"There must be some sort of misunderstanding," Verity pro- tested. "You say there was unpleasantness. Mr. Cole must have believed he was acting in Lady Howell's interests."

Miss Kinsey nodded. "That is how he defended his actions. But they were done in a scheming, underhanded way. He knew his guilt, for when Lord Howell warned of making his behavior public, Mr. Cole left Munro at once, under the pretense of marrying someone in his village. I now understand that was meant to be you. And I am beyond grateful that you did not accept his offer."

Verity felt numb. She did not share in Miss Kinsey's relief. Her world had just slid violently into an abyss. The man she loved, the man she thought she knew, was a conniving, manipulative fiend. He had never cared for her. She had been a distraction from the loss of another he had wanted so fiercely that he had acted in a manner that had been shameful and secretive. Her imagination began to conjure up what form his deviousness may have taken, but she shut these thoughts down at once, for they only deepened the pain of his betrayal.

She didn't know which cut the deepest, the fact that Mr. Cole's courtship of her had been a mockery, or the knowledge that he had loved another with such distorted passion that he would plot to have that woman for himself.

Surely, said a small voice desperate to believe in him, he must have thought he was saving Lady Howell—or Miss Trenton as she had been then—a motive so strong that would drive him to commit such a gross offense. But Verity had seen the viscount and viscountess together. They were happy, content. Whatever had troubled their relationship had not lasted. Mr. Cole had been profoundly mistaken.

And then, in obedience to his parents' wishes, he had made a show of his attentions to Verity. Even bringing a gift to convince everyone he cared. No wonder he had fled at the first obstacle. His heart had never been open to her.

Verity felt the weight of a sob trying to escape her throat.

"Oh, Miss Lockhart, you look quite ill! Let me get you some water." Miss Kinsey—her brow wreathed with lines, her skin paling as she rushed to pour Verity a glass—was at a loss for words. "Oh, dear," was all she managed to say. And again, "Oh, dear."

Verity sipped the water, using the motion to swallow down her tears.

"I am so very sorry," Miss Kinsey said softly, her liveliness quite gone as she wrapped a hand around Verity's shoulder. "I should have considered how this would affect you. I was so eager to protect you from Mr. Cole's wiles, I quite forgot to protect you from the pain of the truth. And you, being such a trusting friend, would feel this deeply. I should have been more careful in my discourse, easing you toward the facts. It was remiss of me. I have been callous. I am so sorry."

A bloom of memory filled Verity's mind. A different apology, equally heartfelt. At the Macraes' ball, Mr. Cole had humbled himself in this way, admitting mistakes of the past and the hurt they had caused. His gift, he had assured her, had been sincerely meant, his intentions honorable, his manner of going about it regrettable. Would he not feel the same about his behavior toward Lady Howell? Had he not grown since then?

Verity was completely torn. She wanted so much to believe in him, and she had seen plenty to give her hope. But knowing that he had been capable of such subterfuge and plotting... Could she ever trust a man like that completely? Perhaps Miss Kinsey was right. It was well they had only been friends. She was better off with an unassuming man like Dr. Westbridge. A man who might not set her pulse racing but who also would not let her down.

As if the heavens approved her thoughts, Dr. Westbridge called across to them. "I have found a treasure trove of them! Come and see!"

He was so excited with his innocent discovery. It seemed to Verity that Dr. Westbridge showed far more enthusiasm in this moment than he ever had toward her as a woman. She sighed. Would this always be his way? And could that be enough?

If only she might live alone and not be a burden on her family, she would not have to make such thankless choices about men.

She stood up, Miss Kinsey's hand slipping from her shoulder. "Are you all right?" Miss Kinsey asked. "I could occupy him while you find your equilibrium."

"I am fine," Verity lied. "Come, let us not waste the rest of the afternoon." She smiled thinly, then proceeded toward the lake once more. A man's voice behind her made her turn briefly to see the footman presenting Miss Kinsey's wrap to her, then, upon her approval, placing it about her shoulders.

At the water's edge, Dr. Westbridge joyfully showed his wondrous find. Verity marveled at the clumps of yellow rice grains that were, in fact, tansy eggs, clinging to the underside of a broad leaf. She had seen them before at her pond, and there was something calming about their familiarity. Nature was predictable, reliable. Unlike men.

A further search produced a warbler nest filled with pale-blue, speckled eggs, and an angry parent nearby, trilling a warning. Meanwhile, Miss Kinsey—who had kept herself somewhat apart, in a likely effort to promote intimacy between Verity and the doctor—had finished braiding her floral wreaths. She now handed them to Dr. Westbridge. "Will you do the honors, sir?" She dipped her head for him to place the circlet over it.

Dr. Westbridge obliged, then readied the next for Verity, who lowered herself into a curtsey. As he lifted his arms to deliver the wreath, Verity looked up and found herself staring right into his eyes. He gave a genial smile. His gaze did not flame with desire, nor did he allow his hand to slip and touch her cheek. But after the daisy chain was settled around her neck, he reached forward delicately and said, "If you'll permit," before removing a wayward strand of hair from her eyes. The movement was neither brisk and businesslike nor slow and sensual. It was kind, considerate... and had no effect on Verity whatsoever.

What is wrong with me? Verity had felt nothing at his touch. Nor had she sensed any feeling emanating from *him*. If any such emotion existed, he had exercised great restraint not to show it. But Verity did not *want* restraint. She wanted his closeness to quicken his heart and hers. Yet he stirred no tingling in her flesh. Just a pleasant feeling of safety, as with one's father or brother.

Oh, just wonderful! Dr. Westbridge feels like a brother! She wanted to bury her face in her hands.

Even if he *was* exercising admirable self-control, *she* had no inclination to do so. Verity was ready to be awoken in love. She wanted to be swept off her feet. But the steady gaze and direct touch of the good doctor had left her feeling... unmoved.

What did it matter if they shared the same passion in science if they did not share it more, well, *carnally?* She had feelings like that for Mr. Cole by the bucketload! But *he*, by Miss Kinsey's account, was not safe.

Bother men! Bother, bother, bother! She wanted neither brother nor cad. At this rate, she was better off on her own. Her mother might be keen to see her married, but Munro's male population was sorely disappointing.

"Thank you," she said to Dr. Westbridge as a courtesy without substance, just as his touch had felt functional and empty. She caught Miss Kinsey's eye and received a surreptitious wink, which she promptly ignored. She was tired of games. Everyone thought they knew what she needed, pushing her toward matches that they believed right for her. Her mother, her sister, Miss Kinsey, even the trio of Cole siblings.

Mr. Cole.

He was either an incredibly talented liar or a misguided fool who had learned his lesson. She could not remain friends with a dishonest man. But a fool she could forgive. A once-selfish boy who was finally becoming a man could earn her respect.

Then again, was friendship enough? Maybe it would be a mercy to despise him. She would finally be able to let him go.

"Sandwiches, anyone?" Miss Kinsey inquired. She looped her arm through Verity's and the other through Dr. Westbridge's. He did not protest. He did not withdraw his arm. The man was completely indifferent as to who should lean upon him. It mattered not. Nor did Verity want his arm. The chance to brush his hand or breathe in his manly scent did not entice her. All she cared about now was to confront William Cole. To love him or loathe him as the truth would dictate.

But how? When?

The picnic! Mrs. Trenton would be there and her brother was staying with her. He would most likely attend with their family. With so many people there, it would be easy to speak to him unaccompanied while still in public, where all could see them without hearing their words. Yes, that was it. She had a plan. The wait felt more bearable with a plan.

Today, she would nibble on crustless sandwiches and talk about tansy beetles. They would paint and revel in the freedom of the outdoors. She would have uninspired conversation with Dr. Westbridge and one-sided interactions with Miss Kinsey.

But next week, there would be a reckoning with William Cole. If he was not the man she thought he was, they were done. It would be a disappointment and a relief. Still, he might have answers she could understand, points of view she had not considered. They could remain friends. Excellent friends. Only friends.

It did not seem to Verity that either outcome was preferable. But she could not look him in the eye again without knowing who he really was.

Perhaps, if he was brave enough to share the truth of his past, and it did not repulse her, she would be bold enough to share her hopes for the future. That she loved him. That she wanted so much for him to be worthy of such feeling. That the thought of losing him—to war, to another woman, to a reputation she could not respect—cut her to the quick.

Next week, she would know. Would she be encouraging William Cole, whose passion may have driven him to great foolishness, or Dr. Westbridge, whose passion had yet to reveal itself?

From deep within, a voice she had forgotten, a whisper she had ignored here in the strangeness of the city of Munro, spoke to her in a moment of clarity. *"First,"* it said, with a love she should not have discarded, *"you must choose yourself."*

CHAPTER NINETEEN

THE MID-MAY SUN beat down on the lawns of Munro Park, which were covered with a patchwork of picnic blankets and ambulating couples. The Trentons had been one of the first to arrive and were seated under the shade of a large, leafy oak, where James amused young Clarence and Charlotte cradled little Jane upon her lap. William, however, stood on high alert, waiting.

When were the Sinclairs going to get here? He had finally worked up the courage to declare himself to Miss Lockhart, but it was gradually draining away as the hour drew to an end with none of her party in sight. Soon the families would eat their packed lunches, and then the games would begin. It would be impossible to speak to her with any modicum of privacy when everyone was seated at their baskets and watching. And the two of them would be constantly interrupted to be drawn into the games if they should wait that long to talk. Now—with children running about and parents keeping a sharp eye on their antics— was the perfect opportunity for a private conversation in public.

The last ounce of William's determination was fading fast when he recognized the particular figure of Miss Lockhart approaching, her pale, blonde hair peeking from her straw bonnet, one of the Sinclair children holding her hand.

William rushed toward them. He did not care if he seemed

eager. Let her see with what joy he welcomed her arrival!

Miss Lockhart certainly seemed startled by his sudden appearance. That was to be expected. But her features did not relax into a calmer state. She appeared uncomfortable in his presence, nodding her acknowledgement of him without a smile, her eyes diverting from his as she steered past him to follow Mr. Sinclair to an open area on the lawn.

William was completely put off his stride. Something must have happened. It was likely the reason they had been late in arriving. He shook himself mentally. Miss Lockhart was simply distracted. She would settle, and he would offer to show her the tadpoles in the stream nearby. It was within sight of everyone yet distant enough to manage a low-voiced conversation without being overheard. He had specially come early to find something of interest to her. It would provide a good reason to call her away. But William also wanted to show her that he acknowledged the things that meant the most to her. He was not going to give her an excuse to reject him this time.

William hovered uncertainly, watching as the Sinclairs laid out their picnic. Then—to his immense frustration—they gathered their children up to play by the stream. Well, *that* wasn't helpful! How was he to speak to Miss Lockhart alone?

The young lady, however, remained seated upon the checkered blanket. She did not join her family with a net and a jar. Nor did she have sketching paper with her. Instead, she sat, unmoving and quiet. Her shoulders stooped as if carrying a great burden. Her eyes were dull and unfocused.

All at once, they flicked up to him. She stared directly at him. No warm, inviting smile to coax him over. But the suggestion was there nonetheless. *Come here,* her focused gaze said. *I am waiting.*

No longer sure of himself, William stepped around the other picnickers until he stood before Miss Lockhart with the nervous apprehension of a boy outside the headmaster's door.

"Mr. Cole," she said blandly, "won't you be seated?" She

gestured toward the opposite end of the broad rug, far apart enough for propriety, yet close enough to talk.

He did as bidden. "Are you well, Miss Lockhart?" he asked, though it was clear she was not. "You do not seem yourself today."

"Indeed, Mr. Cole," she replied, "I am very much myself. The question of the hour is whether *you* are, in fact, *yourself*."

William blinked uncomprehendingly. "What do you mean?"

"I mean, sir, that it appears I have only come to know a very small aspect of your character. And I wonder whether the rest is quite what I've been told it is. Perhaps you would be so kind as to assist me in solving this unpleasant mystery."

William sat down quite suddenly, all thoughts of romantic declarations thoroughly quashed. He had not the faintest notion what, exactly, she was thinking, but he had a terrible idea why she was thinking something troubling at all. She had been to the Howell estate to see Miss Kinsey. Viscount and Viscountess Howell were the only people in Munro with any knowledge about him that he feared having known. His stomach clenched. Was it possible they would share such a distressing secret with her? And why would they have? To warn her off? Might he not even have friends? Would he be punished into eternity for his wrongs of the past?

"I see you do not protest," said Miss Lockhart. "That is a good start. Let us proceed forthwith, then, for our time to talk is in short supply." She glanced at the stream. The Sinclair children splashed happily under their parents' supervision. For now. She turned back to William and pinned him with her stern gaze. "Tell me about Lady Howell," she demanded. "Why are you no longer friends?"

A fist of dread tightened within William's chest. She knew. She knew! Oh, how she must abhor him! There was no chance for him now. All was lost. She would forever regard him with repugnance.

Even worse, he deserved it. What did it help if he was trying to be a better man when the past could not be eradicated? He had done great harm not that many months ago. How could he hope for Miss Lockhart's understanding?

And yet... she had not shunned him. Here he was, sitting with her at her invitation. What did she need from him? What could he offer that would heal this wound between them?

She had asked for the truth. But when she had it, what would she do? Would confirmation of her new knowledge cause Miss Lockhart to denounce him more fully? Or could she accept that his previous mistakes did not reflect who he was trying to become?

There was nothing for it but to bare his soul to her. It was not the secret that he had hoped to share—that he loved her, cherished her idiosyncrasies, desired the touch of her skin. Instead, he must speak of jealousy, arrogance, and deceit. William hung his head.

"I am ashamed to speak of it," he began. "I do not recognize the man who made the choices I am guilty of. Yet I claim responsibility for all of it."

Did he imagine it, or did Miss Lockhart's eyes soften slightly?

"I fancied myself in love with her... with Miss Trenton, for that was her name before marriage."

"Were you then not in love?"

Was there a note of hopefulness in her tone?

"I think..." William hesitated. "I believe I was in love with the idea of being in love. Miss Trenton and I both enjoyed conversation of great wit. She laughed with me, confided in me, in a way she did not do with her betrothed. He'd deeply wounded her feelings more than once within a matter of days. It did not seem a good match for her, whereas..."

"Whereas you thought you were?" Miss Lockhart asked, a touch of insecurity at the edge of her voice.

William wished he could tell her none of it mattered. That these feelings belonged to a different version of him. That he now understood love was more than ownership, or the fulfillment of selfish needs. But such talk was too intimate, and he had not earned that right. Not yet.

What did Miss Lockhart want to know? Only the facts. If, after hearing them, she would still speak with him, he could tell her more.

"Miss Trenton would not end the engagement, even though it brought her much discomfort," William explained. "Her father held too much sway over her life. So, I thought, if she was to be happy, someone else should help to set her free."

How ridiculous it all sounded to him now! How had he ever reasoned like such a child? That was not how the world worked. He saw it clearly now.

"Someone who could then claim her for himself," remarked Miss Lockhart grimly.

"Yes."

"What did you do?"

William writhed uncomfortably within his skin. "Please, Miss Lockhart, I am too ashamed to repeat it. But I will admit it involved deception and betrayal, though, at the time, it felt warranted, even noble. I would readily confess my guilt and regret to both Lady Howell and her husband now if I did not think the subject would cause them fresh pain. Hindsight has taught me a painful lesson... To see myself as others did and likely still do. To understand the extent of my wrongdoing. To carry the shame for the rest of my life."

William struggled to look at her. He was afraid of what he would see. But when he finally lifted his chin and sought out the reprimand in her face, he found none. In fact, Miss Lockhart, too, had her eyes cast down. She picked at a nodule of fuzzy lint on the rug, her actions mechanical, her thoughts seemingly far away.

He ventured a tentative comment. "I am, no doubt, a disappointment to you, Miss Lockhart. Much more so than I was with the butterfly gift, or the way in which I courted you halfheartedly and then abandoned you. I imagine you see a pattern that worries you, even frightens you. You are probably asking yourself what sort of man you have befriended."

There was no response. Miss Lockhart remained focused on her square inch of fabric.

"I can only say that, by the time we became real friends that night at the Macraes' ball, I had already begun my journey toward the sort of man I wish to be. I cannot undo the past. But I do not live in the past. Will you not consider my very real regrets as punishment enough? It would be a far greater penalty to lose your friendship. It was your example that inspired my wish to improve to begin with. Who else has seen me as I am and accepted me despite my errors? You have trusted once before that I have left my loutish attitudes behind. Can you bring yourself to trust me still?"

To William's horror, the eyes that now lifted to him were brimming with tears.

"I want to trust you, Mr. Cole," Miss Lockhart said, her lower lip quivering. "It distresses me profoundly that I have any cause to doubt you. You will, agree, however, that my discovery of your past actions must drive me to far greater caution. I do not wish to be made a fool of. If you were to display any such tendencies again…"

"What sort of gentleman could cause these tears and not despise himself?" William asked bitterly. "I assure you, every choice I make henceforth will depend on your approval. My motivation is to make you proud of me. But how can I do that if you cast me off?"

Miss Lockhart stared at him through wet eyes. "You impose upon me the role of your conscience. I would not have that responsibility. You should do right for right's sake, Mr. Cole. If that pleases me, it is an added benefit."

"You see how you chastise me freely." William threw his palms forward in exasperation. "No one else does that. My father scolds too much and my sister too little. But *you* speak to me plainly. And I listen because I respect and admire you. You are not my conscience, Miss Lockhart. You are my inspiration."

She pressed her lips together. "Mr. Cole, I wish to be nothing but your friend." She looked away suddenly, as if to hold back new tears at these words. "If you are to take on a more inspiring role, you must find the motivation for it within yourself. Else any stumbling on my part will be an excuse for you to do the same."

William grew quiet. Miss Lockhart was right, of course. Even now, he floundered hopelessly in scouting the path forward. He did need her. Without her wisdom, he would make little progress. But the will to forge ahead must come from him.

He was about to acknowledge this when, from amid the multitude of ramblers that milled about on the lawns, an exclamation rang out toward them.

"Well, now! Miss Lockhart and Mr. Cole. Old friends together once more." These words, so innocent on the surface, carried a corrupted meaning, having been uttered by the disagreeable Miss Irene Sangford. As proof of William's suspicions, she raised a conspiratorial eyebrow. "It is well Miss Penrose is not here. She would surely assume there was more going on between you when your faces are so serious."

William and Miss Lockhart both attempted to regulate their expressions, to the obvious amusement of Irene Sangford.

"Miss Penrose," she continued, "is quite the jealous sort, from what I have seen. Sadly, however, her mother would not want her daughter's envy spent on a military gentleman." She shrugged. "I suppose Miss Lockhart's mother does not have the same qualms."

William looked desperately about him for a savior who might spare them from this woman. There was only one other person he knew nearby, and William grabbed the opportunity to call him over.

"Dr. Westbridge!" called William, finding himself gratefully encouraging his rival's presence. "Do come and join us. Tell me all about the insects you discovered on your outing to Munro House last week. Was Lord Howell in attendance?"

Whether it was the mention of the viscount, whom William

knew Miss Sangford particularly despised, or the imminent and possibly detailed discussion of crawling things, William did not know. Nor did he care. All that mattered was that Miss Sangford abruptly found herself no longer interested in lingering.

"Oh. Ah. I think I heard Mama calling. If you'll excuse me…"

The most rewarding part of seeing the back of Miss Sangford was the first hint of a smile on Miss Lockhart's face. William felt the tiniest reconnection between them.

Or was she smiling shyly at the approach of Dr. Westbridge?

"Good afternoon, Mr. Cole, Miss Lockhart," greeted the doctor. "I am pleased to find your new fascination with entomology has not waned, sir. I don't know what I shall say that Miss Lockhart would not already have shared with you, other than it was a very pleasant afternoon, although the ladies no doubt missed your more charming company."

"You do yourself a disservice, Doctor," replied William, obliged to return the compliment. "If the afternoon was pleasant, your own company was surely more than adequate."

"One can only hope," Dr. Westbridge said solemnly, casting a glance at Miss Lockhart. She, in turn, lowered her gaze to the ground.

So, thought William, *there is something there. Perhaps I have missed my chance, after all.*

Should he bow out graciously and leave them to further their acquaintance? Or was there still a chance to win Miss Lockhart's favor?

She did not offer him any encouragement to stay. Her eyes avoided him. Her lips were thin with tension. No, he should not stay.

She needed time to process all that had been said. It was the least he could do. And if, in that period of grace, she grew closer to the doctor, then that was how the fates had willed it. At least Arthur Westbridge would not, on some battlefield far from home, make her a widow.

William stood slowly and offered his vacated spot to the

doctor. "I have taken up enough of Miss Lockhart's time. Perhaps you would keep her company? Or, better yet, the two of you might want to join the Sinclairs by the stream. I noticed a flurry of tadpoles there earlier."

Miss Lockhart stood at once, her hands busily straightening her hem. "That is an excellent suggestion, Mr. Cole," she remarked, her eyes swiveling from her dress directly to him. With her usual warmth, as if the terrible conversation about Lady Howell had not occurred minutes earlier, she said, "Thank you." And then, "It is kind of you to think of others in this way."

William's heart skipped several beats. On any other day, he would have appreciated her sentiment. But today, his soul burdened with regret and grief, her words meant so much more. Indeed, what he truly heard Miss Lockhart say was, *"I forgive you."*

He swallowed down the lump in his throat. They may yet be friends. Was there… Might they… Dare he hope for more?

No, not right now. Above all, he must be patient. He had come within an inch of losing her completely. One step at a time.

"It is my pleasure," he replied. "Perhaps I shall see you at the games later?"

There was the small smile again. "I am sure you shall."

Then she was gone. In the company of Dr. Westbridge. Who was as dependable as a rock. Well, good for him. As for William, he was not ready to be counted out just yet.

He felt the hard presence of the flask at his hip. There was something else he had to do while he waited to see Miss Lockhart again. He had spotted Richard Foyle earlier, much to his surprise. A picnic was not the sort of party the man usually attended, such an event being far too domestic for his usual taste. It did mean, however, that Lieutenant Foyle was remarkably sober and likely in the company of his father, all of which made it the perfect opportunity to return his silver flask. And get the apology the fiend owed him.

It didn't take long to find him. Baron Foyle, his father, had brought two footmen with him. Between them, they had laid out chairs and a table with a spread of food that would never have fit into a humble basket. Baroness Foyle was being spared the bright sun by her lady's maid, who endured the heat to hold a parasol over her mistress's head. William thought they had rather missed the point of a community picnic.

They seemed to have gone out of their way to segregate themselves from the rest of the citizens of Munro, while insisting on being among them. People like the Penroses, who thought themselves too fine for such homely festivities, had not bothered to come. Others, who valued their privacy, like the viscount and viscountess, held their picnics with select friends on their own estate. But the Foyles, it seemed, needed to establish their superiority through vulgar display. No wonder the young lieutenant had so little good sense.

Lieutenant Foyle was the youngest of three sons. There were no sisters whose presence might remind Richard how one should behave around a lady. Each of the Foyle siblings had inherited a decreasing sense of what it was to be a gentleman, with Richard seeming to have mere dregs in supply. While the Foyle heir maintained a measure of honor, the youngest son had been spoiled and allowed to act on every impulse. His parents had protected him from all harm, including that which he created himself. Too late, they had seen the error of their ways, doting on the baby of the family. A military career had been seen as the only recourse to teach him discipline. As such, it had been an abject failure.

None of this was going to stop William from demanding what was due him. Especially when it concerned Miss Lockhart.

Still, he did not want to create a scene. So, William walked quietly up to Richard Foyle and said in a muted voice, "I would speak with you privately, sir."

Young Foyle, however, likely suffering from a hangover and itching for a drink, was in no mood for civilities. "Where's my flask, damn you, Cole?" he demanded loudly. "I've a good mind to report you for theft. That's a hanging offense, you know. And if they won't hang you, they'll strip you of your commission. Then I can order you to be flogged."

Well, so much for privacy. But William was not discouraged. Enough was enough. Today this man-child would be held accountable. "If we're talking about theft," he said, "you've robbed me of an apology. I have come to collect it. Then you may have your flask." He patted his hip.

"Do you hear this?" Foyle turned to his father. "I am to apologize for being robbed. The man steals my silver flask and then demands *I* apologize! Have you ever heard such a thing?"

Lord Foyle, who had been lounging in his chair, now leaned forward. "What nonsense is this? Do you have my son's property?"

"Yes," replied William, "but not his dignity. That he misplaced all by himself."

"How dare you, sir!" Lord Foyle rose, his face reddening with impressive speed. "Return my son's flask or there will be a reckoning."

"That is exactly what I have come for. But the reckoning is his. Unless you support the sort of salacious comments he made about a lady of my acquaintance."

Lord Foyle froze for a moment. William could not imagine this was the first time his son had been guilty of such behavior, but it was unlikely he had ever been called out on it in public. Heads had turned toward them thanks to their own noisy arrogance, and Lord Foyle's response would now have an audience. Even the Sinclairs, with Miss Lockhart and Dr. Westbridge in tow, had meandered back to see what had captured everyone's rapt attention.

Lord Foyle, unsurprisingly, tried to deflect the issue. "Richard would never use the foul manner of speech to which you refer. And certainly not in reference to a lady. I think you are confusing the jocularity among soldiers with serious insult. I would have you withdraw your accusation, sir."

William stood his ground. "Not only did he make explicit

insinuations about the lady to me, he imposed himself upon her directly at the Macraes' ball. In front of several witnesses, I may add."

"And so you stole his flask to punish this perceived slight? That hardly paints you in a nobler light, Mr...."

"Lieutenant William Cole, my lord. And I picked up his flask from where he had dropped it outside Shillington's. I am only too happy to return it. As soon as I have my apology."

"You say you have witnesses of Richard's actions." The baron folded his arms across his chest, then released one of them again to point an accusing finger at William. "But who can corroborate *your* story?" The freed hand now waved in accompaniment to his speech. "It seems you have made up a lie to blacken his name and now hold his own property as extortion." Lord Foyle leaned forward, his fingertips supporting his weight on the table still laden with uneaten food. "I think it far more likely that you seek a better commission and see my son as a rival for it. You would say anything to ruin his reputation. Fie on you, sir!"

William's jaw tightened. "If you imagine such motive, it is because you have become accustomed to this type of low behavior in your own son and believe it equally reasonable to expect it in others."

Lord Foyle's hue deepened to purple, a feat William had not thought possible without the subject suffering an immediate apoplexy.

"Produce your witnesses!" the baron thundered. "Or withdraw your accusation!"

"This is a picnic and not a court of law," William answered. "I will not harass people who are here with their friends and children, especially if it is to repeat the sort of bile that they heard from your son's mouth. *My lord.*"

"But you are happy to malign my son in front of them?"

"I am not. Indeed, I approached him discreetly, but he involved you, and you, my lord, have drawn the crowd."

A gasp went up from the gathering. No one had ever taken

the baron on. Certainly not as calmly and boldly as William did now. A warning slipped down his spine like ice. Had he gone too far? The baron wielded great influence. Even if William bore no guilt, Lord Foyle could make life very difficult for him. Especially if the baron's youngest got away with his actions.

"Lieutenant Foyle has not been maligned, my lord," said a voice from somewhere behind William. It was soft, almost a whisper. But it carried across the hushed onlookers like a clear note, ringing in the air.

Miss Lockhart approached. Her steps were erratic, as if each one had to be forced from her. But her gaze was unyielding. She came at last to stand beside William. He could feel rather than see the nervous tension radiating from her. And yet she stood, unmoving and resolute.

"Who are you, madam?" the baron demanded, though William could hear the uncertainty in his voice.

"I am Verity Lockhart, daughter of the vicar of Fernbridge, sister to Mrs. Daniel Sinclair of Munro, and unhappy recipient of Lieutenant Foyle's inappropriate attentions."

Her voice carried the slightest of tremors, but William only heard the sound of enormous courage.

Lord Foyle visibly deflated. He looked to his son as if seeing him properly for the first time. Then he turned to his wife, who was sizing Miss Lockhart up with her eyes. She gave an almost imperceptible shake of the head to her husband. His indignation subsided further. In fact, it was as if he aged before them.

But Richard Foyle, being of unsound judgement, grew even more brash. "I do not recall meeting with… Miss Lockhart, is it? Besides, a vicar's daughter would never draw my attention. I have my position to think of."

"I only wish my father's occupation might truly have spared me your impropriety at the Macraes' ball, Lieutenant Foyle," said Miss Lockhart. "Though I am not surprised you do not recall the meeting, as you were squarely three sheets to the wind."

"But you *did* recall the meeting, didn't you, Foyle?" William added. "You had plenty to say on the matter at Shillington's. You might have been blind drunk then too, but your memory was not ailing. Only your sense of decency. Now, since the lady in question has been brave enough to speak up, your apology should be directed to her."

"Ahem," began Lord Foyle, "I think we can all agree there has been…"

The sound of hoofbeats caused the heads of the fascinated audience to turn en masse. A uniformed officer was riding directly toward them, slowing as he approached. He halted at the edge of the crowd but did not dismount. William recognized him at once. It was the meticulous figure of Captain Larson.

"I am sorry to interrupt such a happy occasion," said the captain, his horse prancing beneath him before it settled. "Wellington has called up his men to Brussels. Our regiment must report at once. We ship out tomorrow."

There was a moment of absolute silence. Then the picnickers erupted with dismay. There were wails from mothers and young wives, tears from new sweethearts.

Only Lieutenant Foyle saw an opportunity to his advantage. "Father," he said, his back tall and straight, his chin proud. "I must leave to defend our nation against the French. Mother, take this kiss upon your cheek, for it may be my last."

At William's shoulder, Miss Lockhart's trembling now became visible. She—who, but a half hour ago, had doubted his character—had upheld his honor before all, a feat made more remarkable by the fact that she did not like to draw attention to herself. Yet she had sacrificed for William, declared herself a true friend. And Foyle still tried to evade his responsibility, even now. William clenched his teeth. Before they left these shores, Miss Lockhart would have justice.

William stepped forward and placed the silver hip flask upon the amply catered table. "Miss Lockhart awaits her apology, sir."

"What?" Foyle laughed. "Even now, you continue with your false accusations? You are fortunate that we leave for Brussels, else I would have you before a magistrate for theft!"

"Lieutenant!" shouted Captain Larson. "You will withdraw your statement at once! This is a fellow officer. You will be fighting side by side. It is madness to bring trouble to a war that will have plenty of its own."

"But he stole my flask!"

"He did no such thing. You left it on the steps outside Shillington's. I was there when Lieutenant Cole found it. He had hoped to return it to you when you were… more reasonable."

Lord Foyle took his son firmly by the shoulder. "That is settled, then. No harm done. Now apologize to Miss Lockhart. Even if you remember nothing, *she* does, and the insult must be undone."

"But she's lying!" Richard Foyle almost wailed.

"She is not," Captain Larson interjected. "I was a witness to that also, and all the sorrier for it. In fact, I can name several others who were forced to endure your treatment of Miss Lockhart. You disgraced the uniform and your family name, sir."

Lord Foyle squeezed his son's arm more tightly, his voice pure iron. "Apologize. Now."

The reckless foal hesitated. No doubt he was unused to being held to account. Then, all at once, he relented, his entire body taking on the shape of a chastised schoolboy.

"'M sorry," he mumbled.

"Like a man," his father demanded.

Richard Foyle took a breath and rolled his eyes. But he obeyed. "I am very sorry, Miss Lockhart, for offending you."

Squeeze.

"It won't happen again."

Lord Foyle removed his hand from his son's arm. "I too, apologize, Miss Lockhart. Our son should have known better. I assure you, this will be the last of such behavior."

Miss Lockhart merely nodded. She was fully shaking now. William put his arm about her and led her back toward the Sinclairs.

"You were amazing!" he whispered down to her forehead. "I cannot thank you enough. Miss Lockhart," he said as they walked. "Not only for your support, but that you did not believe me to be a thief."

She nodded again but remained silent.

"Can I get you something warm to drink? You are shivering. I fear it's all been too much for you."

She did not answer, except for a whimper that escaped her throat.

"Where is her shawl?" asked William when they reached the Sinclairs. "I think she is in shock."

"Here." Mrs. Sinclair handed him a soft bundle. "Take her to the carriage. We will be there shortly. Everyone is packing to go. Too many families need to say farewell to loved ones for us to eat and play games together as if nothing were happening."

William shook out the cashmere shawl and folded it around Miss Lockhart's shivering frame. His arm once more protectively around her, they made their way to the Sinclair carriage. The footman opened the door and lowered the step, but she did not turn to enter. Instead, she gripped William's lapel and said in a quavering voice, "I am afraid for you, Mr. Cole."

"There now." William spoke warmly, his hand enveloping hers. "All will be well. Lieutenant Foyle is more bark than bite. It will be a while before he risks displeasing his father again. He will not be bothering me. No more than usual, anyway."

"No," she replied, lifting tearful eyes to his. "I fear for your life. I am uneasy about this war. Many good men will not come home."

William's mouth quirked into a smile. "Am I a good man, then, Miss Lockhart?"

"The very best."

"It gladdens my heart to hear it."

Miss Lockhart's other hand now crept to his chest. "How can your heart be glad at a time like this? I might never see you again!"

"Would that matter so much?" His voice grew husky, his skin warming under her touch.

Her tears now flowed freely, and she nodded wordlessly once more.

"What if I promised to return?" he whispered.

"You cannot make such a promise," Miss Lockhart said almost inaudibly.

"No." William sighed. "I suppose I can't. But I should very much like to come back." He tipped her chin up gently with the tip of one finger. "I should very much like to see you again."

She looked upon him without flinching. Her eyes told him… What? That she worried for him as a soldier? That she feared for him as a friend? That she… Did she… *love* him?

His own feelings rose and flamed within him. This might be the last time he saw her. She would never know how deeply he felt for her, loved her, desired her… But here and now, in this moment, he must tell her, find the words, the way…

And then his mouth was upon hers. Hot, and moist, and hungry. She met him with equal fervor, clinging to his coat as if it were a raft upon the sea. Her lips received his like a drowning man received the arms of his rescuer, with a sort of desperation that could have been joy or fear.

William drew back suddenly. His eyes darted to the side, but no one was paying them any mind in their own hurry to depart. "I am so sorry," he said. "I had no right. You must think me…"

But he could say nothing more, for Dr. Westbridge hailed them from a distance, almost running to reach them, his hair made wild with the motion, his hands smoothing it down as he reached them.

"Miss Lockhart," he panted. "Your sister asked me to check on you. She said you were in shock. However, I see the color has returned to your cheeks." He paused to catch his breath. "Is there anything else I can do for you? Perhaps I shall wait with you since Lieutenant Cole must report to his regiment. I hope my company will suffice?"

"You are very kind, as always, Dr. Westbridge," Verity answered, her eyes averted from both men. Her fingertips lifted to her mouth. Did she taste William's kiss still? Or did she wish to wipe it from her lips?

"Miss Lockhart." William bowed formally, the time to part now thrust upon them. "I shall be writing to my sister whenever I can. Will you look in on her while I am away? She will no doubt worry about me. Perhaps she may find comfort in your visits."

"I shall do so gladly," she replied. "I hope that any news she receives from you may say you are well."

She allowed her eyes to meet his. The tears were gone. The walls were up. And yet, he felt she spoke a thousand words in her silence. He reached out and took her hand by the very tips of her fingers, bringing the softness of his lips to them as a reminder.

"I bid you farewell, Miss Lockhart. May the parting be short and the war brief. For the sake of ourselves, and dear old England."

She shook her head slowly. "I shall not say goodbye, Mr. Cole, but rather till we meet again. I wish you a safe journey. May God grant you courage for what lies ahead."

With their parting greetings done, William was forced to turn from her, his beloved, and leave her in the waiting hands of Arthur Westbridge. He willed himself not to look back. He wanted to remember her when her eyes were upon him, not resting upon the doctor.

His legs grew leaden, each step farther from her dragging less and less willingly. A kiss was not enough. It was a thing of the moment, easily misunderstood. Perhaps she had granted it to a man she knew might fall in battle and was saving the one that came from her heart for the man who stayed behind.

He should have told her he loved her, should have asked for her hand. Then they would be engaged and he could write to her directly, receive her precious letters in her hand, her voice.

William ground to a halt. Why should he carry such regret when there was still time? It would make no difference if he took a little longer to report to Larson. But it could make all the difference in the world to his own future.

It mattered not that Westbridge was there. William would declare himself before an entire battalion if necessary. Time was of the essence. And his heart was at stake.

Nervousness and excitement built together. Just a few minutes more, and his life would change forever. No more regrets. Time to move forward. He knew what he wanted, and Miss Lockhart encapsulated it all. All he needed was one little word, a simple "yes," and he would finally have his one true love.

CHAPTER TWENTY

MR. COLE HAD kissed her lips, her fingertips. They were still tingly and warm from his touch. Now that Verity had tasted his mouth, she would have more of him. She wanted to press into his heat, feel his hands upon her.

But already, his dapper form had receded into the distance.

"I wonder, Miss Lockhart," said Dr. Westbridge, "whether I might confide in you?"

"Hmm?" Verity dragged her gaze back to the doctor.

"I have thought much on this, and today, I am quite decided."

"Oh?" She tried her best to concentrate, but her fingers and lips pulsed with recent memory.

"You may remember I mentioned my work at the Royal Hospital for retired soldiers."

"Er, yes?" Verity was certain it was a noble task the doctor fulfilled. But she did not want to think of other soldiers now, retired or otherwise. Mr. Cole was going off to war. He might never have a chance to kiss her again. Never let the wetness of his tongue torment her with a craving for more. If this was to be their first and last…

A terrible realization hit Verity like a brick to the belly. Was *that* why he had kissed her? Because he was leaving to risk his life? Was she someone he'd needed in that moment when emotions had been running high? If so, she could have been *anyone* and he would still have kissed her. It would explain why he'd withdrawn from her so abruptly. If he should come back to England, hale and hearty, he would probably look upon that moment with acute embarrassment.

Her thoughts ran on with her. Mr. Cole's time in Brussels would not be all grime and bloodshed. There would be other mouths to touch with his. Pretty, young things who wanted an adventure with a mysterious foreigner. Would he accommodate them, slake his own thirst with them? After all, he owed her nothing. They were not engaged.

"There will be many more like them when this war is done."

"What?" Verity jerked back to reality.

"Soldiers who can no longer serve."

"Oh." The kiss had probably been meaningless. If Mr. Cole had felt so strongly for her, he would have asked for her hand.

The last of the pleasure his touch had brought now dissipated.

"But when the battles rage," Dr. Westbridge continued, oblivious of the rise and fall of Verity's emotions, "and the surgeons have their hands full, who is caring for those with cholera, infections, amputations that are slow to heal?"

Verity shivered. It was all too easy to imagine a hall full of such men.

"And so," Dr. Westbridge said solemnly, "I have decided to join our good men in Brussels. I wish to serve the king with the skills I have and save as many of his fine soldiers as time and medicine will allow."

"You are leaving too?" Verity murmured. Arthur Westbridge swam back into focus for her. He was abandoning her! Just like Mr. Cole. Nobody wanted her. She was not enough.

"I think I need to sit down," said Verity.

At once, the doctor reached out his hand to offer support as she half-stumbled into the carriage. The dark-leather interior matched her mood. She would have preferred to have been left alone within it. That was what they were doing, anyway, wasn't it? Deserting her, one by one.

"Are you more comfortable now?" asked Dr. Westbridge, hovering at the door.

Verity nodded. Anything not to talk. For her voice would tremble if she tried.

"I'm grateful to hear it. I confess a measure of satisfaction that my departure should affect you so. Naturally, as a physician, I wish no harm to anyone. But a gentleman appreciates when a woman feels faint at the thought of losing him." He swallowed visibly. "The thing is, Miss Lockhart, I should not be speaking so plainly to you. Not yet, anyway. I am a man who likes to take his time in matters of the heart. But this development on the Continent has forced my hand. I must now say in haste what I would have expressed more gradually if there were time. You must know how much I admire you. Even more so, I can see a future with you."

Verity was so startled by the doctor's change in manner toward her that she did not hear the approaching footfalls. She was therefore doubly stunned when the face of William Cole reappeared over the shoulder of Dr. Westbridge just as the latter declared, "And so, my dear Miss Lockhart, I pledge myself to you. And ask you for your hand in marriage."

Verity saw Mr. Cole's face fall as if he had been struck. He stopped dead a few feet from them. Dr. Westbridge must have mistaken the meaning of her wide eyes, for he put a foot upon the carriage step to lean closer to her.

"I understand this is very sudden. I assure you it is not a sign of disrespect that I appear to act so impulsively. I have liked you from our first meeting. Yes, for our shared love of entomology. But also for your strength of character. I would add your beauty to your many fine qualities, but I would not have you think my feelings are so superficial."

Verity watched as Mr. Cole took two steps back.

"I would marry you this moment, but there are banns to be called."

Mr. Cole turned on the ball of his foot like a soldier on parade and marched off so quickly that Verity almost had to pinch herself to believe he had ever been there. Why had he returned at all? It would remain a riddle if she did not call after him.

Should she call? Surely, if it had been important, Mr. Cole would have stayed. Meanwhile, poor Dr. Westbridge was trying his best to propose marriage. It would be very rude to interrupt his efforts.

"And if we call the banns, it will be weeks before I can depart for Brussels."

Mr. Cole had gone. Arthur Westbridge remained. For all his understated manner, it was Arthur Westbridge who was declaring himself. William Cole was charming and witty, his kiss passionate, his friendship precious. But he had not considered her a worthy prize to speak up for.

"I was hoping, if you would honor me and say *yes*, we might at least be engaged. We could write each other without fear of indiscretion. And when I returned, we could be married without further delay. I wish I could offer you more. But my duty calls me to tend to service before self. You are, of course, very much more than duty, dear Miss Lockhart. Yet I must ask for your patience."

His words permeated Verity's heart at last. He truly cared for her. Not with fanfare or displays of affection, but quietly and sincerely. Wasn't that all she really wanted? What need had she of a sensual mouth and lively eyes, or the way a uniform hugged the figure of a man, if that man kept walking away?

Dr. Westbridge continued gently. "I do not mean to press you, but I intend to leave with the regiment tomorrow, if they will allow it. I must have your answer, Miss Lockhart. Would you consider me a tolerable husband? I will accept your answer, whatever it may be, though my hopes are that you will not break my simple heart."

"Yes."

Verity said the word so suddenly, she surprised even herself. But why should she not say it? His was a perfectly good offer. It was real and kind and heartfelt. He would never hurt her, never confuse her with actions he would later be ashamed of. He would not flirt or play games. And she would be able to study and sketch, even be encouraged to do so.

"Yes?" said Dr. Westbridge, his mouth expanding into a broad smile.

"Yes," repeated Verity. "I will marry you. Though I am sorry I must see you off to war. I will worry terribly."

Westbridge took her by the hand. "Do not fear. I will be serving in a hospital, and nowhere near the battlefront. I will be quite safe."

"That is good," she answered, gazing down at the hand that enveloped hers. "Then it is settled."

As if the good news should be shared at once, the Sinclairs now approached the carriage with their baskets and blankets and children. Hope was the first to read the situation and draw the happy conclusion. She saw the doctor's beaming smile, his hand wrapping Verity's, and cried, "You certainly took your time, Dr. Westbridge! We had all but given up on you. Come see, Daniel, you are to have a new brother-in-law!"

Verity blushed. It felt good to have something to celebrate. No more confused feelings. No more wondering if she would ever find a good match. She would not have to fear for *his* life in battle. Her new husband might even have greater passion in the bedroom than he expressed when he was speaking. After all, Daniel was not a flashy fellow, yet her sister seemed very happy.

After congratulatory handshakes and kisses on the cheek, Dr. Westbridge reluctantly bid them adieu. He needed to talk to Captain Larson at once. If his plans were acceptable, there was still much to be organized, letters to be written to the families he tended to. Fortunately, Munro was a big city, and there were sufficient physicians who could take up his medical duties while he was away.

Hope tried to lift the spirits of the newly betrothed couple whose parting was imminent. "We shall take good care of your bride-to-be, Dr. Westbridge. By the time you return, she will be ready to take on the responsibilities of an excellent wife and be aching to do so. No doubt, she will write you every day. And you must do so, too, sir, even if it is but a page and the letters arrive all in a batch after the inevitable delays of wartime post."

"I shall do my very best," agreed the doctor. He cast his eyes warmly upon Verity. "I wonder, would it be possible for Miss Lockhart to come and see me off tomorrow? I would let you know my plans as soon as they are confirmed."

"I should like that very much," Verity said, as much to her sister as her betrothed. "Everything is so rushed in this moment. I would be grateful for another hour with my very own gentleman."

"Arthur," said the doctor. "I would have you call me by my name. Then I may carry the memory of the sound with me abroad."

"Arthur." Verity tested the name upon her tongue. It felt unfamiliar, but not unpleasant. "Will you call me 'Verity'?" she replied shyly.

"I would be happy to, my dearest Verity." Their eyes met briefly before Arthur added, "Now I must make haste. I look forward to seeing you again tomorrow." He released her hand with a perfunctory kiss before turning to Daniel. "Thank you for watching over Miss Lockhart for me. I am most grateful."

"It will be my pleasure," Hope's husband replied. "We wish you well with all that must yet be accomplished in a short space of time."

And then Arthur was off, hastening along the same path Mr. Cole had abandoned her on.

It was a strange feeling, being suddenly engaged. Strange, yet bringing a wonderful sense of purpose. No more time wasted fretting about finding a suitor. She could assemble her *trousseau* in readiness for their life together.

Already, she envisioned herself taking notes of the little flying, hopping, buzzing things in the Sinclairs' garden so that she might report it all to Arthur. Such news would help him think of home. It would be her first act of devotion to the man she would marry.

But was he the man she loved?

Verity glared inwardly at the version of herself that had spoken up. *Be quiet!* she told it. *You are not wanted here. I can be happy. You will not spoil it.*

And yet the little voice niggled at her while the driver steered the carriage home, throughout the excited chatter of her sister, and long after Verity had gone to bed. It whispered of two kisses on her hand, one that roused her to longing and a sense of loss, and one that merely reminded her she was spoken for.

She had said *yes*. And that should be the end of it. And yet, when sleep finally claimed Verity's thoughts, they had still been lingering on the back of Lieutenant William Cole as he had walked out of her life.

CHAPTER TWENTY-ONE

Verity woke up in a cold sweat. Her sleep had been disturbed by the turbulence of numerous nightmares. Shipwreck. War. A wedding with two grooms. A bride stranded with a driverless carriage. A stranger walking away, surrounded by butterflies that fell, motionless, at his feet.

It took some time for the disarray of images and their accompanying distress to subside into some sort of calm. Yet some unease remained. Both a dear friend and her betrothed were to leave for foreign soil this day, their voyage risky, their destiny uncertain. But what made the jumbled emotions more confused was the difficulty in concluding whose absence she would miss most.

She allowed herself a little grace. Arthur's proposal had been sudden and wholly unexpected. Until that moment, her hopes and expectations had been focused on Mr. Cole. It was challenging to reel them in without warning. If Arthur had given some indication beyond mere civility, she might have been better prepared. She would quite possibly have given Mr. Cole no consideration at all. But her betrothed had offered no preamble, nothing exceptional in his attitude toward her to suggest that he was interested in a life with her.

And that was where her thoughts took her on a treacherous detour. What if the same could be said of Mr. Cole? What if, behind his lighthearted veneer and his talk of friendship, he felt a tenderness for her? Could his kiss have meant more? Had he realized it had been his last chance to show his true longing for her? And why had he come back, only to leave again without saying anything? Had it been Arthur's proposal that had shifted his decision?

It had all happened so quickly, and Verity thought she had reasoned it all through adequately. This morning, however, she had more questions than answers.

There was no way to resolve any of it. She could hardly take herself over to the Trentons' home and demand that Mr. Cole declare himself. That was, if he had anything to declare. Nor could she bring herself to call off the engagement on the basis of Mr. Cole's unconfirmed affection. What she really needed was time to think.

She should not have said *yes* so readily. But it had all made perfect sense the day before. To ask Arthur to delay the engagement until his return would be a terrible blow to a man going off to war, even if he only ever saw the aftereffects of battle.

And so it was *without* the uncontained excitement of a newly engaged woman that Verity dressed, had breakfast, and made her way to the docks situated upon the banks of the wide estuary that ran the length of Munro.

Daniel had insisted on accompanying Verity and Hope, saying it was no place for women to visit alone. It was a decision both pragmatic and thoughtful, but Verity did not crave the company. At least it gave Hope someone to talk to when, after a few worried glances at her sister, she gave up trying to draw Verity into the conversation.

The port was busy in a way that appeared haphazard and chaotic, yet boats were systematically being loaded and the number of red coats upon the decks was steadily increasing. Arthur Westbridge—who had no need of uniform and was largely free to wander as he pleased—stood patiently waiting beside the gangplank of the transport to which he had been assigned. As soon as he spied Verity approaching from the carriage, he hastened toward her, his face wreathed in smiles.

"Miss Lockhart." He stopped awkwardly once they were face-to-face, clearly unsure what the appropriate next move should be.

"Dr. Westbridge," Verity replied softly, noting that they had slipped back into old formalities. To set a new tone, she reached across on her toes and planted a gentle kiss on his cheek, balancing herself with her hand upon his arm.

The smile returned.

"I confess I am relieved to receive your affection, Miss Lockhart," he said, running his fingers through his hair.

"Verity," she corrected him.

"Ah, yes, of course. Your name is a privilege I have not yet grown used to."

"We have all the time in the world to become so," Verity replied. "But I am curious. Did you not think I would want to express my fondness for you?" she added, carefully avoiding the word "love."

"My proposal was so sudden," he explained, "I could not imagine you having fully taken it all in. Someone as young as yourself might need time to adjust to the idea. Even I, being close to thirty years of age, am not fully prepared for such a solemn shift in status."

"It may be that our time apart is a hidden blessing," said Verity, "giving us the opportunity to grasp the magnitude of it all." If only Mr. Cole would stay out of her thoughts!

"Perhaps you would like to follow me aboard," Arthur offered the trio. "I could show you where I will be spending the next few days—or the next week, as the weather will have it."

Daniel was quick to intercede. "Have your lady take your arm, sir. There are a great many soldiers and sailors about, with no guarantee that they will show a woman the respect she deserves. We shall have to shield Verity and my wife from rough comments and other bawdy behavior."

"Too right, Mr. Sinclair," Arthur acknowledged. I had not

thought of that. Your experience as a husband is an example to me. I have much to learn. But I am willing, for Miss Lockhart shall have all that is due her."

"Verity," she repeated.

Verity suppressed a sigh, reminding herself that she had chosen this: safety over sentiment, steadiness over passion. She had no right to complain when Arthur continued to behave as he had done throughout their acquaintance.

And yet, she found his commitment to her unsatisfying. All was done as if he checked off a list. He did not express any fervor, only constancy. It *should* have been enough. It could be, if she would let it. But she ached for more. The thought that Mr. Cole might have given her all she now missed gnawed at her.

Even in this moment, when she took the arm of the man who would be her husband, nothing tingled or sang within her heart, her limbs, her womanhood. It was a sturdy arm. It would be there for her whenever she needed it. But she wanted to feel an undercurrent. To know that the owner of that arm wished they were alone, that he might wrap it around her, lifting his other hand to trace her curves, make her shiver with anticipation.

These thoughts fell away as they reached the deck. There were too many watchful eyes. Too many men who might want these very things of her.

She cast her own eyes down, looking only where Arthur pointed, until they reached the opposite side of the boat, the river lapping roughly at the timber frame. The water was deep and dark and murky, reflecting the clouds that gathered ominously above.

An officer approached with a businesslike air. "All non-passengers are to go ashore at once."

Dr. Westbridge made a small protest. "I did ask the captain's permission to bring my betrothed on board. She will leave when we sail."

"Then she must leave now," replied the soldier. "The tide is favorable and there is a storm coming. We are to set out to sea and escape the worst of it."

Arthur turned rather helplessly to Verity. "It seems we are to part sooner than hoped. I am sorry for it." He looked about him for something useful to say. "Let me at least walk you back to your carriage."

They proceeded back down the roughly crafted gangplank. They steered through the mess of hurrying bodies, stacked crates, restless horses, and officers shouting orders as the eight boats transporting the regiment were readied for imminent departure.

Somewhere from within the hubbub, a rushing form bumped into Verity, narrowly prevented from knocking her off her feet by the sturdy arm of Dr. Westbridge.

"I say," Arthur cried, "watch where you're going!" The stranger untangled himself from sword and capsized shako hat, straightening to reveal none other than... "Mr. Cole! Great heavens! What a coincidence!"

But Mr. Cole did not marvel at the coincidence. In fact, he did not seem pleased to see any of them at all. He made no eye contact with Verity, only bowing his head to Arthur and saying, "I believe congratulations are in order, Doctor."

"Ah, yes, indeed. Thank you." Arthur smiled and patted Verity's arm, which lay in the crook of his. "For a time there, I thought it might be *I* who congratulated *you*, especially as I am more the tortoise to your hare in matters of the heart. But I do not begrudge you your friendship with Miss Lockhart. I am not a jealous man."

If Dr. Westbridge thought his words reassuring, he was mistaken. Mr. Cole flushed a deep pink. His eyes remained on Dr. Westbridge by dint of great effort, for they flicked so often toward Verity that it was quite giddying to watch.

"I was never under the impression that Miss Lockhart wished for anything more than friendship from me," Mr. Cole said with a hint of bitterness. "So, your path to her was always clear." He added, with a tone that was more civil than sincere, "I wish you both every happiness. Now you must excuse me. Our fleet is leaving within the hour and there is still much to do."

"We wish you both safe travels," Hope said warmly. "We would have all our menfolk return to England soon, and in good health."

"'Both'?" said Mr. Cole, his brow furrowed.

"Dr. Westbridge has volunteered his services in Brussels," Hope explained. "Though it does not appear you are on the same boat, which is a pity. It is always easier to travel with someone you know."

"I have treated many families and even more soldiers," replied the doctor. "No doubt there will be a familiar face somewhere on board."

Verity did not care if Arthur knew absolutely everyone on the boat to which he was assigned. Her thoughts were slamming into each other at great speed, and the conclusion was nothing less than earth-shattering. She had wondered at Mr. Cole's sudden coldness toward her, heard him say he felt his suit would have been wasted, and realized, with a tearing howl of her heart, that he had wanted her as much as she did him.

His kiss had been real. His friendship had meant everything, for it was all he had allowed himself. And there it was all the feeling she had been missing, tumbling out toward him. She wanted to shake off Arthur's arm and launch herself toward Mr. Cole, clinging to him and feeling her world shift beneath them as they held each other, united in love, forever and ever and ever.

"Cole!" shouted a voice drenched in authority. "Get yourself here on the double!"

William Cole finally lifted his sight to Verity. The flush in his cheeks remained. His brows were lowered, his eyes red-rimmed as if withholding tears. "Goodbye, Miss Lockhart," he said. It sounded so formal, like something Arthur would have said. But Verity could see his heart breaking. She saw it so clearly now. Why had she not done so before? Just one day earlier, that was the wisdom she would have needed. And she would have chosen differently.

How could she tell him she understood at last? That she felt the same, though it could mean nothing now. Such words could never be spoken aloud. Instead, she said, "As I have mentioned before, Mr. Cole, I do not like the word 'goodbye.' There is nothing 'good' about being parted from those we value deeply."

Love! That was the word she wanted to shout! But she could never do so now. Her arm was still entwined with Arthur's, as were the remainder of her days.

"And to you, also, Arthur, I shall not speak that terrible word, for it was meant for separation, and I am unwilling to dwell on what must happen now."

What must happen was to lose, forever, her love. To live a half-life with a man who might tend to all her needs except those of her heart.

No, there was nothing good about it at all.

And then Arthur kissed her.

He chose the corner of her mouth, where cheek and lip met. No doubt it was a thoughtful deed, not to rush her with intimacy. But a man leaving for war should have been consumed with a sense of loss, with no room remaining for such courtesies. Let him shock her with the depth of his anguish, rather than belabor her with his insistence on correctness. She wanted a kiss like Mr. Cole's. One that left her weak and craving more. A testament to his inability to stay away.

But Mr. Cole *had* stayed away. When he should most have been himself, pushing Arthur from the carriage doorway and declaring himself, he had been most like the doctor—restrained, correct, ineffectual.

Oh, these men!

And now these very two departed from her, each to their own ship. Hope stood tightly at Verity's side, offering the comfort of her presence. Verity was grateful for it, though she imagined her sister would be shocked to know what form her sorrow took. For she mourned not for her betrothed, but for the man who was lost to her forever.

They stood thus, watching the dock empty of its people and cargo. They felt the air thicken with damp. Verity would have stood there until the last sight of the ships had faded beyond the bend in the estuary, the wind teasing her hair, the growing darkness brought by the brewing clouds hiding the tears that now dripped down from her nose and chin. But it began to rain. At first, small warning drops. Then the wind whipped up and the drops fell more quickly. Large, plashing things that blurred her view and threatened to soak her clothes.

Daniel bundled the ladies into the carriage and bid the driver head for home. The roof drummed with the onslaught of rain. Somewhere in the storm, Arthur would have made for his tiny private cabin, perhaps to read some academic works. And Mr. Cole... He would have to swallow his pain. He had duties to perform, men to manage. It was only Verity, safe in the guise of grieving bride-to-be, who could cry freely. Until the pain was numbed and the tears dried up. Yes, she mourned the loss of the man she loved. And when those tears were spent, she would have to learn to live with the choice she had made.

CHAPTER TWENTY-TWO

The Duchess of Richmond's ball, Brussels, the early hours of June 16, 1815

IT WAS STRANGE, William thought to himself, how much he had cared about his uniform before. It had mattered so much once upon a time. Here, surrounded by a myriad of lovely ladies for whom he could strut and preen, he would usually have been in his element.

Less than a hundred miles away, the war awaited them. By daybreak, they would be marching into the face of it. But tonight, they danced and feasted. William, Prince of Orange, and their general, the Duke of Wellington, were the honored guests amongst a multitude of dukes, counts, high-ranking military officers, diplomats, a few lucky additions like himself, and—perhaps to offer a blessing on the occasion—one reverend.

The ladies were dressed in unfamiliar fashion, their clothes and hair following the French influence. Their manners, too, were more formal, but that may have had something to do with the caliber of persons attending.

Six months ago, when William had first obtained his commission, it would have mattered that he compared favorably with the other gentlemen. In appearance, that was. His looks and charm were undeniable. The converted carriage-house, now papered with a trellis-rose pattern, was filled to bursting with young women all too eager to forget the horrors that lay less than a day's march from their door. And he would have been more than willing to help them do just that.

But tonight, as with every other night since he'd left England three weeks ago, the food tasted like ash in his mouth. The ladies—despite making every effort to draw his attention—were all but invisible to his moody gaze. William cradled the brandy in his hand. He did not actually drink it but stared morosely into its depths. Eventually, all attempts to engage him ceased. He sat alone, in his shiny uniform, without the one person whose company he sought.

Their farewell haunted him still. Seeing Miss Lockhart upon the arm of Dr. Westbridge had ripped any hope from him that she had rejected the man's proposal. And yet she did not seem happy. Was it simply that her betrothed had been leaving for Brussels? Did she regret not being able to marry him sooner, having to wait for his return? And what sort of man kissed a woman like Miss Lockhart on the edge of her mouth when he was to be parted from her? How did Westbridge restrain himself from claiming all that he could? The man had left her with nothing to long for, save the church bells upon his return.

William had revisited their own kiss over and over again in his mind. She *had* wanted it. He had questioned this from every angle, driven himself to madness to establish the truth of her part in it. He was finally convinced Miss Lockhart had only withdrawn because *he* had done so first. If that accursed doctor had not arrived, she might even have told him so.

Miss Lockhart had called William the best of men, worried for his safety, wordlessly desired his return. And she had met his passion with her own. He had misread her desperate clinging as a sign that she had been overwhelmed, that he had gone too far, but now he feared he had not gone far enough. He should have stayed. Should have sent the doctor on his way. If he had declared his feelings there and then…

But his reasoning had been off-kilter. He had almost lost her friendship an hour earlier at the picnic. He had not wanted to risk it again by claiming too much too soon. Only... now she would never be his.

Worse still, would she truly be happy with Westbridge? Had she accepted the doctor's offer because William had not made one of his own? Was William to blame for her settling in this way?

William may well have spent the rest of the night in this manner, berating himself, scolding the fates, and generally wasting a perfectly good party, had it not been for the arrival of Wellington's aide-de-camp. He delivered a note, the contents of which were soon known to all, even though the general had only spoken them quietly to the prince.

The French army had crossed the River Sambre and were marching toward Quatre Bras, not fifty miles from where the general sat now.

The news was not so much announced as whispered from ear to ear around the dining room, and with it grew the disturbance of many minds and hearts, some of which belonged to those who must fight, while others were those of relatives, friends, and lovers who must watch them go.

The general alone remained undisturbed. He turned to his host and asked in a cool manner, "Do you have a map?"

"Indeed, I do. If you will join me in my study, I shall have it fetched down from the shelf."

Wellington did not stand immediately, but finished his plate of food at an unhurried pace. Several officers who had men camped near Quatre Bras left in far more haste, still dressed in their evening attire, calling for their horses to be readied at once. William could picture their polished boots splashed with mud as they rode furiously to organize their troops. How many of them would return? Too many had danced their last this night.

William remained unmoving in his seat. He had no orders. He had no purpose. No one to whom to say goodbye—not that she would use that word. He sat, staring into the amber liquid at the bottom of his glass.

Twenty minutes later, Wellington placed his cutlery down upon his place, stood, bowed to his hostess, and bid everyone a good night. His host rose also, leading him from the dining room to the study. Across the antechamber that led to the converted carriage house, the sound of music and laughter continued. Evidently, not all young souls understood the gravity of events. It was hard to countenance their frivolity, knowing how many other guests might be brought to dust in the days ahead.

Within half an hour, the general had left the house altogether. In his stead were orders for the officers who remained. Larson was not there, but their commanding officer was. He beckoned to William.

"Time to go, Lieutenant. There is men's work to be done."

William took a last look at his brandy. It would be sorry to waste it. And a little bit of liquid courage wouldn't go amiss. He swirled the sweet liquor about—a last moment of tranquility—before throwing his head back and swallowing the contents in one go. The heat of it was soothing, filling the darkness of his thoughts with its amber light.

He did not remember the ride back to his quarters, nor the scuffling in the dimly lit room to change into his field attire. He vaguely recalled wishing that there were fewer buttons and that he had brought his valet with him. At some point, he must have checked his musket, bayonet, and pistol by the light of the single lamp, for this was his habit whenever joining with the ranks.

What he remembered clearly, though, was the last sunrise as the lines began to march toward Waterloo. His horse was restless, possibly sensing the dread in the hearts of the men about him. But the sunrise bloomed into day, as if great promise lay ahead. And there, flitting haphazardly until it came to rest on his glove, its distinctive color and pattern instantly recognizable, was a large blue.

William scarcely dared breathe. The butterfly pulsed its wings. It appeared in no hurry to leave, perched on his hand, holding on to it with its own tiny claws.

William drew comfort from it, as if Miss Lockhart herself were there with him. As if it were *she* who held on to his hand.

Then his horse shook its mane, and the butterfly was disturbed. It lifted gently into the air, hovered as though contemplating where to go, circled his hat, and disappeared over a scented field of wild rosemary.

William exhaled. For a moment, he thought he had dreamed it. But his heart no longer pounded with angst. His thoughts were quiet—peaceful, even. Slowly, as if the little creature were still perched upon it, he lifted his hand to his chest. The warmth of it spread as it had when Miss Lockhart had clung to him, willing him to stay.

It made him want to pledge himself to her fully. *He* was the right man for her. Not Westbridge. If this war did not kill him, he should insist she break with the doctor. He did not care if there was a scandal. They belonged together. The butterfly was a sign, and he…

William's racing thoughts ground to a halt. This was exactly how he had behaved with Lady Howell. He would not tread this path again.

The lovely large blue was a sign, yes—that he had learned a great many things from Miss Lockhart. The most important of which was to be a better man. If she had chosen, he must respect her choice. If they were to be only friends, he would be the best of them. This was the man she wished him to be. Someone who did right for its own sake, even when there was no reward.

The momentary madness behind him, his equilibrium restored, William focused once more on the dusty road before him, while the face of Miss Lockhart—with her honest eyes and forgiving mouth—lingered with him like the presence of a guardian angel.

And the sound of cannon fire grew louder in the distance.

CHAPTER TWENTY-THREE

Waterloo, June 18, 1815

THE BRITISH INFANTRY had stood their ground since the morning hours, grateful for the sunny day that had followed the sleepless night of heavy rain. The muddy fields of Waterloo slowed the advance of Napoleon's heavy artillery so that the battle only began in earnest shortly before noon. William had lost count of the number of times the French had fired their more than two hundred cannons since then. The whistling sounds and smoke-filled air had lasted for hours, felling thousands of men within range of the shattering cannonballs and flying shrapnel.

But Wellington held his infantry in reserve behind the ridge. They were his most reliable soldiers, disciplined and steady in the face of death. They waited as the day grew warm—hungry, thirsty, tired—before they had even fired a single shot.

Beside William, Lieutenant Richard Foyle's seat on his saddle grew ever less secure. The man had been drinking steadily all night. Even now, he sipped from his hip flask to prevent sobriety from clearing his mind. William would have had pity for the man, for they were all afraid, but the officers were expected to set an example. An enlisted man found drunk on the field was a menace to his comrades and would likely be shot before he even met the enemy. Yet here was Foyle, listing to the left and in grave danger of unseating himself.

"Foyle," William hissed, "Sit up. The men will think you've

been shot."

Richard Foyle lifted his head and looked about him, as if seeing the battlefield for the first time. As more and more detail registered, he reached for his flask.

"Put that away," commanded William more sternly. "Another swig and you'll be on the ground, ready to be trampled. Can you even hold your sword up?"

"Lea' me 'lone," grumbled Foyle, emptying the last of his flask's contents down his throat. He cast an unfocused eye into the neck of the container, shook it, found no joy in his discovery, and thrust it back into his boot leg, where he had kept it hidden. His eyes closed again and William could make out the unmistakable sound of snoring emanating from the man.

It took a few minutes for William to realize that the artillery had stopped. His ears still rang with the echoes of the continuous firing, making it difficult to know whether the sounds were real or imagined. He listened carefully, trying to confirm whether the cannons had merely paused or stopped altogether, when a thundering sound beat through the air and the earth trembled with the hooves of thousands of approaching cavalry horses.

"Hold!" came the order. "Hold!

The screams of French soldiers and their innocent steeds now added to the chaos as Wellington unleashed loose shot into the mass of attacking bodies. The thrumming of hoofbeats continued to bring fresh fodder for the allied artillery, as wave upon wave of Napoleon's cavalry tried to break through the enemy lines.

At last, the British cavalrymen were unleashed, their sabers extended, their mounts holding steady before being urged into a gallop. Barely audible over the shouts and cannon fire came the clashing of swords, though these sounds were brief, the metal blades cutting into flesh before they could be deflected again.

William tried not to imagine the carnage in the field beyond the ridge. The horror of it would reach them soon enough.

It was shortly after six that evening when it did. By now, the infantry was almost desperate to be involved. They had stood for hours, hearing their brethren die by the hundreds, then thousands, choking on the thick smoke that hung over the field of Waterloo. They were tired and scared and helpless. The thought of battle seemed almost a relief. A chance to shake these feelings from them.

As the French finally topped the rise, their faces filled with sweat and mud and blood, the infantry finally heard the words they had waited an entire day for.

"Chaaaaaaaaarge!"

Tens of thousands of soldiers heard the call, braced their muskets, and prepared for the onslaught. The French cavalry plunged through their ranks, heartened by their success and renewing their attack, cutting down the ground troops like stalks of wheat.

A horse whinnied right beside William. He turned to see Foyle's mare rear up, her rider slipping from the saddle toward the ground and hitting his head on an iron ball that had run its course. Bearing down on the fallen figure came a Frenchman who neither saw Foyle nor would have cared if he did.

William kicked his heel into the side of his horse, bringing him broadside before firing his pistol at the rider. The bullet grazed the man's cheek, and still he came at William, his saber raised.

William drew his own sword, ready to block as much as he could of the furious blow that must come at such speed. The shock of the blades connecting reverberated up his arm, the lighter enemy saber raised and ready to strike again before William's heavier sword could match it. His sword was still lifting to defend when the French blade connected with it, sliding upward along the length of it, deflecting away from his shoulder toward his face. William turned his head, the last inch of the saber slipping past his nose across his eye.

He uttered a primal scream as extreme pain shot into his head. The orb of his eye filled with blood, then grew dark. William tried to concentrate, desperately turning his horse so that he might see the enemy with his remaining eye. The French soldier's blade was already in motion, ready to deliver a killing blow. William ducked forward beneath it, thrusting the pointed tip of his sword into the man's throat.

It was his first kill. It was why he was here, on this field, far from home. But he could not stop to think how it made him feel. The agony in his head was almost unbearable, half his face was covered in blood, and yet more riders approached.

He looked through a blur of pain at the figure of Foyle. If he left him there, he would surely die. Perhaps he was already dead. William had but a moment to think.

Every fiber of his being wanted to flee. Instead, he slipped down quickly from his horse. Grunting and struggling, he lifted the figure of Foyle, who groaned slightly as he did so.

"Stand, you useless bastard! Get on my horse!" William shouted through pain and blindness, managing to prop Foyle up against his horse's flank. Precious seconds went by as William manhandled the semi-conscious lieutenant over the back of the animal before grabbing his musket from the ground. He slapped the horse's hide and it set off gratefully away from the noise of the battle.

Once more, William turned to face the French.

"Fooooorm squares!" came the order.

Now on foot, William stumbled to join his regiment. He felt someone grab him around his back and under his arm, running with him toward the cover provided by five hundred men. He did not know who it was, the man being on his blind side, until the voice of Captain Larson said, "Stay with us, Cole. It's not over yet."

The first volley went over their heads. When the second rank took aim, William knelt with the first, trying to ready his weapon. It was nigh impossible. His surviving eye was dimmed with grit. He could not see to aim. He felt his way through the steps necessary to load, touched the arm of the men on either side of him with his elbows to orient himself, and fired when the order came. Round after round he sent toward the enemy before him, not knowing if he made a difference at all. The smoke burned his nostrils, and still, he loaded, sought direction, and fired. He only managed every second round, but he kept at it for what seemed like an eternity.

Until the next order did not come.

"They're retreating!" shouted the soldier next to him.

A new noise exploded. The sound of two thousand riflemen celebrating with shouts and laughter. William felt himself being roughly embraced by many hands.

As if his body had been kept upright by force of will alone, William now sank to the ground.

"Bring a horse!" Larson commanded. "Even a French one will do."

William sensed himself being lifted. He gripped the saddle as soon as his fingers recognized it. Then the bulk of another body climbed up in front of him.

"Can you steer with that shoulder, soldier?" Larson asked. "We don't want the animal taking you behind enemy lines."

"I'll manage, sir," said the nameless man on the horse with William.

"Get going, then. Have them send wagons for the more gravely injured men. Tell them it is safe to do so now."

"Yes, sir. God save the king, sir!"

There was a pause. Then the captain replied solemnly, "God save us all."

For William, the world went black.

CHAPTER TWENTY-FOUR

Munro, June 25, 1815

I T WAS WITH great excitement that the ladies of the Sinclair household awoke that morning. Daniel, having partaken of his breakfast with his newspaper in hand, as was his habit, had scarcely read the headline before throwing down the paper and taking the stairs two at a time to his wife's chamber. A shriek had preceded Hope's rapid departure from the room as she flew along the corridor and burst breathlessly into Verity's bedroom.

"It's done!" she cried. "The war is done! Napoleon, that soggy monster, has abdicated. Our men will be coming home!"

Verity, who had been reading with her back against her pillows and had quite jumped when her door flew open, received the news with equal joy.

"So soon? It's really over? He is safe, then?"

"I am certain the doctor has remained unharmed," said Hope, coming to sit on the edge of the bed. "We are sure to hear from him soon. He will likely stay on to help with the recovery of those who were injured. But he will be in no danger."

Verity nodded silently, unwilling to confess that her thoughts had not been for Dr. Westbridge. She now called him such in her letters to him, for he had never grown comfortable with calling her Verity, blaming the fact that he was an old-fashioned sort. As he had grown busier, his letters had grown fewer, and Verity had again followed his example.

More and more, she regretted their engagement. He was a good man, an excellent man, even. But life with him promised to be very dull. She had believed their shared interest in entomology would fuel enthusiastic conversations—and this might yet occur upon his return—but Verity no longer knew if this would be enough. While in Fernbridge, she had convinced herself that no one would ever support her unusual studies, and her potential husband's acceptance of them had been of the highest concern to her. In recent months, however, she had learned that it was possible to have more than mere acceptance. She had discovered that, when you are loved, *really* loved, that the gentleman in question would embrace you as you were, odd interests and all, even when he did not share them with equal zeal. Moreover— and this made all the difference—he would also make you feel like the most important person in the world.

Dr. Westbridge was the sort of man who made everyone feel important, and, bless him, this was a noble approach. But Verity wanted to be queen of her husband's heart. The way Mr. Cole made her feel.

Verity turned to her sister. "Do you think Charlotte Trenton has heard the news? Maybe she has even had a letter?"

"All of England will know the news by day's end," said Hope. "As for a letter, Mr. Cole is a conscientious writer. If the mail has come in, she will have heard from him."

"Unless…" Verity shivered.

Hope patted her sister's hand. "Then someone else would have notified the family."

"Do you think, perhaps," Verity asked, trying not to show her sense of urgency, "we might call on Mrs. Trenton and see if she has news?"

Hope cocked her head and gave her sister a thoughtful look. "No doubt she will appreciate you looking in on her. She has certainly been very welcoming of your weekly visits."

"Yes," Verity said, "I have enjoyed them too. She is a very kind soul. I have valued her willingness to share Mr. Cole's correspondence with us."

"Indeed." Hope's eyes locked with Verity's. "One could almost say his letters are written with you in mind. I doubt Charlotte finds his clumsy sketches of various caterpillars as enthralling as you do."

"He is a good friend," Verity countered.

"It seems to me," Hope pondered aloud, her voice tinged with reproach, "you wish it had been Mr. Cole who had proposed instead of Dr. Westbridge."

Verity closed her book and put it down next to her on the bed. She could trust her sister, and there was something that needed to be said, for it ate away at her conscience.

"Hope," she began, "there is something you should know. When Dr. Westbridge returns, I am going to break the engagement."

Hope's mouth dropped open. "You don't mean that! What will people say?"

Verity tightened her lips. "I reckon people will be far too busy celebrating the end of the war or mourning lost loved ones to care whether some vicar's daughter has changed her mind about marrying someone."

"What about the doctor?" Hope was aghast. "It will be a terrible embarrassment for him. Everyone knows him."

"And will therefore commiserate with him," countered Verity. She gave a rueful laugh. "Oddly enough, I think Dr. Westbridge will be the most understanding of all. He is such an even-keeled fellow, so reasonable and fair. He knows our betrothal was rushed. No banns have been called. It is only our respective families who even know we are engaged. Still, if the whole of Munro wants to judge me, so be it. I would rather bear the shame of a failed engagement than a lifetime of discontent."

Hope shook her head. "What has gotten into you? Is this because of Mr. Cole? Do you think he will declare himself if you are free once more? Even if he has survived the war, you cannot know how it has changed him. He may very well be ruined by the experience of battle. You are unwise to count on him."

But Verity was not persuaded from her course. "I do not depend on his affection, though I would be lying if I said I did not want it. However, this is not about leaving my betrothed for Mr. Cole. This is about being true to myself. My potential life with Dr. Westbridge does not offer me all I need. I might as well be alone for the feeling of connection he provides. I do not deny it would be a marriage most comfortable, but I want to be with someone who would *not* be civilized when I break the engagement. Someone who would fight for me, fear the loss of me. Can you understand that?"

Hope sighed deeply. "I do understand. But I am not equally assured that *you* grasp the consequences. A broken engagement can hang over your head for a long time. Too long a time. Past the bloom of your youth. It may be a very heavy price to pay for what you perceive as freedom. You may look back at what you see now as a mundane marriage and realize it could have been enough."

Verity shifted across the quilt to lean her head against her sister's shoulder. "You are very good to worry about me. You and Mama have always done your very best in this regard. I know I have been a mystery and a burden to you both. But I have never been more certain of what I want. In Fernbridge, all my actions were driven by fear, and Mama was right to send me here where I might meet broader minds and learn where I fit in. Now I can see clearly what is needed for me to be content. And marriage to Dr. Westbridge is not it. I do not wish for the life of a lonely spinster, nor do I wish to be unhappily married. I must have faith that, if I am comfortable in my own skin, this will attract the right sort of man for me. If I am wrong in this, at least I will have learned to love myself. Will that, at least, not please Mama?"

Hope wrapped her arms around her sister. "You goose," she scolded tenderly, "Mama has only wanted you to be safe and provided for. Dr. Westbridge would have done that very well indeed. But she has never asked you to sacrifice yourself. If your decision disappoints her, it will be because she frets that you will be left to fend for yourself. But Daniel will not let that happen."

Verity let the words sink in. Acceptance. She had craved it all her life. A feeling of belonging. And it had been there all along. In the heart of her parents, the kindness of her sister, the willing duty of her brother-in-law. Relief flooded her body so that she grew heavy with the delicious weight of it, until it siphoned out and left her with a sense of peace.

"Thank you," she said softly, returning her sister's embrace. "You are all so good to me."

"For better or worse, we are family," said Hope. She took a steadying breath. "And that is why I must ask one thing of you."

Verity sat up straight and looked at her sister, a pinch of nerves returning.

"Do not speak of your intentions to anyone else," said Hope, "not until Dr. Westbridge has returned. I know you believe it impossible, but you might yet change your mind. And he deserves to hear it from your lips. He may surprise you. Perhaps there is more to him than you have seen thus far. If, after speaking with him, you are determined to pursue this course of action, then so be it. But grant your betrothed that much."

"I am willing," Verity said immediately. "I shall continue to write to him in the manner in which we have done, which is civil and proper and not demanding in the least. And I shall welcome him home, for he may remain a good friend if he wishes it. I cannot believe he will have changed in a way that will affect my decision, but, as you say, he deserves that much."

"Good," Hope replied. She pushed on her knees to stand. "Now, I think breakfast is in order. I would like to hear the rest of the news Daniel has for us. And then, it seems, we shall have to take the carriage to Thorn Bush Hall and see if the Trentons are in."

Verity bounced up from the bed and hugged her sister once more. Then she grabbed her hands and danced a little jig all in a circle until Hope laughed and protested that it was time to get dressed.

"What shall I wear?" cried Verity. "It is a day for celebration. We must look our best. I know! I shall fetch my favorite hat and add a new ribbon, perhaps even some flowers from the garden. The war is over. Our men are coming home!" And she skipped across to her bell-ribbon to summon her lady's maid.

"Shoo, now!" She waved her hands at her sister, who had been standing still so as not to be knocked over by Verity's energetic motions. "We must clothe and feed ourselves and acquaint ourselves with the details of the news. And then we are off! The streets will be filled with revelers and it shall take forever to reach Thorn Bush Hall. Why are you still standing there?"

She began to push her protesting and laughing sister toward the doorway. As soon as Hope had left, Verity leaned with her back against the door. She sighed a happy, satisfied sigh. It was a beautiful day! And, more wonderful than any other thought, Mr. Cole could be coming home!

CHAPTER TWENTY-FIVE

Brussels, June 26, 1815

I T TOOK TWO full days to transport all the wounded from the field of Waterloo. The mayor of Brussels had declared the entire city a military hospital. When the existing hospital buildings overflowed, churches and residences filled with damaged soldiers. All local surgeons and physicians had been called in to assist. Those not actively engaged with amputations or other urgent care had been sent from house to house to tend to the lesser injuries. As the week dragged on, the number of men to care for grew less, and the number of graves filled the countryside, a testament to the price paid for victory.

Outside a farmhouse, less than a mile from the now-deserted battlefield, William sat on a chair in the courtyard. He had been unconscious when the surgeon had cleaned out the mess where the orbit of his eye had been, sewing the lid shut and sealing all with a bandage. He'd been lucky, he had been told when he'd awoken. There was very little risk of infection. He would survive.

It seemed a very small compensation for a life now bereft of all that had given it purpose. There was a good chance William would have no use for his commission, now that the war was at an end. And his ruined face would limit the chances of finding a woman to love. Not that any of this mattered anymore. Miss Lockhart was spoken for. Even if she wasn't, what could he now offer her? He had no prospects, no fine looks, and his heart was brittle with all he had witnessed.

As if to rub salt in his very fresh wound, of all the medical staff available in Brussels, Dr. Westbridge had come by to check on him. Dr. Westbridge, who was whole in body, well established in his career, and who would return to England to claim his bride. William supposed he should have been grateful to see a friendly face, but he was not ready to see that face in particular.

"You are healing well," said the doctor as he changed the dressing. "Those stitches should be able to come out in another week. Let's hope they see fit to transport you home and not to France, where some regiments are chasing after the enemy."

"There is nothing for me in England," William said morosely. "They might as well put me to use while I have any."

Dr. Westbridge frowned. "You don't mean that. You have family and friends who await your safe return. And you have been luckier than most. This," he said, indicating William's bandaged eye, "is nothing. You have another one like it that works just as well. You have your full quota of limbs. You have been spared your life. There are many who would wish to be in your place."

William turned his head away. He didn't care, even if it was true. The doctor had not seen what he had seen, experienced the horror, pain, and loss. He wanted to be left alone.

But the universe would not grant him this.

"There you are, Cole!" It was the last voice on the entire Earth that William wanted to hear, except, perhaps, that of a Frenchman. "I've been searching through this whole wretched city for you."

Lieutenant Richard Foyle—his head bandaged, his slight stagger suggesting he was already mildly intoxicated—pointed an accusing finger at William as if he had been purposefully hiding from the man.

"What do you want?" William snapped. He was in no mood for Foyle's nonsense.

"I want you to withdraw your report to Larson."

"What are you talking about?"

"In your written report on Waterloo… You said I was too drunk to fight. I want you to tell Larson you were mistaken."

"Why would I do that? I told the truth."

Foyle waved a hand about. "You think, with all that has happened, he needs to know the so-called truth about such an insignificant detail? Isn't it bad enough that I was injured?" His mouth pouted into a sulk. "Suffered a concussion, the doctor said. Could have been trampled to death."

"Would have served you right," William grumbled. "I should have left you there to get your just deserts."

"So you pulled me from battle that you may ruin my reputation?" Foyle snarled.

William laughed roughly. "What reputation? Everyone knows you're a drunk. But this time, your lack of sobriety could have cost men their lives. You should have been ready to fight, to defend our troops. Instead, you lay on the ground like a sack of flour with an injury you had brought upon yourself."

"Why, you little…" Foyle charged at Cole, but Westbridge interceded, stretching his arm across the space between the two agitated men.

"Still got fight in you?" Westbridge said, his voice shaking slightly. "You haven't seen enough death and destruction to last you two lifetimes? Back here," he said, indicating the farmhouse, "behind these walls, men lie in agony, undecided whether to pray for life or death. And you would attack a fellow officer who saved your life?"

"Stay out of it, doctor!" growled Foyle. "There are fates worse than death. My father is all but poised to cut my allowance if I disgrace him one more time."

"Reduced funds?" William scowled. "*That's* what you're worried about? Not the behavior that causes it? You have no honor, man. If your father had had any sense, he should have cut you off completely a long time ago."

"Shut up!" shouted Foyle, putting the heels of his palms to his ears. "I don't want to hear it! You sound just like him. Always telling me I'm worthless and shaming the family and how thankful he was that I was not the eldest, for he would never want me to be his heir." His voice pitched higher, his eyes roving wildly. "He almost cut me off after the picnic, thanks to you! Said it was my last chance." Foyle's eyes settled back onto William, changing abruptly from the edge of hysteria to a menacing glare. "*You!* Ever in my way. Always harping on about honor. Always bringing my father's attention to the details of my life. And now you would ruin me."

William rose from his simple wooden chair. He was still several inches shorter than Foyle, but the man backed away half a step at the suddenness with which William stood. "Anything that befalls you now is your own doing," he told Foyle. "Your very demand that I should lie to cover your indiscretion is further proof of your unworthiness. And I have a witness to attest to your continued dishonorable conduct." William gestured toward Dr. Westbridge, who stood ready to intervene if his patient were at risk of being injured again. "If I were you," William continued, "I would start thinking what you will say to your father to explain your actions. A little humility and a change of heart on your part might win him over."

Lieutenant Foyle blinked rapidly as if trying to understand what he had been told. He looked at the doctor, then back at William. And then, to William's utter astonishment, Foyle smiled. It was a very disconcerting sort of smile and did not belong among the features of a sane man.

"So it's that simple, then," said Foyle, drawing his sword with worrying calm. "Just two witnesses to remove. There will be no evidence of this conversation. And no one to cross-examine in a court martial. The report becomes worthless. I don't know why I bothered to ask for your help. This is so much cleaner. No more Lieutenant William Cole to be a thorn in my flesh."

William raised his palms to the madman before him. "Think what you are saying, Foyle. I have nothing to lose. My life is as pointless as yours. But leave Westbridge out of it."

"No," Foyle responded, looking at his blade that now swung free from its scabbard. "I don't think I will."

"Look," said William, rather more desperately now, "I'll withdraw the report. It's not worth a man's life. This is between you and me."

"You should have said that earlier," came Foyle's sinister answer, "before the doctor heard everything. What happens now is *your* doing, Cole."

Before William could say another word or think to act, Foyle pulled back his sword arm and thrust it forcefully away from him to the right where Dr. Westbridge stood. He did it without looking, without hesitation, without a tinge of conscience.

The sword scarcely made a sound. Westbridge, too, did little more than exhale a plosive "UH!" before the blood began to seep through his shirt.

Foyle slid the blade out smoothly, keeping his eyes on William, then lunged forward to repeat his fatal strike.

William grabbed the blade instinctively. It sliced through the flesh of his palm and fingers, mingling his blood with the doctor's. He twisted his body to the side, pulling the sword farther forward so that Richard Foyle was jerked off-balance and fell forward, his face planting into the mud at William's feet, his sword hilt bouncing once as it touched the ground.

"Murder!" shouted William. And then again, a sob rising in his chest as Westbridge sank to the same muddy courtyard floor as his killer, "Murder!"

Boots clattered as those well enough to run came from the stables and kitchen, stopping in their tracks as they beheld the scene. A young woman with greater presence of mind knelt by the doctor, looking for the wound under his shirt. Upon seeing the extent of the damage, she lifted his head to her lap to offer compassion in his dying moments. Two of the men grabbed Foyle and wrenched his arms behind his back, forcing the struggling, swearing wastrel to his knees while another fetched rope to bind him.

"You're bleeding, sir," said one of the kitchen maids. Come with me. We will wash and bind your hand."

But William barely heard her. He threw himself down next to the form of Westbridge, whose face had grown pale, his breath raspy. William grabbed his hand. There was nothing else he could do.

"This is my fault," William said through hot tears. "It should have been me. You have so much more to live for." He dropped his forehead against the almost lifeless hand of Westbridge. "Miss Lockhart will never forgive me," he said in whispered torment. William felt the mildest of pressure as the failing doctor tried to squeeze his hand.

"You are…" Westbridge struggled against death. "…a…good man." He closed his eyes, as if the energy of keeping them open robbed him of speech. "You must…marry…her." His head sagged as his last breath left him.

"No, no, no, *no!*" William cried with rising panic. "This is all wrong!" He looked about him, seeking help where none could be found. Instead, his gaze fell upon Foyle, still held between two men, though he no longer struggled against them.

William launched across the small space between them, his fist flying at Richard Foyle's jaw. "You bastard!" he almost screamed. "You selfish, murderous bastard!" And then he was raining blows upon the man's head and body, the sight of Foyle's bloodied nose and cheek not even registering in his rage. Several men had to pull William off him, but he kept shouting and flailing until eventually, they found it easier to remove Foyle from his sight and thus calm the distraught William a little.

He stood hunched, panting heavily, the entire scene burnt into his mind with more ferocity than the horrors of Waterloo. Someone placed a chair behind him and gently guided him to sit. Another figure brought a basin of water and began to tend to his wound. They moved about him like ghosts, for he was barely conscious of their presence.

Eventually, William's hand was bound with clean linen. But not by Westbridge. Never again would he give of his time and skill as he had always done with such devotion. A good man had been lost. And a bride waited for his return.

"Marry her." The last words of Arthur Westbridge. Always he had thought of the wellbeing of others. But how could William honor such a wish? Miss Lockhart was not a commodity to be passed along from one man to another. Besides, he had nothing left to offer her.

William sat in the courtyard, far from home, and wept.

CHAPTER TWENTY-SIX

Munro, early July 1815

TWO LETTERS HAD arrived within a week of each other. First, the tremendous announcement that William had survived the war. This letter was addressed to Charlotte Trenton and had been sent by a clerk in the British Army. An injury was mentioned, but William was said to be recovering well. Charlotte Trenton shared the news with great enthusiasm, and Verity and her sister received it equally so at their next visit.

The absence of any tidings from Dr. Westbridge had not raised any alarm, as Verity had grown used to his work demanding the majority of his attention. But the second letter—a black-rimmed correspondence written to Miss Verity Lockhart from an unknown address—created much consternation, so that Verity had sat down and unfolded the page with a trembling hand.

It was from the parents of Arthur Westbridge. Their son, they were deeply sorry to inform her, was dead. They were grief-stricken, of course, and, assuming she would be too, they had pledged their desire to fulfill any promises their Arthur had made her. The letter was short, sincere, and so utterly unforeseen that its contents took a very long time for Verity to absorb. She only sat numbly and stared at the words as if they did not, in any way, apply to her.

Eventually, she rose and walked, as though in a trance, to where her sister sat working on some embroidery and placed the letter wordlessly in her lap.

Hope noticed the black borders of the paper at once. Her hand flew to her mouth. "It's not Papa, is it?" she asked, her voice filled with trepidation.

Verity shook her head. "Read," was all she said.

Hope raced through the contents, her eyes like a pendulum as she rushed from one line to the next. She quickly reached the part where the death of Arthur Westbridge was announced.

"Oh, Verity, I am so sorry," she said, looking up with a mournful gaze. But Verity did not respond. Hope waited a few moments, but when the silence dragged on, she decided it best to finish reading the letter.

"So that is where Dr. Westbridge formed his generous nature," murmured Hope, as she learned of the Westbridges' earnest commitment to their son's wishes. "To think of others while feeling their own loss…" She looked up at her sister. "Are you all right? I know you did not yet love him as a wife might, but you were fond of him. This must be a terrible shock."

Verity perched on the edge of one of the upholstered chairs in the drawing room, her hands clasped tightly where they rested on her knees. "I never expected the war would claim *him*," she said softly. "My emotions are all in a jumble. I know I should be much more distraught." Her voice began to rise. "The fact that I am *not*, that I knew I was to break with him upon his return…" Verity wrapped her arms around herself to ward off the hollowness inside. "I feel a deep guilt, Hope. He was not loved as he ought to have been when he died."

Hope crossed the space between them in a fleeting movement, bending slightly to place her arm about her sister's shoulder and rest her cheek against Verity's white-blonde hair. "His parents loved him true enough," Hope said. "And he was doing what he most wanted. He was happy. It is well he did not know of your intentions, for he went to his grave believing all was as it should have been. It is better this way."

Verity shivered and rubbed her arms in a soothing motion.

"Do you think he suffered? I would not want him to have suffered."

"It does not say if he was ill or injured," Hope noticed, re-reading the letter that was still in her hand. "Mrs. Westbridge writes that the army only mentioned he served them well as a volunteer. I suppose they have many such letters to write. Let us not imagine the worst. Instead, we shall remember him as the man he was: kind, generous, honest. Perhaps we can find a way to honor his memory. A donation to the Entomological Society comes to mind."

"I think I owe him more than that," said Verity, whose self-soothing movements had calmed at the thought of doing something productive. "There is the Royal Hospital." Her head lifted quickly. "Do you think Papa would allow me to volunteer there, as Dr. Westbridge did? I would not have his skills, but I could still be useful. It would help take my mind off everything that has happened. Could we ask Papa?"

Hope smiled gently. "We shall certainly do so. He would no doubt be happy for you to serve the community in some way. His only concern would be that you are kept safe. We shall make inquiries and reassure him."

Verity nodded, but her body remained stiff and her lips pressed tightly together.

"I confess," Hope remarked, "you have taken this news far more to heart than I would have expected. Maybe, after all, your feelings for the doctor were not thoroughly explored."

"To my shame," answered Verity, "I must say my sorrow for his loss is as for a friend, and nothing more."

"Then what ails you? You have done nothing wrong, you know. One cannot force love where it does not grow naturally. And you did not break your engagement or his heart."

Verity reached inside the pocket of her underlay and drew out another letter. "There is this…"

"Who is it from?" asked Hope.

"It was sent from Thorn Bush Hall. The hand is Mrs. Trenton's." Verity looked at her sister with some consternation. "Why would she write me? We visit on the regular. She would only write if…if something could not wait, or was too awkward to be spoken of in person, or both." She thrust the unopened paper at Hope. "You read it. I am too afraid."

Hope sat down again and carefully unfolded the page. "Shall I read it aloud?"

Verity shook her head. "First determine the contents. Then you shall impart them to me. You will know better how to tell me bad news than the author of this letter would."

Hope lowered her eyes to the words that had created such apprehension in her sister. The clock ticked in the background. Verity watched her face for any clues, but her sister read only with concentration. Until…

"Oh, my!" Hope cupped her hand to her mouth. "What a vile man! What a terrible deed! Poor Dr. Westbridge! And poor Mr. Cole! How helpless he must have felt!"

Hope lifted wide eyes to her sister. "Oh, my dear, you must read this for yourself. I could never speak such things to you." She held out the page from her as if it would strike her like a serpent.

Verity hesitated, then took it gingerly from Hope. She felt that nothing in all the world could coax her to read the words that had so affected her sister.

But she must.

Cautiously, as if taking her first steps, Verity read the first sentence. Then the next. Before she knew it, the fearful truth had been revealed and her heart was thundering in her chest so hard, she could feel it without lifting her hand to her bosom.

"That fiend Foyle!" Verity cried. "He would have killed them both!"

At last, the tears fell for Westbridge. "Poor Arthur," Verity whispered as the reservoir of her eyes overflowed, shedding teardrops onto her cheeks, the shock finally giving way to sorrow. "He did not deserve this. Poor, poor Arthur."

"It appears Mr. Cole's courage saved him from a similar fate," said Hope. "His hand should heal. It is a pity his eye will not. But it could have been so much worse."

"Who cares for his hand or eye?" Verity said almost angrily. "Such things are nothing compared to a life. How grateful we should be! Mr. Cole has been spared twice over. He will come home to his family, his friends." Verity began to sob. Relief took the place of sorrow. She could not fix the broken past. A terrible crime had occurred, a good man lost. But William Cole remained. He would return.

"But when?" she wondered aloud, fiercely wiping the tears away so that she might once again study the letter.

"I don't think Mrs. Trenton knows," said Hope.

Verity finished her examination of the letter and lowered the hand that held it in disappointment. "No, the letter does not say if she does. But she will inform us when that changes, I am certain of it."

"Agreed." Hope stood and stroked the creases from her skirts. "Meanwhile, you will want to reply to Mr. and Mrs. Westbridge and send your condolences. And I shall write to Mama and have her petition Papa regarding your volunteering at the hospital."

Verity nodded. It was good to have something to do. She could not bring back Arthur Westbridge. She could not make Mr. Cole whole again. But she could be of use in other ways. If only her father would let her.

Being busy might also help to distract her from the way her heart skipped a beat at the thought of William Cole's return, and the very honest conversation she was determined to have with him as soon as the opportunity availed itself.

A pang of guilt toward Dr. Westbridge resurfaced, but Verity quelched it. She would honor the memory of a man she had heartily respected. But she was done throwing away her chance at love. If anything, the death of Dr. Westbridge had taught her that life was unpredictable, and she should not waste a minute of it.

William Cole had survived all that the fates had thrown at him thus far. He deserved the truth. She would have him know her heart. At the very least, he would understand what he was worth to her. It might heal some of the pain he must surely be suffering from his all-too-recent experiences.

What she hoped, so very much, was that he felt the same. The hints for and doubts against had tortured her long enough. If there was the slightest chance that they might know happiness together, Verity wanted to find out, once and for all.

CHAPTER TWENTY-SEVEN

Munro, late August 1815

WILLIAM HAD BEEN home over a month, though he still felt a stranger to it.

Napoleon had been sent into exile once more, and Britain had begun to pick up the pieces left from the war. For William, this meant being placed on half-pay, as the government could not afford to keep an army four hundred thousand men strong when there was no one to fight. All around, the news was that of misery. Those who were lucky enough to return to the bosoms of their families did not always do so whole, nor was there employment waiting for them all. There was talk of famine and riots. General despair ruled the mood.

William had refrained from visiting his parents. His mother would have fussed and his father would have tried to give him a sense of purpose. He wanted none of it. At Thorn Bush Hall, where he had chosen to hide himself away, James Trenton was refreshingly insensitive, feeling no need to coddle William, instead inviting him to the usual cigar and a game of cards as if nothing had changed. Charlotte worried, William could tell, but she let him be.

Mostly, he occupied himself with long walks in Munro Park or sat in the garden and read. The sweet domesticity of his sister's household contrasted too sharply with his memories of the fields and streets of Brussels and beyond. Outside, he could breathe.

The reliable constancy of nature was reassuring. It needed nothing from him. He could just exist.

Though she gave him much room to recover himself, Charlotte still received the occasional visitors, all of whom he had avoided successfully. It was the weekly tea with Miss Lockhart and her sister that had proved more challenging.

"But they will want to see you," Charlotte had explained when William headed to the stables just as the Sinclair carriage had arrived. "They have been a great support to me while you were away and shared my concern for your wellbeing. Let them at least greet you and welcome you home."

"I do not wish to be put on display as some curiosity from the infamous Waterloo," had been William's surly reply.

"That is an unkind thing to say," Charlotte had scolded. "They deserve better from you."

"Which is why it is best I make myself scarce, for I have no social graces at present."

Charlotte had pursed her lips and said no more, and William had made his escape. Yet the ride had given him no satisfaction. He knew it would hurt Miss Lockhart when he refused to see her. But he could not bear to have her pity. For pity him she must.

If she did not already hate him.

Because of him, Westbridge was no more. His animosity with Foyle had cost the doctor his life, and Miss Lockhart had been robbed of her betrothed. No good could come of meeting her. He would spare her the painful reminder that he lived while Westbridge was lost.

At the second visit, the two sisters had arrived early. William had just been coming in from the garden to pre-empt running into them when the two ladies took their seats in the drawing room. Miss Lockhart had spied him in the hallway and jumped up from her chair, calling after him as he fled to his rooms. Her cries, bold and urgent, grew sad and faint as he widened the distance between them.

William could not face her. Images of the war still flashed

before him. His scarred hand and silken eye patch were a constant reminder. And Arthur Westbridge lay buried in Brussels. The world was an ugly place. All his dreams and hopes were shattered. The last thing he was capable of was looking into the fearless eyes of Miss Lockhart.

In this fashion, four visits had come and gone, and William believed himself settled into a tolerable pattern of solitude and quiet. His days consisted of largely meaningless conversations with his brother-in-law, meals that filled his stomach without demanding much by way of social intercourse, reading, and the outdoors. Slowly, the burdensome aspect of being alive was lifting. He even allowed Charlotte to arrange a picnic with the children where he would be included.

On that cloudless day, William and the footman carried the wicker baskets and blanket to the clearing that Charlotte pointed out to them while the nurse carried baby Jane and led Clarence by the hand. Charlotte had chosen a surprisingly secluded spot in Munro Park for the picnic. Trees formed a natural boundary that blocked the view William thought she might otherwise have enjoyed.

"I do not want Clarence to go near the stream or fountain," she explained. "Here he can run for a hundred yards while I watch him, without any other sights to tempt him further."

William accepted her explanation and settled upon the blanket, lying on his back, his head cradled in his hands with fingers interlocked to support it. The sun was bright, but the trees kept it from blinding him as he lay staring up at the heavens, at peace, and grateful for it.

It had never occurred to him that Charlotte, his patient and kindhearted sister, could conspire against him. Nor that she had, in fact, chosen this spot for a different reason altogether. Indeed, the trees blocked his view of anyone's approach, the footfalls muffled by the grass, so that he had no chance to flee before a newcomer was almost upon him.

A soft shadow fell over him just before a familiar voice he had been avoiding said, "Good afternoon, Mr. Cole. How lovely to see you out and about."

William sprang up, his senses now on high alert, but no obvious escape presented itself. He blamed the jolt of surprise for the clumsy greeting he now gave.

"Miss Lockhart, what are you doing here?"

She looked down at herself with an appraising air, then up at him again, and replied, "Preparing to make a fool of myself, Mr. Cole."

"Take Miss Lockhart for a stroll, William," his sister commanded. "I can chaperone you just as well from here, though you may be walking a hundred yards away. The line of sight is quite clear."

So, it was an ambush, planned and orchestrated by the two women he trusted the most.

"I do not feel in a mood to walk," he protested stubbornly. "Why don't *you* take a turn together while I read my book?"

Charlotte glared at him, then sighed. "Very well, if you're going to behave in that way, I shall invite Miss Lockhart to stay for the entire picnic rather than for the short conversation she had hoped for."

William turned from Miss Lockhart so that she might not stare at his covered eye. She promptly circled around until she was facing him once more.

"I see you are well," she said, gazing directly into his face, brazen and unflinching. "Certainly well enough to listen. That is all I ask."

Confronted now with her presence, William found his resolve slipping. Her clear, blue eyes were like pools of peace, *sans* judgment or hatred or pity. They saw him and were content. The sun lit up her pale hair so that it shone like a halo about her face. He felt his resistance melt away.

"I will hear you," he said in a low voice.

"Will you not offer me your arm, that we may walk?"

William complied by offering his right arm so that his damaged left eye might be largely hidden from view. They set off in a wide circle that followed the edge of the clearing.

"You have been somewhat of a recluse," began Miss Lockhart, straight to the heart of the matter, as it was in her nature to do.

William did not argue. It was the truth. With Charlotte, he may have been defensive, but Miss Lockhart, he knew, would not tolerate it.

"That is so."

"Understandable, of course," said Miss Lockhart. "You have experienced tragedy that most would take every measure to avoid. You have sacrificed for the lives of others. You deserve time to recover from the pain it surely inflicted upon your person and mind."

William had expected a rebuke, bitterness, dismay. Not this. Not wholehearted understanding.

"I... Yes... It has been a difficult adjustment."

"I understood this," Miss Lockhart said, suddenly shy, "yet I confess it has been a challenge to be patient in waiting to see you. We worried so for your welfare while you were away. And then we worried, it seems, in equal measure when you returned."

"I am sorry you felt neglected."

Miss Lockhart stopped and turned to him. "Being kept from your company was not neglect, Mr. Cole." Her voice hitched. "It was agony." Her lashes were cast low, as if she were afraid of his response.

"I have been a poor friend," said William. "I... I could not face you. Not after..."

Her eyes lifted. "There is nothing for you to fear, Mr. Cole."

"But Westbridge... It was my doing..."

"What?" Miss Lockhart frowned. "How have you reached that morbid conclusion?"

"I was stubborn," William said wretchedly. "I should have let Foyle have his way." William hung his head. "Your betrothed paid the price for my sense of honor."

Miss Lockhart was silent for a while. Perhaps she pondered his words. Perhaps she refrained from uttering her disgust. When she did finally speak, it was with an unexpected edge of urgency. "Hear me, sir." Her voice was almost pleading. "You carry no blame. None at all. Lieutenant Foyle is a foul creature. He has brought nothing but shame upon his family, now more than ever. I pity his father and mother. You had every right to insist the truth be heard about him. Only a monster like Foyle could think, in his depravity, of murder as a solution to his petty, self-inflicted problems."

Miss Lockhart grabbed a quick breath and continued. "Furthermore, Dr. Westbridge was himself a man of honor. If the roles had been reversed, he would have acted exactly as you did. The crime is Foyle's, and no one else's."

William had not expected such complete exoneration from her. How noble a woman she was, despite her great loss! "I can hardly believe," he replied, "that you have such grace for me when you have lost your engagement in so brutal a fashion."

For the first time, Miss Lockhart seemed unsure of herself. He followed her line of sight toward Charlotte, her eyes seeking, as if answers might be found there. She inhaled deeply and sighed it out. "There is something you should know," she said before pausing again.

"Yes?"

"My engagement… It was not what you might think."

"No?" William's heartbeat increased its pace.

"Dr. Westbridge was a good man. I was fortunate to be asked to be his wife."

"Certainly." William held his breath.

"However…" Another pause.

"Yes?" William thought he might scream with anticipation.

"I did not love him." Miss Lockhart looked away, as though ashamed of what she had said.

"I see." William's heart now sped a mile a minute.

"Do you?" Her eyes searched his face. "Then you should

know I intended to break the engagement upon his return."

William thought his heart would burst right out of his chest.

"So you see," said Miss Lockhart, her lips curling as if the words tasted sour, "I have my own guilt to bear."

"Westbridge had no idea," William said rather than asked.

"No."

"Then you caused him no pain."

"But I would have."

"You must have felt very strongly to make such a decision…" William's voice had grown thick with restrained emotion.

Miss Lockhart shook her head. "I should never have agreed to the marriage in the first place. It all happened so quickly. I would not even have considered it if…"

William waited for her to finish the thought. But she did not. Instead, she twisted her fingers into the folds of her dress and kept her gaze focused in the distance.

"If *what*, Miss Lockhart? You may speak freely to me." William's entire frame was fit to burst. He kept his feelings under control by the most fierce effort.

"If…" Her eyes roved from tree to tree." "If…" Her fingers grew frantic in their assault upon the fine muslin of her skirt. "If… *you* had asked first." Her crystal-blue eyes locked on to his, searching, asking.

"You *wanted* me to ask?" All the pent-up hope, restraint, denial now crashed down like a wave, briefly overwhelming him before releasing him from its torturous presence, then receding into a waning tide that trickled puddles around the foundations of his soul.

"So very much," Miss Lockhart whispered.

William asked in a voice hoarse with rising ardor. "You knew I loved you?"

"I hoped," she said, sounding very small. "I could not be sure. And when I wanted to ask you these past weeks, you would not see me. So I thought I would declare myself and find out if…"

She could say no more. William's lips had pressed into hers.

His mouth molded with the soft, yielding warmth of her own. William heard the groan escape his throat. His hands wrapped around her waist, pulling her against him, the skin of his palm savoring the feel of her closeness, the shape of her body. Her hands clung to him as they had once before, an unmistakable expression of desire. No more doubt. No more ambiguity. Only this: a blending of mutual yearning, the outflowing of a love that was shared and certain.

Miss Lockhart—though surely his heart now called her "Verity"—released her lips from his and panted, her breasts heaving against his chest as she caught her breath. But she did not let go. Oh, she must never again let go!

He had been such a fool. He had always sought *this* first. This great passion. He had believed it would be a sign of that one great love he had wanted more than anything else. But William understood now—such passion was the *outcome* of love, not the foundation upon which to build it. True love, he had realized at last, was honesty even when it hurt, acceptance despite being undeserved, trust because one knew that person well, ferocity in their defense—all qualities Miss Lockhart had by the bucketload. *That* was why he'd been drawn to her, long before he'd desired her. He had—he could hardly believe it now—walked away from it all, not once, but twice. And yet, here she was, in his arms.

Years of self-loathing, hidden under layers of superficial nonchalance, now fell away like the enormous weight of a great stone. All his fears, his disappointments, his sense of worthlessness were wiped from the table by the unassuming arm of Miss Lockhart. Relief bubbled up from deep within, shaking free from him in an involuntary sob. "Verity," he cried, pulling her even tighter to him, his head hidden in the curve of her neck. "My own love." Tears now wrenched from him in gasps. His wasted years pretending he didn't care what people thought of him. The blood and screams and smoke of Waterloo. The terrible death of Arthur Westbridge. He released them all to her. And she took him in, cradled him as if she could hold the whole world at bay with the power of her love.

At last, emptied of all that had dragged him under, William surfaced, renewed. Verity wiped his wet cheeks gently with the back of her fingers. He cupped her hands to his mouth, pouring his gratitude into them with kisses and murmurs of contentment.

"I love you." He breathed the words against her palms.

"And I you… William."

He lifted his head in happy surprise. "Say it again."

Verity smiled coyly. "William."

"Again." He kissed her eyelids, her cheeks, her mouth.

"William," Verity purred against his lips before sealing them with her own.

He thought he would consume her with his desire, but she held her own, returning his passion with equal measure, until…

A hand that was not Verity's tugged at William's coat.

"Mama says to come and sit," little Clarence said before turning and running back to the picnic blanket where Charlotte sat watching them. "Mama, I told them to come and sit! Did I do it right?"

"That was well done indeed, Clarence." Charlotte smiled proudly at her son, then cast a more meaningful look at the lovers. "I have sandwiches," she called, "and you seem to have a healthy appetite, William."

William plaited his fingers through Verity's, drawing her forward while he walked in reverse, still facing her. "I suppose you'll have to marry me now," he teased. "We can't have your lips neglected now that I have claimed them. Do you think you might say *yes* if I asked?"

"You will have to ask me to find out," she answered, quirking her mouth playfully.

William stopped at once and dropped quickly to one knee, her hand still in his but now pulled closer to rest upon his heart. "Miss Lockhart, will you do me the most profound honor of being my wife, to cherish me and scold me, to tell me about beetles even when I don't remember their names, as long as we both shall live?"

"I will."

William beamed. He stood and embraced his betrothed, though he did naught else, for Charlotte would surely have had his hide if he did not restrain himself in public.

When they sat, William was obliged to let go of Verity's hand. But his gaze stayed upon her and she glowed under his constant attention.

"Am I to understand I will have a new sister?" Charlotte asked pleasantly while she poured a glass of lemonade for Verity.

"You will indeed." William winked. "Are you pleased someone has finally tamed me?"

"I don't believe that is what Miss Lockhart has done at all," Charlotte objected. "For you were never the wild thing you pictured yourself to be, dear brother. She has merely shown you it is enough to be yourself, and for that, I thank her from the bottom of my heart."

"Oh, do call me 'Verity,' for we are to be sisters now."

"Not until I have had the honor first," interrupted William. He hesitated a moment to savor the imminent experience. Then he breathed her name. "Verity."

She lowered her lashes and a smile crept upon her face. Shy at first, her lips quirked into a playful pout. "Does this mean I can come to tea and you will not run and hide?" Verity teased him.

"How does tomorrow sound?" asked William. "I promise to stay close." He coughed mockingly toward Charlotte. "But not *too* close, of course."

"You will have to write to my parents to secure my hand," Verity reminded him, "though I can think of nothing they would want more."

"Unless," Charlotte pointed out, "you were to also claim the position as vicar."

William grew suddenly still. In the blur of emotions, he had quite forgotten his lack of prospects.

"I think," said Verity slowly, as if contemplating every word, "you would make a splendid vicar after all. You have learned to value life and forgive yourself. You would have much to teach your congregation."

"I could not bear to watch people fall asleep while I am talking," William answered wryly. "That is," he continued, tapping his eyepatch, "if this does not frighten them away first."

Verity shrugged. "Then you will make your sermons shorter. And your roguish charm is not lessened by your new accessory. Being a vicar does not need to be tedious. Think of all the families who have been touched by the war. You would be a comfort and an inspiration to them."

William had not thought of that. Purpose. He needed a sense of purpose. Else he would soon grow tired of his own company and frustrate the woman he loved.

"I will think on it," he promised.

Charlotte clapped her hands. "Excellent! Now, how about those sandwiches? Even though 'Man cannot live on bread alone,' a sandwich has much to offer an empty stomach."

The afternoon progressed with much talking, eating, and laughter. William felt as though he had a new lease on life. He watched Verity snuggle little Jane in her arms and imagined their own precious babes with their father's dark hair and their mother's clear, blue eyes. His heart swelled at the thought. His great love had not yet reached capacity. Verity had swung the door wide open and so much joy was ready to march right in.

Tomorrow, he would see her again. And every day thereafter if Mrs. Sinclair would permit it. The banns would be called. His bride would stand by his side and they would pledge themselves to each other. For she had chosen him. And he could want for nothing more.

EPILOGUE

One month later

VERITY SQUEALED AS William lifted her over the threshold of their cottage. It was a stone's throw from the vicarage, where they could have stayed at no cost, but the new Mr. and Mrs. William Cole were determined to live alone and follow their own dictates. Mr. Lockhart, on the verge of retirement, had employed William as curate. This meager income, plus his father's allowance and the savings from his time in the military, made it possible for William and his bride to reside in the tiny abode, close to his duties, while granting the couple their independence.

The rooms were sparsely furnished, and Verity had returned to wearing her simple country clothes, which she much preferred, anyway. The smell of freshly baked bread filled the room. Mrs. MacTavish, delighted that young Miss Lockhart had found a match, and no doubt grateful she would no longer be dragging mud into her kitchen, had baked a loaf for them and left it in the window to cool. A little pot of her best preserves stood on the table. Next to it lay a silver spoon, previously a wedding gift to Verity's mother and now passed onto the new Mrs. Cole.

Verity's feet slipped down to the floor, but she did not step away. William was holding her close, his smile widening as she slipped her arms around his waist.

"Welcome home," she said, pressing her cheek to his heart.

William stroked her hair and planted a kiss in its loose waves. "I have a surprise for you," he said, looking rather pleased with himself. "But you will need to take off your shoes and stockings."

"Will you have me undress in the doorway, Husband?" she whispered in his ear.

William's eye danced. "Do not distract me from my surprise, you minx. I only need you to remove your footwear. For now…"

"Very well." Verity sat down upon the nearest chair and slipped her shoes from her feet before rolling down her stockings and placing them carefully to one side. She wriggled her toes. "I have not gone barefoot for months. I have missed it." She tilted her head at William. "What now? Where will you have me?"

William swallowed hard. "I would have you here and now, Mrs. Cole," he growled. "But there is something else we will do first."

He reached behind the door and drew out two large nets, as well as Verity's portfolio and pencil. "It is a day for new beginnings," said William. "And I would have it remembered as the happiest you have ever been."

Verity leaped up and crossed the floor in an instant, throwing her arms about his neck. "You magnificent man, I am already fit to bursting with happiness."

"Then, perhaps, we may immortalize this day with a sketch. We shall find the rarest insect with a name I shall likely not remember, and you shall record it for posterity. We will show it to our children and say, 'This is from the day your mama and papa were married. Do you see the beauty of these colors your talented mama has painted? They are as nothing compared to her eyes.' And then we shall all run down to the pond and see who can find a tansy beetle first."

"Shall we let our children drag their muddy feet into our parlor?" Verity giggled.

"No, indeed not," William replied sternly, "for I shall be a respectable vicar." His lips parted in a grin. "They will have to drag their mud in through the kitchen like the rest of us."

Verity hugged William. "You will be a wonderful father. And I the most blessed of wives."

William stepped back and reached for Verity's hand. "Come, Wife, let us go and show the neighbors what eccentric manners we have."

Hand in hand, they strolled along the grassy path, their laughter ringing out into the bright, sunny day. Verity felt grounded by the earth beneath her, and the hand that held hers, while her heart… Her heart soared to the heavens.

Acknowledgements

My deepest thanks go to my mother, who takes phone calls in the middle of the day that go something like this: "You know when a person feels sort of, you know, and then they want to express that in one word? What's that word? It's on the tip of my tongue. *You* know. It's driving me bonkers." (Yes, first drafts do sound this rough.) Thank you, Mamma. You are still my go-to person after all these decades.

To my husband, who proudly tells everyone—whether they are interested or not—that his wife is a published author. And for reading my books, even though you don't like fiction. You're a keeper!

To my editor, Amy McNulty, who is insanely knowledgeable and cares about helping me succeed. I am so blessed to have you in my corner.

To Evelyn Adams, for holding my hand as I navigate a writer's worst nightmare: self-promotion. You make it feel easy, especially knowing there is someone who's got my back.

Thanks also to the Regency Fiction Writers organization, of which I have been a member for four years. Your forums and classes have been an invaluable resource for my Regency fact-checking, not to mention the wonderful camaraderie found among such a warm, talented group of authors.

As always, though, my greatest thanks go to you, my readers. Without you, my efforts have no purpose. I often imagine the readers as I write, hoping I've made you smile, cry, or shake your fist at the villain. If you've spoken aloud to a character, even better! When I don't feel up to starting a new chapter, I remember you are waiting for it and sit my butt back down in the chair. Bless your hearts for making it all worthwhile!

About the Author

Elizabeth Donne writes sweet Regency romance, a natural outpouring of a lifelong love affair with English literature.

She has spent most of her life in Cape Town, South Africa. In 2015, she moved to Iowa with her husband, their two children, two cats, and their African bush dog. When she's not writing, or discovering the secret wonders of the Midwest, she is enthusiastically introducing her visitors to the joys of drinking *rooibos* tea. With a biscuit, of course.